The Kingdom Where Nobody Dies

By Audrey Borenstein

ISBN (Softcover): 978-621-434-005-7
ISBN (Hardcover): 978-621-434-006-7
ISBN (eBook): 978-621-434-007-1

Printed in New York by:

OMNIBOOK CO.
99 Wall Street, Suite 118
New York, NY 10005
USA
+1 202-738-1322
www.omnibookcompany.com

First Edition

For e-book purchase: Kindle on Amazon, Barnes and Noble
Book purchase: Amazon.com, Barnes & Noble, and www.omnibookcompany.com
Omnibook titles may be purchased in bulk for educational, business, fund-raising, or sales promotional use. For more information please e-mail info@omnibookcompany.com

The Kingdom Where Nobody Dies is a collection of seven short fictions written with the support of a Fellowship from The National Endowment for the Arts in Literature awarded Audrey Borenstein in June 1976. Although events in this work are a matter of the historical record, the characters portrayed herein are fictional, composites drawn from several individuals combined with the literary imagination. No reference to any living person is intended or should be inferred.

for Walter

"revocate animos maestumque timorem mittite; forsan et haec olim meminisse juvabit"

--Virgil, *Aeneid,* Book I, 202-203

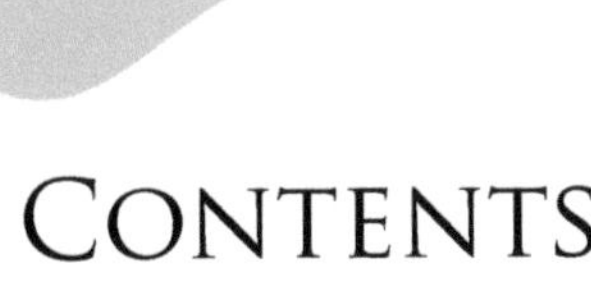

CONTENTS

"Sowing In the Shadows" was published in *Bloodroot,* No. 7 (The Special Fiction Issue (Spring 1980), pp. 2-9.

"Blue Sunday" was published in *Webster Review,* Vol. VI, No. 1 (Spring 1981), pp. 81-97.

Author's Book Description

Lives and loves crisscross and intertwine in these seven stories of natives and sojourners in Louisiana at a critical point during the civil rights era and the trauma of the death of President Kennedy. *The Kingdom Where Nobody Dies* takes its title from a poem by Edna St. Vincent Millay, "Childhood Is the Kingdom Where Nobody Dies," as expressive of the theme of these tales of the loss of innocence in the aftermath of the assassination of the nation's youngest President. The search for the meaning of the public events of the era becomes a crucible for the characters in these seven tales as they strive to make sense of their lives at this historic moment during "the American century."

In the title novella, a young artist from Chicago who was awarded a fellowship from the art department of the state university in 1961 narrates a retrospective of paintings from his "Louisiana period." He recalls the luxuriant beauty of "Belle Ville," the singularities and high spirits of the mixed company of his new-found friends, and his lovers' quarrel with a student of the state university's theatre arts department. Torn between her passion for him and for a Southern-born civil rights activist, she told him *that artists are vain and frivolous people, and that, however appealing she found me to be, she could never live with me, that I was selfish and self-indulgent. Did I ever think, she demanded, of the world that the Negroes I was painting had inherited? This infuriated me then, as it would now....The artist will do anything to buy freedom; he will amuse the wicked of the world to earn the freedom, the independence to create. And every creation mocks all that by which the wicked rule, visiting their cruelty and peonage and suffering on most of humanity. Every act of creation is made of the artist's blood and bone; every creation is a defiance of bestiality and ugliness, all that she professed to abhor. And this she called vain and frivolous!*

"Passing the Goal" takes its title from the lines in *Oedipus the King:* "speak of no man's happiness/Till, without sorrow, he hath passed the goal of life." On the Saturday after the assassination, a schoolteacher soon to be married prepares for a party she will be giving that night after the college football game, one of the very few that had not been cancelled because of the assassination. Her mother comes by for a visit, and they talk about the shattering of the dream of the rich, full life the young Kennedy family might have had, and about the death of dreams and the dreams they refuse to allow to die.

In "Blue Sunday," a young man who had been crippled in an accident is day-dreaming alone while watching the news on television, and brooding over his disability and his loveless, joyless marriage. Jolted awake as he witnesses the shooting of Oswald on the screen, he telephones his sister in Alabama, and finds only his eleven-year-old nephew at home. He realizes he did not even *know* he could feel the violence coming until after he remembers shouting into the receiver, *History is being made right now, and there's a lot more to come, I can* feel *it, hear me?.... We'll see what they'll all do when it all blows up.* After his wife and the neighbor who covets her return to the apartment, there is a vicious quarrel. Toward late afternoon, he feels that the *blue, blue quiet* is pervaded with foreboding. *The day of judgment tomorrow,...and none of 'em prepared, none of 'em feeling it coming ....whatever there was in Dallas, he must've caught some of it.... the blue light deepening, the cold blue November light at dusk, coming in like a growing shadow.*

For a prominent lawyer in Belle Ville, his birthday on November 22nd, 1963 is "A Time To Be Far From Embraces" as he relives the death of his beloved wife, a daughter of the Old South, in the death of the young President in Dallas. His mother was a native Southerner who married a farmer in Iowa where, after being widowed, she made her home with her other son. The lawyer reflects that his brother *had it right, it was better that Mother stay up there with him and his family, there was so much stirring down here, so much uncertainty about what might be coming...at her age, it was best Mother stay with what was lasting, with what would never change so long as the country lasted.*

In "Sowing In the Shadows," an older black woman pours out her heart to her dead mother in the rural church where her husband is the preacher. In mourning the death of the President she agonizes for her son Will, a civil rights activist. *They didn't let our President have his rightful time on earth. They took it away from him. Just like that, they took it. So it's too late to pray, now, about that. But it's not too late for Will, no more'n it's too late for those two brothers he left behind him, nor for the Reverend King, they still got a chance, oh, let them have their life! Mama, all the mothers prayin'. You'd think all heaven'd just melt on down, listenin' to us all.*

A woman tells a cautionary tale of her discovery that, since a house feels scorned by people when they decide to move out of it, it's apt to try to pull them back if they haven't performed some ceremony of leave-taking on Moving Day. In their "Flight From a Phantom" during the Freedom Summer of 1964, a family moves away from Louisiana not long after the bodies of the three slain civil rights workers are found in Mississippi, and the spirit of the place pursues them. Too late for her to turn their car around, she takes the only way she knows to make their escape.

"Creatures of a Day," a woman's memoir of life in Louisiana at the time of the civil rights struggle, takes its title from Marcus Aurelius's "All of us are creatures of a day; the rememberer and the remembered" *(Meditations).* Her remembering commences with the 1950s, when the memorialist, Moira, moves with her husband from their native Midwest to "Belle Ville," Louisiana, where he joins the faculty of the English Department at the state university. Enthralled by the haunting beauty of the place and delighted by the amusements of the repartée exchanged by the convivial souls they meet on the campus, the young couple fall in with their *divertissements* of making salacious witticisms and irreverent wordplay about the manners and morals of officialdom. After she becomes a reporter for the local newspaper, Moira sees that this was her merrymaking friends' way of fending off the omens of malice and menace in the atmosphere. Belle Ville emerges anew for her as a microcosm of the region of the country where critical issues of the times converge and where deep changes are in the making. In the early 1960s, her life is transformed by motherhood and by the rending of her deeply felt bonds with the South when her husband joins the faculty at a private college in the Midwest. By the late 1980's, her children are grown, and her marriage is over. Now the owner of a newspaper in a village in upstate New York, she reaps her losses. The bright figures of the boon companions of her youth emerge from the deepening shadows of its afterlife. They beckon to her as she measures a portion of her gleanings and leaves them to lie fallow for the sowing of promise in times to come, recommencing her journey back to "the kingdom where nobody dies."

To read a book is to keep its light in this world. But first it must be brought to light by a publisher before it can be offered as to whatever readers it may find. In her Afterword, the author reviews her strenuous and steadfast efforts since 1977 to bring this collection of fiction to light. For three decades, her perseverant efforts have been unavailing. Now, in her imagination she hears the ghosts of her characters rustling about in her files. Clamoring for life in this last season of hers, they have unearthed evidence that she knew very well all along the challenges she would face in searching for a publisher for these tales; and they remind her that she had vowed she would prove undaunted by them. They lay a fading copy on her writing-desk of a letter she had written in February of 1976. The letter was her response to a request the Director of the NEA's Literature Program had made of all its Fellowship applicants for recommendations that might benefit future Programs. Her revenants draw her attention to certain passages of that screed: "having read through many 'littles' over the years, I am aware that much is being lost, much work of meaning and value; and I feel that those who come after us will not have a fully rounded or clear grasp of our time because...certain sensibilities, certain perspectives...will be silenced...,certain unique ways of seeing things will fall into oblivion...,and certain understandings of our time will be lost to those who will search through the archives and records for some grasp of what we were really about, of what our 'age' really was."

In recounting the travels of this collection from one publishing house to another during the past three decades, the author of this Afterword asks a question she leaves to its readers to consider: What has happened to the implicit covenant between writers and publishers of literary fiction during the last decades of "the American century"? What has happened to their sense of a calling to a common cause it is the mission of both parties to serve in partnership as keepers of the flame, to bring worthy works of literature before readers who understand their irreplaceable value for humanity? The author asks this question in presenting the facts of her experience, and finds that her question begets further questions concerning the future of the transformative arts of writing and reading in the aftertime of "the American century."

In the course of deciding she must see this book into print in her own lifetime so that it might be granted life beyond hers, the author revisits her plump files of her correspondence with agents and with editors at trade houses, small presses and university presses throughout the United States since 1977. Only one agent, now deceased, sought to represent the collection; and after her death, the author's strenuous efforts to recover her manuscript were unavailing. Of the editors, a fair number praised the literary quality of the writing and the power of its evocations of a time and place at an historic moment in the life of the country. Yet not one of them offered to publish this book.

Time is a god who devours his children. The civil rights movement and the assassination of President Kennedy are watersheds of "the American century." This collection of fiction tells a tale yet to be told of a time and place that is a vital part of the American experience and that cannot come again. In her Afterword, the author reflects that another might read her struggle as a cautionary tale for aspiring fiction writers or as a case study of one writer's experience during the last third of "the American century." Instead, she has chosen to offer it to such readers as it may find, in commemoration of the dream proclaimed by Martin Luther King in Washington, D.C., in August of 1963, and of the ideal of public service inspired by America's youngest President whose loss we suffered in November of that same year; and in tribute to the courage of the leaders and the unsung heroes, Southerners and Northerners alike, of the civil rights struggle. It is her testament to the fighting heart a lover of creating literary fiction must have in order to persevere on behalf of what Montaigne wrote of as our "second selves," the "works our soul engenders, the issue of our understanding, heart, and abilities."

AUTHOR BIOGRAPHY

Audrey Borenstein's short fiction has appeared in a variety of America's literary publications since the 1960s, among them *Prima Materia* (2003); the Transition issue of *Kansas Quarterly/Arkansas Review* (1996); *The MacGuffin* (1989); *The Albany Review* (1988); *Ais-Eiri, The Magazine of Irish America* (1978); *Creel, A Catch From the Mainstream* (1976); *Ascent* (1975); *Jewish Heritage* (1969); *The Arlington Quarterly* (1967); *The University Review* (1966); *Nimrod* (1966) and *The Carolina Quarterly* (1961.) Her stories and excerpts from her novels also have been published in the collections *Paradise* (Florida Literary Foundation, 1994); *Women and Aging: An Anthology By Women* (Calyx Books, 1986); *Womanblood: Portraits of Women In Poetry and Prose* (San Francisco: Continuing SAGA Press, 1981); and *Pioneer Letters: The Letter as Literature* (Northwest Review Books, 1981). A story she published in *North Dakota Quarterly* was nominated by the editors for a Pushcart Prize in Fiction, as was her story in *Womanblood.* Her story "The Visions" *(Kansas Quarterly,* 1973), was selected as one of the "Distinctive Short Stories, 1973" in *The Best American Short Stories 1974,* edited by Martha Foley. In 1988, a story she published in *The Arlington Quarterly* in 1967 received the Award for Excellence in Fiction, Fiction Prize for New York State in The National League of American Pen Women's annual competition in published or unpublished fiction and poetry. A story she published in *Zeitgeist* in 1966-67 was awarded First Prize for Fiction by that magazine. A story she published in December 1961 in *The Reconstructionist Magazine* was included in *May My Words Feed Others: An Anthology of Verse and Fiction from The Reconstructionist* Magazine (South Brunswick and New York: A. S. Barnes and Co.; London: Thomas Yoseloff Ltd., 1974.). *Critical Survey of Short Fiction: Current Writers*, edited by Frank N. Magill, includes a discussion of her fiction.

The recipient of a Fellowship from The National Endowment for the Arts awarded her in June 1976, Borenstein wrote a collection of seven works of fiction during her Fellowship year about people living in Louisiana at the time of the civil rights era and the assassination of President Kennedy. Two of these stories have been published, "Sowing In the Shadows" in *Bloodroot* in 1980; and "Blue Sunday" in *Webster Review* in 1981. This collection, entitled *The Kingdom Where Nobody Dies,* was completed in 1977, and includes her "Afterword," written in November 2008. Her "Afterword" is a review of her steadfast, strenuous efforts over the past three decades to find a publisher for this volume of short fiction, which she has decided to publish herself in 2009.

In 1978, Borenstein was awarded a Rockefeller Foundation Humanities Fellowship in support of her research project to examine the woman's experience of aging through an inquiry into historical, literary and social scientific materials on this subject. The outcome of her Fellowship year includes two books, *Chimes of Change and Hours: Views of Older Women In 20th-Century America* (Fairleigh Dickinson University Press/Associated University Presses, 1983) and the reference work *Older Women In 20th-Century America: A Selected Annotated Bibliography* (Garland Publishing, Inc., 1982); and essays published in *Women In the Eighties,* Selected Papers from the 1983 New York State Women's Studies Conference, and in *Human Values and Aging Newsletter,* published by the Brookdale Center on Aging of Hunter College in 1981.

Borenstein also is the author of *Redeeming the Sin: Social Science and Literature,* published by Columbia University Press in 1978; co-author with her husband Professor Walter Borenstein of *Through the Years: A Chronicle of Congregation Ahavath Achim, 5725-5750* (Franklin Printing, 1989); and translator of Ferdinand Tönnies's *Die Sitte,* published as *Custom: An Essay on Social Codes* by The Free Press of Glencoe in 1961. Her essays have appeared in *The Diarist's Journal* ("Journal Shares," Spring 2003), the *Antioch Review* ("The Spy In the Citadel," Summer 2003), *The South Atlantic Quarterly* ("Knowing the Poor: Thoughts of a Sometime Social Scientist," Winter 1970), and other literary publications. "The Spy In the Citadel" was nominated for Pushcart recognition. Her essay, "Saving Words: Old Letters and Journals" is published at the web site of The Life Writing Connection (LWC; www.lifewriting.org).

Borenstein has published her poetry in *Bridges,* an anthology of works by Hudson Valley poets (Springtown Press, 1989); in *The Croton Review* (1978); and in other literary magazines. In 2008, her poem "Dreamscape: One" and an entry in her 2002 Journal, "On Journey," were published in "Around the Ponds," a newsletter published by Heritage Village in Southbury, Connecticut. She also is the author of "Field Notes of the Simurgh" a humor column, in The Stone House Press Newspaper, New Paltz, New York (1973).

In 2002, Borenstein's book, *One Journal's Life: A Meditation on Journal-Keeping,* was published by Impassio Press in Seattle. Reviews are posted on Impassio's Web Site, www.impassio.com. Her Journal writings have been published in the anthology *Darkness and Light: Private Writing as Art,* edited by Olivia Dresher and Victor Muñoz, 2000) and in *Messages From the Heart* (1999)*; Journal Shares* 1998 and 1997)*; Medicinal Purposes Literary Review* (1996)*; The Journey: A Quarterly for Journal Writers and Journal Lovers* (1995); *Life Scribes* (1995); the anthology, *Women of the Fourteenth Moon* edited by Dena Taylor and Amber Coverdale Sumerall, 1991)*;* and *Resoundings*, a literary publication of Temple Emanuel in Kingston, New York. Her manuscript of fragmentary writings, "Shards," is included in the anthology of fragmentary writing, *In Pieces,* edited by Olivia Dresher and published by Impassio Press in 2006. Her "Journal-Keepings: Spring Into Summer, 2006," is forthcoming in the March 2009 issue of *Passager: A Journal of Remembrance and Discovery.*

In 1980, Borenstein completed a trilogy of novels, innovative forms of the genre, "novels-in-the-round." These are fictional explorations of alternate lives in "Palatine," a community in the Mid-Hudson Valley founded by French Huguenots in 1677. Excerpts from these novels have been published in *Oxalis, The Albany Review, Resoundings,* and *The MacGuffin*'s Special Issue on Experimental Fiction; in the anthology *Paradise;* and in *Prima Materia*'s "Short Fiction by Writers from the Hudson Valley, New York," Volume 2 (2003.) Borenstein continues her search for a publisher of these novels. In 1991, she produced fifty copies of the third novel, *Simurgh,* and donated them to special libraries throughout the United States with collections of Jewish fiction, and to friends of her literary estate.

In November 1992, Borenstein presented a lecture, "In the Field of Boaz: Writing Jewish Fiction," in the Fall 1992 series of The Resnick Distinguished Lectureships in Jewish Studies at the State University of New York College at New Paltz. The subject of the 1992 Fourth Annual series of the Lectureships was "Jewish Literature Through the Ages." *In the Field of Boaz: Writing Jewish Fiction* was published as an Occasional Paper In Jewish Life, No. 3, by The Louis and Mildred Resnick Institute for the Study of Modern Jewish Life, in 1999.

Borenstein is co-founder with Olivia Dresher of The Life Writing Connection, which sees value in helping to preserve privately-held, unpublished life writings by 20th-century Americans. Dresher, who serves as Director of LWC (www.lifewriting.org), compiles and maintains the Life Writing Directory, an annotated registry of 20th-century American life writings, which functions as a resource for facilitating public access to copies of unpublished, privately-held journals, diaries, letters, autobiographies and memoirs written in English during "the American century." Borenstein has listed four volumes of her Journals and three volumes of her collected letters in the Life Writing Directory.

A member of Poets and Writers, Borenstein read her fiction at the Mercantile Library in New York City in October 1988, at Barrett House in Poughkeepsie in September 1988, and at Val-Kill, the Eleanor Roosevelt Center, Hyde Park, New York, in April 1988. She also read her fiction at Adriance Memorial Library in Poughkeepsie in October 1987; and in May of 1986, Poets and Writers and The Stone Ridge Poetry Society co-sponsored her solo program of literary readings at The Stone Ridge Public Library. Earlier in the 1980s and also in the 1970s, she read her fiction at the Dancing Theatre in New Paltz, the Ulster County Council for the Arts Cultural Center in Kingston, the County-wide Arts Festival in West Hurley, New York, and in a number of programs of literary readings in the Mid-Hudson Valley. Borenstein was interviewed by poet Shirley Powell about her novels-in-the-round on Woodstock ACCESS TV on September 23, 1988, and read excerpts from her trilogy on this program. Poets and Writers sponsored her in a solo program of readings from her trilogy in March 1989 at Congregation Ahavath Achim's synagogue in New Paltz. And on October 4, 1989, Borenstein presented a solo program of literary readings of excerpts from her trilogy at The Stone Ridge Public Library in Stone Ridge, New York.

A native of Chicago, Borenstein received the Bachelor's and Master's degrees in Sociology at the University of Illinois in 1953 and 1954, respectively; and the Ph.D. degree in Sociology at Louisiana State University in 1958. She served as assistant professor on the faculty at LSU, and as adjunct professor at Cornell College in Mount Vernon, Iowa, where she taught Anthropology; and from 1970 to 1986, at the State University College at New Paltz, New York, where she taught Sociology. She and her husband, Walter Borenstein, Professor Emeritus of Spanish, are the parents of two grown children. In 2007 they moved from New Paltz, New York to Southbury, Connecticut.

The Kingdom Where Nobody Dies

Of those years I have only one painting to show you, this group portrait. It's different from all my other work; you can't make out the faces. To me it's not art, precisely. This frame is a window-frame. When I look through it I can hear slow, sweet Southern syllables rising and falling, I can feel the sky shuddering as it comes down. These shadowy figures are somewhere between the world of the living and the spirit world. They are attending their dying king. Kennedy is dying, and they are gathering around him in this gleaming white barge here in the rushes. The wind has a human voice in these cypresses. You can feel the dampness of this roan-colored gloom, you can feel the warmth of the light veining these misted figures. Remember Tennyson's words? *The old order changeth, yielding place to new* This is at the moment of its changing. Now. In this place.

Sally was married not long after the assassination, married in a rose organdy dress and white linen slippers. One romance had ended; did another begin? I, gallant Maury, wished her the best. My last kiss was a father's and brother's kiss in one, solemn and clean, cool lips upon cool lips; I held her shoulders lightly. Whatever her perfume was, whatever the flowers were that Hannah had set out on her table and in vases around the living room, there was a heavy fragrance, a mixing of jasmine and pittisporum and sweet olive, that followed me for a long time after that. It was in her hair, and it was in the wood of the bookshelves in the living room, and in the wine punch, and in the spun sugar icing on the wedding cake. Later I found it in my hands, and in my brushes. After I made this group portrait, it began to fade. The same thing happens, of course, with these sandalwood boxes from Mexico. Once, they had a very strong incense.

The sweet olive is like apricots, ripe apricots.

Her skin was luminous. On my canvas, it was incandescent. Her breasts shone. Sometimes the eyes in them were pink, and sometimes amber. Her right breast was smaller than her left, and the eye in it tilted toward her armpit. She had a small mole, a flake of cinnamon, right on the edge of her navel. There were mauve shadows in the folds there, and blue shading in the place where her belly rimmed the upper ridge of the hip-bone, and in the clefts of her thighs. Under the mossy rise, the flesh was a blue so tender it was almost white. Once, I painted her nude on apricot-colored velveteen. Her body glowed on the canvas. But it was as nothing compared to the radiance of her skin against that velvet cloth. The brightness of her figure hurt my eyes. When I began the painting, she was remote. Then something--a thought, or a dream she remembered--lighted her from inside. We made love; and I painted her; and when I was painting her, I was making love to her, and when I was making love to her, I was painting her. We were more than ourselves that afternoon. We were in another region. I left that painting, with all the others, in Louisiana.

An old friend of mine, Mark Gibbs, was living in the French Quarter in New Orleans, making a career, he wrote me, out of being a kept man, the foundling and household pet of girls in the university. *"I ravish them, they ravish me; we carry each other home from the Drinkatorium. They lie down and rise up for me before and after, and sometimes during, a sitting. I'm in a cafeteria, Maury; I can have anything that appeals to me. It's my beaten look; these girls can't resist me."*

He sent me a flyer with that letter, an announcement of a competition for a fellowship for artists. The award winners would spend two years on the campus in Belle Ville, painting and studying. *"Send your portfolio down, Emil and the Mexicans, and that one of your mother in the rocking-chair by the window, what have you got to lose? The Midwest will dry you up. You want to paint? Come down here and have a look at some of this tropical flesh, I can paint it with my toes, and that way every part of me is busy. These chestnut beauties, these honey-blondes, all these low-slung asses swaying in the lazy Southern breezes, you can do it all justice if anybody can."* I know that crazy letter by heart.

It was the right time to tempt me to break away. After the bakery closed, I bellhopped for a while, and I did some bartending. I even gave shampoos in a beauty parlor. *"You're twenty-five!"* my parents shouted, and then, *"You're twenty-six!"* I gave them money for my board, and they kept it in an old canister in the pantry. *"It's yours,"* they said. *"We wouldn't touch it."* After a while, my mother would hold out the canister for me to put a few bills in on Fridays before she lighted the candles. *"For your education,"* she'd say. Or, *"For your future."* And she'd look at me with that old mother-sadness.

I crated the paintings of Emil, of the Mexicans, of my mother, and my self-portraits, and I sent them to Belle Ville. *"I never liked that guy, that Mark!"* my father shouted. *"If you'll win,"* my mother said, *"then I'll know you'll never grow up."* The gods were with me, or maybe against me. I won that Fellowship. I took the train months early from Chicago to New Orleans. This was in 1961, in January. I left winter behind, somewhere in Tennessee.

There was a slender girl standing at the window of the front room in Mark's apartment. She was playing with the venetian blinds, opening and closing the slats, twisting the cords around her wrists. Evelyn. I painted her, not long after I left New Orleans for Belle Ville. There was a pulse of melancholy in her that caused the small breasts under her white blouse to lift and fall in a steady, quiet sighing. Her thighs and hips, in a straight black skirt, were taut, defensive. Her crinkly black hair was alive with anger. But her brown eyes were warm and receiving. *"She's a genuine octoroon,"* Mark boasted, *"and she'll sit for you, she'll lay for you, she has many talents."* Evelyn shared the place with Mark and a red-haired beauty by the name of JoAnne, and Harry, a drummer with a jazz band. We had supper in the apartment that night. Mark talked too much, drank too much wine, played host with what was not his, probably. He and JoAnne put on a display of slapping and teasing and pushing, for nobody in particular. Evelyn said nothing. Harry devoured his soup and his plate of red beans and rice, half a loaf of French bread and a quarter of a pecan pie, like a man who had paid his board in full. Once, when I looked over at him in the middle of one of Mark's stories, I caught his eyes. They were resting on my face without any curiosity. I saw a reptilian ancestry under those heavy-lidded eyes, and in the thin, long lips that were drawn over sharp white teeth. I saw a fierce intelligence in his slate-blue eyes. He tore portions of bread from the loaf and buttered them tenderly. When he bit into the crusts, I could taste them, feel them melt down under the roof of my mouth. He left after supper, and Mark and JoAnne went into the back bedroom and shut the door. Evelyn started clearing the table, and I asked her if she wanted my help. *"Your choice,"* she said. Her feet were bare; she was humming to herself. She washed, I dried; I found out that she waited on tables in a restaurant in the Quarter, that she was a dance instructor, that she had grown up in Charleston, South Carolina, that she had a twin brother in the merchant marines. Her skin gave off a dry, herbal scent. When I went back to Mark's again, just a month later, she'd left. I painted her in the white blouse and black skirt, with stripes of light across her face and hair; her eyes are soft and huge, the eyes of a deer. That painting is in Louisiana too.

That week-end, Mark took me around the Quarter. The buildings ran almost into the street. The sidewalks were so narrow that two could just about walk abreast in some places. You can imagine how exotic it all looked to a Chicagoan, the lacy iron grillwork around the balconies, the passageways between the buildings that led into the patios with their stone fountains and banana trees and flower gardens. The cold down there has no winter in it. Even in January there was that sickly sweetness on the wind that makes you feel languid and at the same time restless. There's an aching in that air, a kind of torment I never felt anywhere else. By April, when it turns balmy, you can sense it in your bones. Mark and I drank dark roast coffee and talked about art and wandered in and out of the shops together. The whites looked the same to me as they look anywhere else, but the Negroes were new, their faces were new to me. Their skin was dark honey; their smiles were gentle; they moved like you move in a dream. Every face had its own story to tell. I saw a man, about my father's age, with a kind of Celtic mischief in his eyes and mouth. The brim of his hat was pulled down over his forehead, and his silver glasses frames flashed in the sunlight. He had a strong nose with flaring nostrils, and a brush moustache. I still remember that he caught me staring at him, and he gave me a piercing look that drove into me and stayed. He brought to mind the holiness of each person, the sanctity and completeness and privacy of every human being. There was great humor in that man, and great peace.

Later, when I made trips to New Orleans by myself, I walked around Jackson Square and took pictures, like any tourist would, of St. Louis Cathedral, and of the Cabildo and the Presbytere and the Pontalba Buildings, and of the French Market. These photographs were all for my parents. I have a sketchbook of my work in New Orleans. The paintings, though, except for three, were of the Negroes I met in Belle Ville. Of those three, two were done in New Orleans, and one in St. Francisville.

But my art work is another story.

On Sunday afternoon of that first week-end, I took the bus to Belle Ville. A heavy rain was washing down. I was wilting in my overcoat. But when I took it off, I felt that chill dampness go right through me. The air had a dankness to it. It smelled of mold and sodden earth and the rank sweetness of rotting vegetation. When it cleared, we were riding past swamps, and I remembered that we were in Evangeline country when I saw the cypresses and the heavy willows. You could see the small silverfish of raindrops flashing on the Spanish moss and crackling along the withes. The light foamed, café-au-lait, in the thick entryways to the swamps. There was one rest stop, at a white frame chicken coop of a place. The two Negroes riding at the back of the bus didn't get off. There was a FOR WHITES sign on the bathroom door.

We rode into Belle Ville through the old part of town. The frame houses crowded the edges of the streets; there weren't any sidewalks. I learned the lay of the land about a week after: the middle-class neighborhood on one side of the campus, and the poor white and Negro section on the other. And they were actually divided by a railroad track. They called the campus town Cougar Alley, after their football mascot. I saw the houses and a few estates of the really wealthy, out on the eastern edge of town, and the Negro shantytown on the far north. And, up at the northern tip of Belle Ville, the oil refineries. They glow red and orange in the night, a modern prophet's vision of Hell.

Carruthers and I found one another by reading messages on the bulletin board in Gates Hall. We both were looking for someone to share one of the more livable apartments off Hyacinth Drive near Cougar Alley. He was nearly six and a half feet tall, and ramrod straight, with wispy hair the color of dark mustard. He always kept it combed neatly back from his high forehead. His face was sprinkled with pock marks and freckles. His eyes changed color; sometimes they were a clear grey, sometimes a pale green, other times almost blue. His face was long and thin and wistful. When he laughed, he held an open hand over his heart, mocking a kind of horror at my impieties. He was organist at the First Episcopal Church, and an adjunct piano professor at the college. He gave lessons to his private students on campus and at the Church. Every other day or so, he'd say, *"No organ is quite like the organ at our First Episcopal."* Carruthers had no parents, or so he said. Perhaps they had died; perhaps they had disappeared. He told of a childhood presided over by a maiden aunt whose upswept, rich hair never turned grey, not even when she was nearly sixty and in failing health, who entertained the parson on Sunday afternoons, and who kept a parrot who had once relieved himself on the reverend's balding head when he arrived at the gate for his weekly call. Aunt Caroline wore peach-colored gowns, and pearls, and Chanel Number 5 cologne. When he was in high school, which he said had been a *dreadful* experience, *horrible, obscene,* he used to take her out rowing on the lake. *"For the pure purpose of maintainin' sanity."* Creating his past, he created this composition: Carruthers, smiling at her, the sun searching out the silver granules in his eyes, his bony elbows flapping up and down as he worked the oars, like the plucked wings of a great, clumsy and affectionate bird touching down at his roost. She lay back against her bolster pillow, her gown of pale orange lifting and falling with the gentle winds playing over the lake, and with the rhythm of his rowing. Her leghorn hat lay in her lap. She shaded her eyes, smoothed back a few loose strands flying free from her elegant French roll and grazing her cheek. From time to time, with a graceful motion of her wrist, she would reach down and let her hand float, a delicate flower, in the quiet water.

Carruthers had few possessions: his jackets and pants and one good suit for playing at funerals and weddings took up little space in our closet. His bedding and towels were frayed and worn from twice-weekly ceremonial ablutions at the Laundromat; he outfitted our kitchen with pots and pans and utensils from Montgomery Ward, *circa* 1955, and the remnants of a grand set of china that, he said with reverence, was *"real ol' family."* He had put himself under the shadow of debtors' prison to buy a Bechstein; and now that he had an apartment he planned to have it moved from his office in the college. One afternoon four moving men appeared with the glorious instrument trussed with padding and rope, in a Belle Ville Transfer Van. I called the Church and left the message for him that his Bechstein had arrived. He came running down the street a quarter of an hour later, with his tie and his hair streaming in the wind, his face pale, his armpits soaked with terror; and knelt and genuflected and leaped and wrung his hands, and screamed at the workmen. They rolled the gleaming splendor from the truck and waited, smoking lazily, while Carruthers circled his treasure looming on the sidewalk in front of the apartment house, caressing it, crooning to it, examining it minutely for the merest scratch, evidence of abuse by the profane world. When he was satisfied that his beauty had survived the transplant from the campus, he began his dance of entreaty once more, praying and sobbing and threatening the movers as they rolled the shining majesty to the door and, their backs creaking and snapping under their magnificent maneuvers, lifted it over the threshold and into the hallway. From there, while Carruthers wept and died and was born again seven times over, they ushered the Bechstein into our apartment, and installed it in our living room that now--with this extravagance--was fully furnished. We squeezed in two wicker chairs and a lamp and a reading table; now we were ready for callers.

"You do the scullery, Maury," Carruthers decreed, *"and I shall cook. And we'll take turns sweepin' up."* I painted in my studio on the campus in the mornings, and had most of my classes in early afternoon. These were the hours that Carruthers practiced. He was never around in late afternoons--that was Church and lesson time; so I had the place to myself then to take a siesta. Carruthers usually had our supper on the table by seven. He broiled fish and tossed salads and cooked potfulls of wild rice. *"I just* love *those dressings on salad that make you completely sick all next day,"* he exulted.

His peppered stews, his bean salads left me frothing at the eyes and mouth; his gumbos turned my skin a kind of ochre; my tongue had a chronic fever; I padded back and forth to the bathroom, to pass water that had a metallic odor. Whether it was from Carruthers's fare or from the oppressive heat down there, I got into the habit of lying down after I cleared away the ruins of his suppers, and I had dreams that I can only call my Louisiana period. The black eyes of giant sunflowers looked gravely into mine; griffins and centaurs strolled through orchards with dark purple trees, braying my name. If you have ever read of the tortures of the martyrs of the Catholic Church, you might remember the practice of tying them to stone altars. And every day, they'd lower a stone on them, a huge block of stone, pressing down on them more and more, until they were crushed to pulp. Every evening, I could feel that stone descending. I felt the weight of it on my face, my chest, my groin, my thighs. Every evening I lost my will, and I sank into a scarlet and vermillion dying; I surrendered to that squashing; I felt happy to release my soul from that terrible exhaustion. This went on until nine o'clock or so. Then I'd get up and read for a while. Carruthers, a real homebody, never practiced after sundown. You could always find him in his wicker chair, wearing Bermudas and sandals, with one hairy leg swinging in rhythm as he read aloud--Baudelaire, Rimbaud, St. John Perse, first in French and then in English. *"My own cookin' does me just right,"* he claimed. Only once do I remember that he suffered any distress from eating the wrong thing in his own kitchen. He lay awake all night tossing, beating his pillow half to death, over an Italian plum one of his students had given him.

When he and I both stayed in Belle Ville over the week-end, Carruthers would go downtown with me and wander through the drugstore and look over all the doodads made in Japan, and read the labels on the medicines and deodorants and boxes of shampoo, and put in some time at the magazine and paperback racks. Then we'd go over to the counter, and Carruthers would ask for *"two nice tall lemon cokes, please";* and afterwards, we'd walk up and down the main street, looking in the windows of the jewelry and hardware and department stores. Other times we'd stay on campus, see a film or play or hear a concert if there was anything on; if not, we'd go to the drugstore there. You had to push past a crowd of Latin American students--they were down there in great numbers those years, and they were always making *piropos,* comments about the attributes of the girls passing by--and Carruthers always waited until we were inside and seated at the counter before he would translate these for me. Saturdays, Carruthers said, ought to be for doing trashy things like hanging out in drugstores, or sweeping up, or going to the picture show. Sundays, of course, were for the First Episcopal.

I painted all morning in my studio, and he always turned out a big dinner by mid-afternoon.

Carruthers always had the correct change. For an ascetic and a musician, this worldliness surprised me. Never, absolutely never, was he without the correct change--for waitresses, telephones, meter boxes, beggars. I could see him in my imagination, both hands and feet busily engaged at the organ, and then, without once glancing up or missing a beat, reaching into his pocket, coming up with the proper amount of money, and dropping it into the collection basket making the rounds up in the choir loft. Somehow he managed to have the crumpled, sweat-stained checks of his private students, and the salary check from the university, converted into rent money--always paid a week in advance--and into ones and fives and tens for the grocery store and the barber shop and the Laundromat; and into perfect change in his pockets. Money was tabooed as a topic of conversation. I pointed this out to him once, and he told me that once his Aunt Caroline had found herself in a meadow with great, fresh patches of steaming cow-plops. and she had lifted her peach-colored skirts and her genteel eyebrows, and stepped around them. Without once acknowledging that they were there.

When Carruthers used the bathroom, there was never the slightest evidence of a human presence afterwards. I told him with gloom when we first met that I am flatulence itself, and he laughed, arms crossed over his chest, heels pounding the floor. But out of respect for his refinement, I used to shore up my discomfort until he left in the morning, and then open all the windows and discharge at ease. He was solicitous about my *"pore li'l ole Jewish stomach";* he had cures for headaches, colds, athlete's foot, constipation, diarrhea, boils. Once, when I had a terrible earache, he made hot compresses of herbal tea for me, and played chess with me while I held them in place. *"Don't fret,"* he said, *"we'll change them every fifteen minutes or so, and won't be long before ole earache will be gone."* He was right; I was cured after a few changes; and he and I celebrated by drinking the rest of the tea and eating some of his home-made praline pie.

About a mile from the campus there were two lakes--you could almost take them for bayous. Except that they were in town. Well, Belle Ville was more country than town. It was built over swampland, and wherever you walked you felt the ground squish and give way, and you felt that it could all fall in from one good storm; we'd be swallowed up in marshland. You have to get up early down there if you want to breathe a few real draughts of air once spring comes; and I used to get up around five, five-thirty, and wander around. That's how I found the lakes and the Negroes I painted. In early morning, there was a soft grey light over the trees, and the water was pink. The birds whistled and sang. The air was almost cool, and very sweet. I met Will Jackson down there, and Roger Cunningham and Vernon Blue, and the others I painted. They had a long day of work ahead of them, but they said that passing the time first was more refreshing than sleep. Sometimes they fished. Most of the time, they just visited. They laughed at me, at the ignorance of a city boy, when I asked them to tell me about the different trees; I wanted to get them talking. But their laughing was good-natured enough; we felt easy all around; and they knew I wanted them to talk about themselves and what they knew, so that I could sketch them and later paint them as they really were. They thought I was a harmless crazy, I guess. I had no skills of any kind, nothing I could do with my hands besides draw pictures of people or paint portraits of them. *"Talk,"* I'd ask them, *"talk about anything that comes to mind." "What comes to mind,"* Vernon Blue said, *"is that you're workin' awful hard to draw my face when nobody but my mother'd want to look at it."* They wanted me to talk--about the city, about *up North;* they asked me how I felt about the South, and why I wanted to paint Negroes rather than whites. They talked to me about their wives, their work, their worries. But they would not talk with me about color, about race, not when I asked them about it directly, nor when I asked them how they felt about the little children in New Orleans, taunted day upon day upon day as they braved the mobs to go to school. Whenever I brought up the subject, they turned away from me, an inward kind of turning away, and sat there, quiet, looking at the water and listening to the birds and the wind in the cypresses. If you could see my paintings, you would find that look there. It came into my own eyes since then. Sometimes it comes back to me through mirrors.

There was one man...Andrew Harris...he had a powerful body, a head like a god's. There was a steadiness in his eyes, a courage and a love and a hurt, that when he looked at you, you felt something inside yourself crumbling. He told me that he had been in the Army in the Second World War, that he was now a cook for a wealthy family, that he had a wife and a daughter and his own home, that he felt two ways about religion, that he had been up North and found it too fast, too cold, but that he might move up there to stay anyway, because of the anger that choked him sometimes. He said that he had two fine parents who had kept him from violence. He told me all this and more. But he told me the most when he said nothing, when he sat in front of me on the wet grass and looked into me with that sorrowful knowing.

There were two other Fellowship winners--Vivian Holcomb, a sculptor, who was never around much. And John Gomez, from Texas. *A sky-watcher* his wife Marta called him. Gomez invited me over for supper a number of times. His family lived in the barracks just south of the stadium, a quadrangle of low tin buildings. The place reminded me of the tenements in Chicago. There was a brown patch of lawn with washing lines always strung with diapers and kids' clothing. The walk was cluttered with rusted trikes and bikes and wagons and skates and scooters. Kids ran around--the toddlers bare-bottomed and drooling, the older ones fighting or playing ball or jumping rope. There was always a mother around, giving some kid a smack or a yell.

"Home sweet home," Gomez smiled, *"you'd never know you were anywhere in particular here. And every one of us brought the rags and tatters of our former lives with us, and made ourselves right at home."* When we walked over that first evening, Gomez said the Texas skies had brought him here, and that the Louisiana skies would keep him here, maybe forever. He said that the heat was sucking him down, that the place was devouring him, that he was losing the will to do anything, even to get up in the morning anymore, but that Marta had enough will for both of them.

Marta's belly was swollen, as if she'd swallowed a pumpkin whole. She and John could have been twins. Her eyes were as black and deep as his--eyes you could drown in before you'd ever find out what was sealed in there. Both of them twisted their full lips when they talked. They both had the gift of irony; they both had plump hands and tiny feet. John saluted you every once in a while, raising his hand to his right temple and then lifting off, slicing the air at a right angle. Either that, or he shrugged and drew circles with his right hand, palm up. The salutes told you to go on talking, and the shrugs were in answer to your questions; the circles said, *"You know how it is; you can say it better than I can."* Marta used her hands to serve at the table; to pick up the baby, Gilberto, who was just learning how to walk and who was going through his wobbly paces between his attentive brothers, John, Jr., and Martin, on the concrete floor; to wave the world away in anger; and to sew.

The children set on us as soon as John and I came in the door, rifling our pockets, sliding down our legs after we sat down, and putting Gilberto down on all fours and having him crawl over our feet and chew on our shoelaces. Later on, Gilberto climbed up on his father's back and sat on his head, and John squeezed his ankles and growled at his bare feet, and pretended to munch on his toes. After we had a supper of chicken and spaghetti, Marta put the baby to bed and sent the two older boys outside. *"I have to fill up my yard with boys before I get my daughter,"* she laughed. She colonized a corner of the couch with her sewing basket, and darned socks and sewed rips in the boys' clothes. She pulled the needle in and out of the sun-bleached, faded garments of her brood, sewing by the light of an imitation Tiffany lamp with a crimson lampshade. The hairs on her arm gleamed red; sparks of fire came and went in her thimble. *"Down here,"* she said, *"Mexicans are colored, Mexicans are Spanish-speaking Nigras, Catholic Nigras. Jews are Nigras, too, you found that out? You learn all that in Texas, it's your body they despise, the rest comes after that. All this talk about mixed housing, putting coloreds and whites together so they'll learn to love one another, discover that they're all brothers and sisters in Christ, this is the talk of people who don't know what's inside. To white people, most white people, we've got a different smell, our pores give off something they fear and they despise. People in the stores--it hurts them to serve us, they stand back away from us, they're afraid we'll breathe too near their faces. It pains them to have to look at thick lips and fuzzy heads and chocolate-colored skin and big, bumpy noses. They cheat us, they keep us down, nobody can tell me it's not physical."*

John brought out a bottle of wine and a plate of cheese and crackers. Throughout his wife's impassioned speech he sat gazing at the wall, at her, at me, then back to the wall again. There was nothing in his eyes for either of us: A great, soft black flower spread its petals and devoured them. I asked him what he thought about what Marta was saying, and he spread his hands and mumbled, *"Too easy. It's too easy."*

Martin Luther King, Marta said, was the only man of God you could find anywhere in the country today. Kennedy spoke the words of a politician, she said. He was white and rich, no matter how you turned it; he would do things for the Negroes down South because that would bring him votes. But he would do it in his good time and in his slow way, because he knew he'd lose a lot of votes, too--maybe enough to lose the election in '64. He was playing both sides, she said, and the Southerners knew this, knew he wouldn't use his power to the full. So they'd keep right on lynching and burning and beating and oppressing, because they knew they could get away with it. And even Kennedy was too much for them; they despised him, the whites in power; he was all the wrong things to them. A Catholic. An Easterner. A man who believed in the centralization of power. Well, they all better watch out, the Kennedy people *and* the Southern powers-that-be. They all had something they didn't bargain for, in Martin Luther King. In *his* mouth, beautiful words had substance. He was standing his ground in front of the sons of bitches, they would have to shoot him down before he would kneel for any of them. There was nothing could stop him, and he's got a following none of them bargained for. *"You wait,"* she said, *"you just wait and see."* There was no way anybody could touch him without dirtying themselves even more. Every time they throw him in jail, they get weaker. *"The Negroes down here, in fact all over the South, are stirring themselves,"* she said. *"Used to be a time when I went to the Catholic Church to pray for justice and brotherly love. Well, down here I went to Mass one Sunday, and it was my last Mass. The priest said a few lukewarm words about racial justice, and more than half the hypocrites in there got up and walked right out. Don't think they came back later, either. And if a Catholic misses the Communion, it's like he never attended Mass at all. It's a mortal sin. You think those sons of bitches believe in God? You think they're afraid to die in a state of mortal sin?"*

She put down her sewing, and poured herself a glass of wine. Her hands were trembling; her violence thrilled me. I feared for the child inside her, almost fully ripened. Not once did John's hand reach out to restrain her; not once did his eyes flicker, either in pride or in reproof. When she stopped speaking, you could hear the whirring of the small fan they'd set on the table that lifted wisps of her hair away from her temples, and stirred the papers on the table in front of us. Only that, and the calls of the children outside.

The damp breath of late evening murmured in this room; it became a cell, with its concrete floor and tin walls and single window cut high up in one of them. I felt that John might be praying, praying for our souls. Either that, or dreaming of his skies. The wine was sour and dry, and it worked a fever in me--that and the heat crawling through the narrow window, trickling down the walls, sighing through our skins. John had confided to me less than a month after all of us came to Belle Ville, that he was being bled of his will, that he felt what dying must be like. I felt that then too. Only Marta, swollen up with a life that was beating its wings against her insides, a life already fighting for release...only Marta believed she was alive. What were we all doing here, in this room, in this place, in this life?

Hundreds of years ago, Marta was saying, they would have known what to do with that woman in St. Gabriel's Parish who shouted that she'd rather burn in hell for all eternity than ride in a bus next to a Nigra, than sit herself down in a restaurant where they serve Nigras, than send her children to school with Nigras, she'd as soon be excommunicated from the Church than let the Nigra lovers and Yankee agitators tell her how to live, that woman, do you know what they would do with her back there in the Middle Ages? They'd cut out her tongue, they'd roast her alive, they'd give her a one-way ride on their rack, Marta told us. *"And that son of a bitch that owns half the Parish west of here, that's building his concentration camps for anyone who preaches race mixing, they'd roast* his *hide too. Instead of that, they turn brutes into heroes; they put their pictures in the paper; they turn them into movie stars! We'll get ourselves organized not too long from now. Never thought I'd see the day that Marta Guiterrez Gomez would go to a Baptist Church, but there's a Negro one not too far from here where our Committee on Human Relations meets. It's mixed company. Of course, these people see me go in there, to them I'm another Nigra. But the white people that come--Southern whites--that eats them up. They harass us, those cowards, you ought to see what they do. In fact, you ought to come with me some time, Maury. We talk about the real meaning of being Christian, but don't let that bother you, it's just a cover. Religion's always been a cover. For both sides."*

It wasn't too long after that night that Marta appeared to me in a dream. Her face was cloven in two, and blood was foaming on her upper lip. I began my painting of her after that; on Sunday afternoons, she sat for me in my studio and talked to me about the things she had said that first evening. I had the idea that my painting would heal that dream's vision of her face, and I hurried, because her baby was to be born soon and she'd have no time to sit for me then. John wanted it; so after I put it on exhibit with the others, I gave it to him. A work of art is, after all, an offering. No more than that, but no less, either.

Carruthers would go off to *check* kinfolk and friends, sometimes over a long week-end, other times during the holidays. There were cousins to check, from one to several degrees removed. There were marriages to check, and the welfare of growing children, and the state of small businesses. Everybody's health and well-being had to be inquired into, and this took real dedication. I think these avuncular concerns kept Carruthers on this earth, that this human touch was his gravity. He told me about Jody, Cousin Jane's oldest boy, who worked so hard in law school that the pore ole thing's mind went, and he was arguin' cases with every lamp post in town. He told me about Willie, with his weakness for gamblin'; and Fred's whole family prosperous and bloomin' from his good investments; and pore sweet Aunt Melissa, with her husband in an institution for the mentally disturbed for over thirty years, and her one son, the brilliant one, a suicide, and the other a little soft in the head, makin' his way, drivin' a taxicab in Greensboro. Aunt Melissa took her comfort in long walks (few people, Carruthers maintained, really knew how to walk *well),* and Hershey's milk chocolate bars with almonds, and king-size filter tip cigarettes, when nobody was lookin'. Little Catherine Ann, Cousin Rhys and Laura June's little girl, was so brave and sweet about her affliction, half-blind since birth, but doin' so *well* in school. And everybody's favorite, Melanie, decidin' to get married again, they were all so pleased; she'd had a foolish romance in her third year of high school, and run off and married a sweet silly boy, it wasn't but a month after they were secretly married that he took polio and would have to spend the rest of his long days in an iron lung. Melanie had cried and cried when they had her marriage annulled; she felt so guilty about Ted, she visited him faithfully every week-end for two years and more, and she vowed she never would look at another boy. But she fell in love, and Ted was the very first person to insist that she go on and get herself married and live the kind of life *they* would have had if such misfortune had not befallen him; and Melanie cried, but she listened, and here she would be getting married, and everyone agreed it was the thing to do.

"The Jewish people value family just like we do, don't they, Maury? But, you know, you couldn't get on without family, why, we wouldn't even be up to the animals, without family."

Through Gomez, I met Miller Lee Sexton; and through Miller Lee, I found Sally. Miller Lee shared stories and family concerns with Carruthers, whose music made him, or so he claimed, believe in God. A graduate student in Anthropology, Miller Lee had been a devout worshipper of Carruthers' music at the First Episcopal for a long time, and he was *so happy to make your-all acquaintance.* He had straight black hair so long that it brushed his collar, and he wore it in a page-boy--Carruthers said that this made him look princely, but Miller Lee said he did it to look Indian--and his eyes, set very far apart, were long-lashed and beautiful, *shamelessly so,* Carruthers did declare. He was built close to the ground, as if he had a very low center of gravity, with a narrow chest and wide, sprawling hips, and big, stocky legs. He claimed that he had Indian ancestors though his immediate family denied this, and he said that the Indians, if they knew his immediate family, would be right grateful for the denial. Carruthers said it all sounded very like family.

Miller Lee had a party that spring, not long after the Bay of Pigs fiasco, I remember, because there was a lot of talk about where the country was going. His landlady received us in the foyer of his apartment, like a proper mother would receive her son's guests, she said; and she sat all evening in a velvet chair, *gloryin'* in all our youth, and in havin' visitors from all over the world in her *home*--apple-cheeked Klaus from Freiburg, and the dark beauty Laura from Bologna, and all Miller Lee's Latin American friends, and the lovely girls in their fluttery party dresses. Miller Lee told us we were on our own, to find out which girls were claimed and which were not. One of them, Sue Ellen, was a genuine Rubens, and she wore a strapless white lacy dress you could just about see through. She got drunk, and she danced with Miller Lee, and with Klaus, and with me; and some time that evening she sat down in a platter of caviar and crackers. Rafael brought along his guitar, and he played and sang some love songs for us. The landlady held a pleated white fan in her fingers, and her rings sparkled when she fluttered it. Klaus kept the wine punch bowl filled, and Miller Lee showed us slides of his People, still lifes no outsider but he would have been permitted to take, because they believe there's an Evil Eye in the camera. There were women in bright velvet blouses and full calico skirts, festooned with beads and silver jewelry, sitting at their looms on the dry, dusty earth or tending to their infants, tilting their cradle-boards to keep them shaded from the harsh sunlight. The men, the healers, in somber shirts and with orange headbands tied around their foreheads, sat cross-legged in a semicircle around a sand painting of a mandala. The warriors looked out at us impassively, dressed in ponchos and buckskin leggings, and with black stripes painted on their faces; they stood, legs far apart and planted in the dust, grasping their shields under one arm, and driving their tall quivers into the earth with the other. There were slides of their lodges with the domed roofs baking in the sun, of their bright blankets strung up on a rope between the trees, of their masks and beaded bags, of their baskets and jugs and head-dresses. *"They allowed me to take pictures of their rain dance,"* he said, *"but only on condition I never showed them to anyone." "Miller Lee,"* Carruthers said softly, *"and your sweet li'l ole Indians."*

Miller Lee said that his People had told him that he could come and live with them if he so chose, at any time, that he should know he would always have a home with them, that if the white rulers, drunk with their mightiness, began a great war, he was to come to them for shelter. They had underground hiding-places long before *we* ever thought of the idea, Miller Lee said, and what is more, they had ways to restore harmony between humankind and the gods. *"And you know,"* Miller Lee went on, *"I think the time has just about come."* There were two big dinosaurs in the world now, he said, and they were roaring at each other, the two big K's drunk with power-lust, hiring outright criminals and murderers to lead their armies against one another, havin' the fantasy that their secret police would do *their* biddin' when, it should be clear now from the Bay of Pigs, who was runnin' things. *"What a dark view,"* Klaus sighed. *"Don't you think that your country is in danger, that Kennedy had to do what he did to defend your hemisphere?"* Miller Lee replied that attacking small countries was always done in the name of defending the big ones. Kennedy, he said, was whippin' everybody into a froth over a missile gap till he came to believe in his own nightmares, and for that reason was listenin' to some very evil people. *"Mind, I don't deny that the people runnin' things in the Soviet Union are out to devour the world. But when you have the two dinosaurs linin' up their forces, there's about to be some very big bloodshed."* Miller Lee said he did not care to choose between Batista and Castro, that was no choice for a feelin' human being, no more than the choice of placin' your trust in one big K or the other. He said there are evil forces in the world in every age, and that they kept themselves invisible, that was how they won all their battles against the good. His people knew this, they knew that those everybody think are the rulers are only their instruments, their mouthpieces, that they would keep Kennedy only so long as he would do their biddin' *"Mercy,"* the landlady cried, *"mercy me, is this any way for a young person to look at the world? You make it sound like we're all completely powerless."* Miller Lee said there were things we could do, we could keep them fightin' between themselves. And we could learn to pray like his people knew how to pray. Laura argued that he was making things sound much too simple. In her opinion, the Bay of Pigs invasion might have worked, with better planning and a better sense of timing. Not that she thought it was moral, she told us; political maneuvers are one thing, morality is another. In her opinion, the Alliance For Progress could accomplish some good both for the South Americans *and* the North Americans.

This made Rafael laugh hysterically. He said that if Kennedy and Krushchev could both be put into space, instead of Yuri Gagarin and Alan Shepard, they might see how small and helpless the earth really is. This was a lesson his people had learned when the Spaniards first found them. *That* was an Alliance For Progress too, he said. Alliance For Progress meant Indians would be killed, that's all it meant. It was a new slogan for a very old European game. If the killers don't come from one side of the sea, Rafael said, they'll come from the other side. Alliance For Progress meant killing Indians. Organization of American States meant killing Indians. Communist revolutions in Latin America meant killing Indians. No matter who does what, there will be a lot of dead Indians. *"Mercy,"* the landlady cried again, *"mercy me, you with all your fresh faces, and all so intelligent, why, I refuse to listen to such pure despair."* Klaus, who had spent the entire Second World War in a sanatorium in Zurich, said that if a person concentrated, really concentrated, he could make all the brutality and ugliness and war and death disappear, that if we chose not to believe in evil, then it would vanish. Carruthers declared that after listening to us all, he was going to go off and live with Miller Lee's Indians forevermore, but only on condition that they would allow him to bring along his Bechstein.

Rafael played his guitar, and Miller Lee danced for us, with the cheese knife clenched in his teeth and his long, black hair falling over his cheeks. His eyes were fierce with joy. He thrust his head at the landlady, and she covered her face in mock terror. He lunged at Carruthers, who pounded his knees with his fists in appreciation. He lifted Sue Ellen up and swung her back and forth, and then set her down in my lap. He made low cries in the back of his throat. All around us, you could feel the earth shaking; Kennedy and Krushchev were bouncing the globe back and forth between themselves; Indians were weaving a blanket for all the dead.... Klaus took

Laura's hand, and she looked at him in surprise, but she let it lay in both his hands. The landlady was falling asleep. Sue Ellen was leading me out the back door into the steaming night with its nameless fragrances. I remember that the moon's light lay a silver glisten along the tips of the dark tiers of the junipers and on the little hollow in Sue Ellen's throat, and that it drew us in its tides and we rode its rhythms, climbing the blue path to its white flare.

Soon after, at a party at Rafael's, I met Sally and her sidekick, J.J. Rafael got us all drunk on sangría, and then he sat us down at card tables to a feast of guacamole and enchiladas. Carruthers and I were sick the whole next day. I fell out of bed that night, and when the phone rang the next morning I crawled over the floor to answer it. I had a terrible fever, and my throat felt like it was full of ashes; I think that was the time that I first knew I had a slipped disc. Carruthers kept moaning that he was dying, and I remember lying on the floor, bruised and sick and thinking that I had already died. That was the kind of party we had. Rafael brought out a box of colored scarves, and turned off all the lamps but one, which he called his whore light, and Sally danced to a record of Ravel's *Bolero.* She whirled and leaped and did a few entrechats. And then she fainted. J.J., Carruthers and I carried her home. I was in love with her that first night I met her. *"She has been spoken for,"* J.J. told me. He said that she was to marry one George Hutchins, whom everybody hated just because of that, besides which he was a deluded idealist, a civil rights worker who had turned his back on a good career in law, left school, and was wandering all over the Southern states, agitatin'. *This* had laid claim to our Sally, Queen of the Theatre and Music Department, our darling Sally.

Beauty and the beasts! J.J. would greet her when we called for her at her little apartment on Wisteria. She was Woman in her infinite possibilities--a young girl in a pinafore, her long hair flowing over her shoulders. Or regal, with her hair in an elaborate up-do and wearing a dark coachman-style dress with a white ruffled ascot. She was The Student wearing braids and a blouse and peasant skirt, a Matron in a chemise and high-heeled shoes, a Nun, demure and pale in crisp white linens. She was the proud lady-not-for-burning, she was Stella in *Streetcar Named Desire,* she was the doomed daughter of Mother Courage. She would be herself, completely, J.J. said, only in the play that he was writing, his Sally play. He and Sally always walked in front of Carruthers and me, holding hands. They had consulted charts and secret books, and they had discovered that they had been brother and sister in former lives. Once he had died by the sword defending her honor. Once they ruled a small green kingdom off the Cornish coast. Once they had been sealed in a tomb together for refusing to obey the stern orders of their father, preferring death in one another's arms to separation. J.J. said that he had been the younger brother, the last of the wild geese, for whom she had sewn so valiantly on what might well have been her last day on earth. *"This is the arm that is more wing than limb,"* he would say, flapping his right arm. Sometimes he forgot and flapped the left one. Once, too, as castaways from cruel parents, they had wandered through a dark forest and come upon a gingerbread house, and there Sally had pushed the wicked witch inside the stove and made black-bottom pie out of her, and freed J.J. from the cage where he was slowly fattening for the bitch's dinner. *"Our devotion to one another,"* J.J. said, *"would be unnatural, if it weren't for this bond between us."*

He was as fair as she was dark. His eyes were a faded, weeping blue; Sally's were furiously bright, the blue of cornflowers. His mouth was comical, a cartoon mouth, with the points of the upper lip sharp and high. Sally's was too fleshy for her small face. The upper lip curved in a crescent. She wore a perpetual pout. She loved to kiss; she never greeted or parted from J.J. without exchanging these chaste kisses. She and Carruthers kissed hello and goodbye too. Her mouth was sweet; when she first gave it to me, in that first innocence, her taste was fresh. like lime; her lips were cool, and new.

Sally was a Texan. She claimed she was part Cherokee, part French, part *Arsh,* part Anglo-Saxon and part Swedish. *"People think I'm a black Swede and that's that,"* she said. *"They don't know the* half *of it. There's Indian in me; there's my Jewish grandfather; there's French, not Cajun, though there might as well be, and the Arsh, and the British, probably came in with the Romans back then."* I gave her a different nose every time she sat for me. She said that Jews are obsessed with noses, and that she was obsessed with Jews. *"Don't take advantage of me, Maury."* Later, she explained that she had meant two things that afternoon. She had meant to tell me that she was *powerfully attracted* to me. At the same time, she had meant to say that those who had been consigned by society to a group that was persecuted, oppressed, those were people to whom she was *powerfully attracted.* I sensed the second meaning, but I didn't care to dwell on it. I told her I had every intention of taking advantage of her, that if she would say one word I would put down my brush. *"Please go on painting,"* she pleaded; she told me she was afraid of what she felt, that she was confused. *"There are two of me, you know."* I told her I only wished it were that simple, that I had counted seven or eight Sallys just in the last half hour.

I had covered her with jewelry, like Rembrandt his Saskia, and I sat her in a velvet chair wearing one of the fine gowns from the theatre wardrobe cabinet. She was silent for a while, and then she said, fiercely, *"I am going to burn down the theatre inside of me, Maury. I am going to burn it to the ground."* I wanted to tell her that, at that moment at least, the theatre was all around her, inside perhaps, but certainly outside also, that she had made my entire studio a set. Instead of this, I told her from across the room that I loved her and that I had every intention of winning her away from this Hutchins J.J. had told me about who, as far as I was concerned, was a ghost-lover. I told her that she should choose me over him, because I would not place any cause above the pleasure of being with her.

We had what you would call a lovers' quarrel that afternoon, though we had not yet become lovers. I remember that she said that artists are vain and frivolous people and that, however appealing she found me to be, she could never live with me, that I was selfish and self-indulgent. Did I ever think, she demanded, of the world that the Negroes I was painting had inherited? Had I in my imagination ever followed them to their work, to their homes? She too had once been a spoiled child of the city, she too had refused to see beyond the play world of the artist. But Hutchins had awakened her to the fact that her life was a fairy tale, that the stage, just like my studio, was a pleasure island in a sea of poverty and peonage and cruelty.

How can one remember the workings of an argument that raged so many years ago? We all know what happened in the years that followed. It is impossible for me to go back to that afternoon with innocence. I know I felt that whatever we said and did would be decisive for both of us. And I know too that I was arguing with myself as much as with her, and that it was the same for Sally. I felt exaltation that she cared so passionately about me; but at the same time, I felt I had already lost her. I remember that I told her she lived beautifully, that the role of the reformer did not suit her, that her gifts lay elsewhere. I had seen how her eyes shone when the final curtain fell; I had seen the ecstasy in them when the audience applauded her. I told her that sackcloth and ashes did not become her.

She strode up and down my studio, smoking, swearing, pulling off the fake jewelry and throwing it on my desk, jabbing her finger at me. She asked me how I could justify my life, how I would earn my keep, my right to be on this earth. This infuriated me then, as it would now. To whom must one justify one's life? The artist is a kept person, no more and no less than anyone else, I told her. The only morality to which the artist submits is the code that will allow him to go on working. The artist will do anything to buy freedom; he will amuse the wicked of the world to earn the freedom, the independence to create. And every creation mocks all that by which the wicked rule, visiting their cruelty and peonage and suffering on most of humanity. Every act of creation is made of the artist's blood and bone;

every creation is a defiance of bestiality and ugliness, all that she professed to abhor. And this she called vain and frivolous!

We didn't see one another for a long time after that. I went on painting. Sometimes, when I dozed, I saw the movie of the first part of my life. I remembered autumn, and winter, and snow, and Emil. And the synagogue on *Erev* Yom Kippur, the old men *dahvening,* the rabbi's voice off-key but strong, and my father swaying at my side, his glasses falling down his nose. And my mother covering the kitchen table with her strudel dough. Now I was in a region where the seasons did not change. The fates had given me a reprieve from life's grim business, had set me down in this studio in a white stucco building with a red thatched roof, in this tropical dream of long afternoons of painting, of working while the sky moved down, its blue darkening into black. There was a hush, a stillness, before the storms broke. The hot air thickened, and the light was swallowed up; and human flesh wilted on the bone, and thoughts, half-formed, wrapped the mind in a sodden fog.

One evening I found her sitting on the top step in the hallway. Carruthers hadn't come home yet; she'd knocked and knocked. *"I knew you'd come back eventually,"* she said. I unlocked the door; she came in, looking penitent. She sat down at the table and leaned her forehead on her hand, and her loose hair fell over her face. I got Cokes out for us; I sat down across from her. We sat there, not speaking. Then she laughed, and I was laughing too. She said she missed me. I reminded her that my door was always open to her. *"I can't make up my mind what I'm doing,"* she told me. She asked me if she could come back a while, if I still wanted to paint her.

It started all over again. We stumbled down the rickety steps of her apartment on Wisteria after a Sunday brunch of eggs and gin, on our way to rout Miller Lee out of his bed for partying. We shared her, our little sister, in a polyandrous bond of protectiveness and adoration. We sent her flowers; we took the first row in the theatre to cheer her triumph in *Lysistrata.* We were a united front against her critics. On closing night, we lifted her up on our shoulders in a human toast. Miller Lee invented a Sally Cocktail, composed of gin and bitters and vodka and quinine water. We drank down her spirit and lay, sprawled against cushions, on the bare floor of her living room, our eyes rolling free in our heads, our bodies turning to warm stone, our lips swollen and numb with Sally-praise. Carruthers composed a song cycle in her honor; J.J. created a rapturous Sally-dance.

That first night that she gave me to know I could lie down with her in love, I felt their presence; when her tender body, pale blue in the half-light, turned with mine, and when my tongue licked at her tears, they were there, in my gentleness with her; their kiss was in mine on her eyelids; and when I entered the moist meadows of her, when I lifted her hips and carried her with me up that steep bright climb. I remember J.J.'s grave look, and Carruthers' delicacy when he understood that I would not be leaving with him; and Miller Lee's soft *"g'night, y'all,"* and then the click of the lock in the closing door. She would never belong to me; I knew that most keenly when I was deep inside her, when she was all around me; I felt that sorrowing. In those hours, with the venetian blinds clacking against the window sill and the jasmine and pittisporum soaked with night dew burdening the blue smoke of oncoming light, I knew she was not mine, she was not ours, nor even her own, this living dream of woman who moved with me, so warm with desire that she wept of it. I could no more hope to reach and hold her than Gomez the Louisiana sky.

There were two Kennedys--Miller Lee's. And Hutchins'. Miller Lee kept vigil with Carruthers and me every evening of the week of the Cuban missile crisis. He wondered if we understood that we were about to turn into nice bright primary colors and gases at any minute. *"All-out, global war,"* he prophesied, *"they're gettin' their firecrackers all lined up for that final display."* And *"Whew, whew,"* when it appeared that it was over; followed by his having us to *know* that it could burst wide open at any moment again, and we'd best be prepared for our final judgment. Castro told Secretary-General U Thant that he would not allow any inspection of the Cuban bases. And he was demanding that we give up the Naval base in Guantánamo Bay. Castro had all to know that we are pirates. And we all know what pirates do. *"Mercy,"* Carruthers worried, and *"O Lord,"* he didn't want the whole world, and his Bechstein along with it, to turn into dust, no matter how lovely the colors might be. Kennedy, Miller Lee decreed, was a most dangerous man; watch we didn't let ourselves be carried away by all that charm and good looks, there was something in him itched for a showdown. And the Russians would love nothin' better. He'd go back to his People straight away, if he wasn't so ashamed to look them in the face. After all, he was as responsible as the next person; he had voted for the man. Not that he had much choice. *Nor* that Kennedy was doin' any more than obeyin' those invisible evil forces.

The other Kennedy, the champion of civil rights, the man who said that race has no part in our life or in our law, the man who had brought in hundreds of marshals and thousands of troops on the campus at Oxford, Mississippi so that James Meredith might be enrolled, *this* Kennedy we met at the Thanksgiving Party at Felix and Hannah Mannheim's. This Kennedy we met through Hutchins. *"We're living in very exciting times,"* Hutchins said softly. He spoke of the revolution in the South, of the sweeping changes that would be taking place before our very eyes. He was leaning against the mantelpiece, and the mirror was just over his head, and in it you could see Felix, tall and thin, in his armchair next to the fireplace, listening attentively as he stroked one of the household's hundred cats. You could see Miller Lee cross-legged on the carpet, his eyes watchful, never leaving Hutchins' face. And Carruthers bent over his plate of goodies. And Sally, intense, and clearly, clearly in love.

Carruthers had won me this invitation to the Mannheims, me and Miller Lee. They had met Hutchins through some other people; and that, of course, was why Sally was there. Carruthers explained why he revered, why he adored the Mannheims, why he would abide their talking about political, about public affairs when he would not abide this in anyone else, not even in Miller Lee, when there were more than two or three close friends gathered together. It simply wasn't done. But the Mannheims--well, Felix was a European, and a philosopher; he had had to contend with the Third Reich. He had lost his home; he was an immigrant, and a most honored guest here. Felix was a man of vast, if difficult experience. He understood things in a way that no one else could. And he never spoke but what he had long considered beforehand. And whatever he said, it was well worth attending to. And Hannah--well, she was Carruthers' mother-away-from-home; a lot of people had made her their adoptive mother. And when she went to the legislature and stood up in front of them all and said they were behaving and talking like Nazis, why, they'd best sit up and pay attention, this dear brave forthright woman knew what she was speaking about. *"I have never held with certain things you hear of as the Southern way of life."*

Hutchins was tall and graceful; he had the blonde good looks and easy smile of some of the fraternity boys I saw at Illinois. Except for his eyes, you would have thought of him as just another executive-lawyer type, which is what J.J. had called him. His eyes were silvery grey, and frank and compassionate. There was no reserve in him, no guile. When he spoke with you, you could not look at him, and you could not look away either. His manner was calm and at the same time hesitant. I had been prepared to meet a fanatic, an evangel, an angry prophet. Hutchins was none of these things. I remember thinking that he belonged exactly to that time and to that place. *"When he comes back,"* I had told Sally, *"you'll have to come to a decision."* Not long after that, she said that we should not see one another anymore.

"We're makin' progress," Hutchins told us. He spoke of the past year when he had lived in Atlanta, lived with Negroes, going from door to door talking to people, telling them over and over that they must vote, that it

would make all the difference in their lives, that the time was Now, that Negroes and whites must organize and march together, and boycott together, and that their children must share the same schoolrooms, that there was a man in the White House now who would support them in their struggle for what was theirs by birthright, their citizenship. There was no mistaking the powerful emotions in him, there was no mistaking the unabashed love for the people whose cause he served, and for the South, and for the three men he believed were wholly dedicated to The Cause--Martin Luther King, and John and Robert Kennedy. *"The hour has come,"* he said again and again; *"the time is Now."* What we had seen of it--the sit-ins, the marches, the boycotts, the voter registration drives--all these were only the beginning of a bloodless, a non-violent revolution.

He had broken with his family; he had quit law school; he was living with Negroes; he would live out the Christian principles by which he had been raised, and his kin would not forgive him for this. None of this could be helped. There was no turning back. The South was undergoing a sea-change; all its beauty and its suffering, its tragedy and its glory, made it the place, the only place, for real transformation. *"The South has history; it has a soul; its sons and daughters, Negroes and whites, are brothers and sisters in a common household. And at long last there is a man in the White House who fervently believes in the equality of all people everywhere. We will do all that has to be done, and he will not desert us."* Did we understand, Hutchins asked us, what this meant to people who had come out of slavery only to live for a hundred years in fear and darkness? Who had been terrorized by the club and the whip, by police dogs and lynch mobs, pushed to the back of buses and given the business-end of a broom when they were hired with a high school diploma, even with a college degree, did we understand this? People who had been reviled for nothing more than the color of their skin, taunted, mocked, humiliated, kept in conditions of hunger and squalor that you find in newspaper photographs of underdeveloped countries, did we understand what this meant? At long last we had a President who would see to it that the Bill of Rights was made a living reality, who would firmly assert the authority of the federal government over the authority of the separate states, a President who gave more than lip service to the freedom we won in the American revolution. He showed his determination in Montgomery; he showed it again in Oxford, Mississippi; he would *go on* showing it; he would turn a bright light on the places where the terrorists took their victims and beat them and whipped them and mutilated them and killed them. There wouldn't be any *way* the violators of the law could escape full justice anymore.

Miller Lee had quiet words with Hutchins. *"I want to believe in Kennedy,"* he said, *"and I am tryin'. But do you know, last month, if Krushchev ate the wrong thing for breakfast, we wouldn't be here discussin' domestic policy."* But Carruthers decreed that we had all had enough of politics for Thanksgivin', and that now that we had had our turkey and fixin's it was time for him to pay his respects to Hannah's piano, so come on, crowd around, and we'll all sing some Christmas carols.

Sally was away most week-ends after that. In early spring she told me that she and Hutchins would be married some time late that summer or in early fall. J.J. came around sometimes, and he missed her sorely; he spoke of her as if she'd been hypnotized by Hutchins, as if in some way we had to release her from his spell. *"She's got King fever, she's got Kennedy fever, she's caught it from him. Willin' to throw all that great talent to the stars. For what, for what indeed. You know yourself, Maury, what's waitin' for the Nigras when they move North, you've seen yourself how we live together without any fuss, how we've been goin' along right well, until all those agitators came around and stirred up a real mess o' trouble."* He'd go on and *on,* Carruthers sighed, if we'd let him; oughtn't we all to go to a picture show, or see what's doin' in campus town.

Gomez's fourth son was almost out of babyhood now. He raced over the concrete floor of the barracks in a second-hand walker Marta bought for him. There was no time for her to go to the meetings anymore, she told me, but that didn't matter; in less than a year they'd be gone, gone back to Texas where the *real* work was to be done. She would just mark time now until she could get back to her casework in San Antonio. John was having his season now. The colors of an evening sky, she said, of cypresses, of grapes in a white bowl, that's what touched him. Never the colors of human skin, even of his own. If you threw him in prison he wouldn't know or ask why; he'd only think of how he could paint the view from his cell window.

That night, when John walked me part-way back, he said that Marta had everything he had always lacked. Passion. Feeling. Will. This was what he had loved in her. He had asked her what it was she had loved in him, he told me, and she had said she couldn't remember anymore. *"It's worse now than it was before. Maybe it's this place. Something about it...it sucks you under. The heat in Texas is dry; you can tolerate it. Here, you feel you're living on the bottom of a lake. I had more energy before we came. Maybe I just want to think that. Anyway, it's ruined. Things always get ruined. We'll leave, but it won't get any better."*

It wouldn't get any better for any of us. Gomez was looking away from this place; it was time I did too. I walked around by myself that night after he left me. I breathed in the jasmine and the detritus rotting in the stream near our apartment house, and the wet, warm night winds, the sweetness mixed with decay. The heavy branches of the trees reached down to stroke my back and touch my neck as I walked; I caught my face more than once in a freshly-spun spider's web. That night was alive with the music of insects. I admitted to myself for the first time that I would be leaving, that I had a life before now, and that another life would have to come after it.

In early June we exhibited our works in the university gallery. Marta brought a following from the barracks; Vivian had a crowd of friends from, she said, as far away as Georgia. I had my loyal circle; I'd lost touch with Mark, but I sent him an announcement anyway. I wasn't surprised that he didn't come. There was Louisiana, there were its people, up there on the walls: the skies, the bayous, the live-oak and cypresses. The Negroes fishing. The Negroes walking in the early morning. And my portraits of Evelyn, and of Marta, and of Sally. Three of Sally.

She was wearing a yellow dress. Her black hair shone. *"There are three Sallys on the wall,"* she said. There were tears in her eyes. I told her she could choose, that I'd make her a gift of one of them, the one that she liked best. When she took my hand, her incense was all around me. I remembered the slope of her back when she lay turned away from me, the press of her warm hips against my belly. I remembered how the wine of her sang in my blood.

There was a little pond in the copse of pines and evergreens outside the old science building. On Sunday evenings it was the most private place on campus. She held my hand and walked very close to me. The sun was still so bright at supper-time that I saw jewelled spirals in her hair, and silver wheels turning in her eyes. She was a living daffodil floating next to me. The sun was in her voice too. A steady fire.

It was very hard for J.J., she said. *"I never cottoned to magic in any person except you,"* he had told her. But she had never claimed that anyone was magic! She had been searching all her life for what it was she was meant to do. And she had found it.

"I've been arrested," she told me. *"First time for everything."* It was on Independence Day, in a demonstration at Gwynn Oaks, in Maryland. She sat next to me on the grass, spreading her yellow skirts around her, and she was saying that when she was a child she played with the things of a child, but now she was a woman, a grown woman. Politics over art, she was saying. It had to be, a person has to grow up. A life of action over a life of play. *"But even politics isn't everything. Only love, only love is everything."* I understood that none of this cruelty was intended, that she was not even aware of how what she was saying sounded to me. She was too full of the

life that she had chosen. I told her that I wished her well. I was thinking that nothing is everything, that there is no everything.

They were to be married on Thanksgiving Day by a Unitarian minister in Belle Ville. It was her only home, Sally said. Her family had expressed their disappointment in her; she doubted they would come to the wedding. In late August, she and Hutchins were among the hundreds of thousands who made the Freedom March in Washington. Not long after school opened at the end of September, the Mannheims held a party for them, to announce their engagement and to tell their plans for the future. Sally would stay on campus until February, when she was to receive her Master's degree in Theatre Arts. Then she would join Hutchins "in the field." They were going to work in Mississippi the following summer, and to stay working in the Movement for at least two years after that. Then they wanted to serve in the Peace Corps.

The Mannheims' house overflowed with people that late September, a gathering of Belle Ville town and gown, of people whose paths crossed one another's only at the Mannheims' front door. Felix and Hannah believed in mixing people from the university with business people and lawyers and doctors and sales clerks from around town, ardent segregationists with moderates and radicals, Eastern with Western Europeans, foreigners with America Firsters; in the Mannheims' house there were many mansions. There was teasing, laughter, the exchange of civilities. But the air was electric with the shock waves of the murder of Medgar Evers that June, the Freedom March, and--little more than a week before--the deaths of four Negro girls in a church that had been bombed in Birmingham. Miller Lee was full of the news that the Senate had ratified the test-ban treaty; but when he tried to talk with people about this they so much as told him that nuclear bombs and trips to the moon and fallout shelters were all very far removed from the real issues, namely, what was going on down home. A lady from South Africa held forth on the innate inferiority of colored people; and Hannah chose to argue with her. A little circle gathered around them. Another formed around Felix and an executive from one of the oil corporations--they had begun by talking about the cold war but from this they moved to the development of the Southern economy, and from there to the plight of the Southern poor, and from there to the issue of segregation. *"The North,"* someone said, *"is tryin' to make the South into a battleground again, tryin' to move in on us again, stirrin' up, agitatin', usin' the Nigras for their own purposes."* Someone else spoke of how well the Negroes and whites had got on before all this agitation, and said that it was well known that Martin Luther King was being encouraged by power-hungry politicians in Washington, and that any bombings in churches and fire hoses and police dogs turned onto crowds and shootings from ambush were the clear responsibility of the crowd in Washington; the blood of deluded colored people would be on *their* hands. A number of people argued that this was too simple-minded a view, that people on *both* sides were using the colored and the young students of both races, Northerners and Southerners, for their own purposes. *"You can't blame everythin' on the Kennedys,"* one woman said, *"it's just too easy."* Another woman said she thought highly of them, that they were refined people, whatever their political views. Earlier this month, she reminded everyone, they had their tenth wedding anniversary. They were a good couple, devoted to their children, *that* could not be denied. And how sad it was last month, when little Patrick Bouvier died. *"Now if only Mother Rose could have had a mishap like that some forty 'n' more years ago,"* her husband laughed. Later I saw Hutchins closeted with this man, engaged in earnest discussion.

Sally wore a white tunic, and gold bracelets high on her arms. They had thought of marrying on Christmas, she said, but the Mannheims' children would be home then and it would be an imposition to have the reception in their home, with family there. *"We'll only live apart from one another one little month,"* she said. Hutchins advised us all to look our fill of her all clean and brushed. *"She has no idea of how she'll have to live,"* he said. *"You're lucky if you can get to brush your teeth every day, never mind get a shower once a week!"* She laughed, *"He's still tryin' to scare me off."*

The Fellowship had run out some months before, and here I was, and here Gomez was. Carruthers told me, *"You* can *stay on, you know. No law says you have to pick up 'n' go off. B'sides, where will you go--back to the Midwest?"* I shook my head. Chicago was Emil in his wheelchair rolling down Clark Street at my side. And the Mexicans leaning against the glass windows of the bars, their brandywine faces, their eyes of black narcissus, their brownstone lips parting over the white flares of their smiles. And my mother in her rocker by the window. Whatever I had to say about them I had said, and it had given me passage to this place. And now the Negroes by the lakes in early morning, Roger Cunningham and Andrew Harris and Will Jackson and the others; and Marta with the red lights flashing in her eyes and in her thimble; and Sally, turning towards me, on apricot velveteen--they had said to me whatever it was they had wanted to say. Those canvasses were my harvest. Whomever it belonged to, it didn't belong to me. I went in to Buford, the head of the art department, and told him I'd like to donate my work to the university. *"That makes two of you,"* he said. *"Now I have your humans and Gomez's skies. We can see ourselves as others see us, eh? You've both been very generous."* Of course I'll never know how Buford meant that.

Marta had a job with a social agency. She said that John could stay home and chase his four sons around the house for a while, or get a job himself and hire a nursemaid; she'd had enough of sitting by while he painted the sky, the sky was falling down.

They left the campus in late October. I helped them move out of the barracks and onto a U-Haul truck. It was a terrible day, the sun burning the senses right out of our skulls, so that we sweated and shouted at each other, carrying bedding and books and runaway little boys back and forth in that devouring heat, thirsting, drinking soda, thirsting again. Nothing can quench that kind of thirst. We ate Marta's tuna fish sandwiches at the sink. It was piled with stuff, dishes and rusted tools, a lampshade, a bath brush, a cellophane bag full of diapers, our Coke bottles. The sight of it took the heart out of you; I swore I'd never get married after I saw that sink that day.

Marta made sure that I put their new address in my wallet. She took down my parents', and said she'd write to me. She said that people shouldn't lose each other, and that maybe we'd meet again. Gomez shook my hand, and then punched me in the shoulder. He and Marta looked straight ahead once they got the car started; but the boys waved, all four of them, until the truck disappeared.

I stopped going to the lakes in the morning. I knew I'd stay around for the wedding, that much I had promised Sally. I marked time at the library, and I took in a few classes. One week-end in November, Carruthers and I decided to go in to New Orleans. We had a ride that would be leaving that Friday afternoon.

You remember trivial details with perfect clarity. I had slept late that morning. When I finally did get up, I cleaned the apartment and then I took our wash over to the Laundromat. It was pouring, so I packed everything in a plastic bag. I didn't pay much attention to the time, but it must have been somewhere between noon and one o'clock. I was sitting in the Laundromat reading, reading, I remember, Pirandello's *Six Characters in Search of an Author,* when a woman came running in, soaking wet and crying, and I thought, *"My God, maybe she's lost a child, or had an accident, or is crazy."* And she screamed at us: *"They've killed the President! You-all hear? Somebody shot the President in Dallas, and he's dead! You-all hear? Kennedy is dead! They just killed him in Dallas!"* And she ran to the drugstore next to us, this town crier, and then to the barber shop and the hardware store, and on down the line, to tell everyone that the President of the United States had just been assassinated.

There was no wedding at Thanksgiving, not even a Thanksgiving at Thanksgiving, only a small gathering at the Mannheims'; the voices were muted; all you heard was the dull talk of the newly bereaved. Sally's face looked beaten; her eyes brimmed over. She said they couldn't think of getting married so soon after, that they'd wait, now, till after Christmas. *"I grew up last week-end,"* she said. *"I think we all did."* She quoted a line from one of Edna St. Vincent Millay's poems: "Childhood is the kingdom where nobody dies." She said that it was impossible that he was dead; she asked us if she was dreaming all this.

Hannah said she could not remember a harder time in America. Hutchins, head down, arms folded, was standing again in front of the mirror over the mantelpiece. They had warned him not to go to Dallas, he said to Felix. Many of his associates were convinced that it was a right-wing conspiracy, that there were many, many people involved, and that all this business with Lee Harvey Oswald and Jack Ruby and Officer Tippitt was just show business. People in high places were involved, he said, and some say this isn't the end of it. Felix shook his head; in their grief, he said, people tend to see ghosts; in any case, there would be a review of the assassination by a panel of honest, irreproachable men. Hutchins wondered bitterly if there was such a person. But, Felix asked him, surely you do trust some people implicitly? For instance, John Kennedy's own brother? Surely, if there had been a conspiracy, Robert Kennedy would not hesitate to expose it? And Hutchins said he no longer knew how *any* person might choose, when given the choice between family loyalty and civic duty. When he closed his eyes at night, he said, all he could see were these posters that the Freedom marchers carried so high, with the three Freedom Fighters on them--John Kennedy and Martin Luther King and Robert Kennedy. The Negroes believed in these three, believed that they were the defenders of their faith in justice and human brotherhood. The message they had brought to all those shacks on those back roads, and all the run-down neighborhoods in the cities, was that they had a President now who was firmly resolved to enforce the laws of this nation, to see to it that they would enjoy the rights that were theirs by birthright, that had for so long been denied them. These three were to have led them out of their bondage and their suffering. Could anyone wonder that these people would feel he had been killed by the very forces that had for so long oppressed them? What could he tell them now? Yet he would not desert them. The battle lines had been drawn, the struggle must go forward.

And Felix sighed. So much vitality, so much talent, snuffed out in a single, terrible moment, torn out of the world! *"We have lost so much,"* he said, laying his hand on Hutchins' shoulder. *"A part of ourselves,"* Hutchins answered. *"More than we even know now. But the Cause is greater than any one person, even the person of the President. King will lead us, King's dream will not die, not even now, not ever. And there are other Kennedys. And the circle of men he had gathered around himself will go on working. Fighting. The Movement is sweeping across the South; it will be felt in the most remote hamlet in the country."* They had come too far, he said, to turn back. They would go on.

"Johnson is a good man," someone was saying. And someone else replied, *"That remains to be seen." "I can't believe that John Kennedy is gone,"* this one said, then that one echoed. *"Johnny, we hardly knew ye,"* a woman murmured. There were others vexed that he might now be canonized, that streets and schools and airports and hospitals would be named after him. But they were stared down. The violence was still too new, too raw, for engagement in the old arguments. *"Charisma,"* Felix told us all, *"carries a high risk, for the one who possesses it, and for all those who are touched by it. It can make all the difference. But it is a danger, just the same."* And Sally said softly, *"We have a legacy."* And Hannah sighed, *"Ja, but it would be better still to have the man."*

We had witnessed his death as many times as the reel of film was played over; we saw him wave; we saw him turn; then we saw him slump over. There was that crazy veering of the camera. Hutchins and Sally had gone to Washington to mourn, to walk past his bier. The rest of us had mourned in front of the glass screen, had become part of the crowds lining the streets that Monday, viewing the funeral procession from the White House to St. Matthew's Cathedral. We saw the flag draping the casket flutter in the wind as they carried it up the steps. We watched the chiefs of state, the heads of government, the monarchs and dignitaries enter the cathedral: Prince Philip and Prime Minister Alec Douglas-Home, General Charles De Gaulle, Emperor Haile Selassie, Prime Minister Lester Pearson, Crown Prince Akihito, President Eamon De Valera, King Baudouin, Chancellor Erhard, First Deputy Anastas Mikoyan....

We watched the Cardinal bless the coffin: "For those who are faithful to You, oh Lord, life is not taken away; it is transformed."

We saw the casket borne from the cathedral, the pallbearers lifting it up to the caisson. We saw Jacqueline Kennedy lean down to whisper something to her son and take a pamphlet from his hand. We saw the little boy salute his dead father. We saw the heads of state, the visiting foreign dignitaries waiting for the cars to bring them in procession to the cemetery. We heard the muffled drums beating in the clear, bright air. The horses drawing the caisson began their trot. In the silence, we heard their hoofs clacking smartly, in keeping with the drum-beat. The family cars followed.

The camera swept over the procession from Arlington National Cemetery. Lincoln Memorial stood majestic in the background.

We saw the funeral cortege cross over Arlington Memorial Bridge and enter the cemetery. The bagpipes wailed. The Irish Guard was standing at the graveside. The jet planes zoomed overhead, shattering the silence of the skies. The President's personal plane flew over the grave, and dipped its wings in a last tribute to the Chief Executive. It had borne him on many missions.

We heard the Cardinal praying in his dry, nasal tones: "Oh, God, through Whose mercy souls of the faithful find rest, be pleased to bless this grave and Thy holy angels to keep it...."

We saw the face of his widow transfigured by grief and loss. We heard the 21-gun salute. Then they played taps, and the wrong note sounded--a sob, a flaw, a human break in the voice of the final farewell.

White-gloved hands fluttered in the bright sunlight, folding the flag swiftly, neatly. It was passed from hands to hands until it was placed in the hands of the widow.

The Cardinal's voice surged in his last blessing of "the *won*derful man we bury here today."

We saw the flare of the eternal light. And then Jacqueline Kennedy turned to leave the grave, and she stumbled, and then caught her balance. She leaned on the arm of Robert Kennedy.

At Felix's that last Thanksgiving, we looked in one another's eyes, and we saw these films playing there. And then we went home to our Kennedy dreams.

They were married on New Year's Eve, and I gave her my last kiss, a chaste kiss, the kiss of kin to kin at time of parting. Carruthers had gone back home for the holidays, so when I left Belle Ville a few days later there was no one to see me off. I took a bus to Hammond, and then the train back to Chicago. After a few weeks with my parents, I went to Brownsville. I've been moving back and forth over the border since then. This kind of work gives me just the release and the freedom I need so that I can go on painting. The rest of the Sixties and into the Seventies, it seemed from where I lived that the whole country was set on giving a continual fireworks display, the greatest show on earth, maybe the last show on earth. The rioting in the cities, the marches and demonstrations, the steel birds of war pouring liquid fire down on a country not much more than the size of two Louisianas.... I used to read the papers from time to time, but they seemed like horror comics to me, they seemed unreal. When I read about those brutal murders of the three civil rights workers in Mississippi that first June, I dreamed about them both night after night, about Sally and Hutchins; and again, when Martin Luther King was assassinated in April and Robert Kennedy in June of the same year, I had these violent dreams. I kept thinking of the poster Hutchins told Felix about on that Thanksgiving in 1963. Well, people have been talking about conspiracies ever since. Some of the Anglos I know who live in Mexico can talk about these things endlessly. Some are convinced that Cuba was the issue; some say it was the Mafia; others insist it had to do with the Movement. What do I think? To tell the truth, I don't know what to think. I never did. I listen, and I go on painting Indians.

Sometimes I play with the idea of looking up Gomez, but I probably won't ever go through with it. He belonged to another life. They all did. The only name that came up in all those years between then and now is Miller Lee Sexton's. I went over to the university to see an art show, and I read that Miller Lee was giving a series of lectures on some archaeological subject. The announcement said that he's teaching at some private college up in New England. If I hadn't seen his name on the poster, I would have walked right by. You could never have recognized him from the photograph. He doesn't wear his hair Indian-style any more. He's grown a beard. And his eyes could have been anybody's eyes. But that's probably because, as his People know, the eye of the camera is an Evil Eye; there are only ghosts on film.

"speak of no man's happiness   Till, without sorrow, he hath passed the goal of life."

--*Oedipus the King*
Tr. J.T. Sheppard

Passing the Goal

Saturday, sweet free Saturday, with all the trashy things to do she had put by during the week. The mesh bag of delicates dangling from the hamper, waiting to be rinsed out. The recipe for gumbo scotch-taped to the kitchen cabinet for that big pot for the crowd after the game, that had to be set up by late morning. And three letters to write. And all that ironin'. B. J.'d best go easy tonight on the liquor and on *her*, she had all those papers to grade over the week-end. Lord God, what would she do without Izola comin' this morning to pick up this mess around here, and her with an appointment for a wash-and-set at noon. Izola could make up a tuna salad sandwich for her to have under the dryer. And there'd be time for one letter, Mother's, to get written there.

Nine twenty-five. Up, *up* you lazy girl. She forced her eyes open, her honeybee eyes B.J. said they were, and she laughed by herself there, in the bed, her rip-roarin' laugh accordin' to that madman, never *mind* rememberin' the outrageous things he said about the rest of her. She stretched, waved her hands at herself, and then brought them down over her breasts and caressed their plumpness, and teased her nipples until they started to harden. Then she spanned her waist, and stretched again, and lay her hands over her sleep-warm center, feeling the muscles tighten deliciously. In the slow tide of pleasure, her back arched slightly. There was a low drumming in her thighs; she could all but hear it.

Yellow hair and honeybee eyes, and down beneath her sweet surprise. A new little rhyme every day, he promised her. Oh, no way to start out! She was about to close her eyes again when she heard someone opening the refrigerator door.

"Izola? That you?"

"Nome. It's Ruby. My mother cain't come today. I'm startin' in the kitchen, if it's all right with you."

She sighed. Now she had to get up, truly. "Never mind the fridge, do the stove first, Ruby. And put some coffee on for me, first, hear?"

"Yes'm."

Jane got herself up out of bed and into her robe. On her way to the bathroom, she called down the hallway:

"It isn't *like* your mother not to call and tell me! She sick?"

"Nome. She said you'd understand, she'll be here next Sattiday."

"If she's not sick, then what? Never mind. I'll talk to you once I'm dressed."

She took her first shower for the day, rubbing her scalp without mercy because she knew she'd be having her hair done, and got into a blouse and the wool suit skirt. Felt chillier today than most Novembers. She called Ruby to turn on the gas heater, and stripped down her bed. She could take the laundry out back after breakfast, if one of those fool machines was workin' and everybody else could be counted on for oversleeping more than *she* did.

Ruby had set out the cup and saucer, and plugged in the toaster, and remembered to make the dark roast coffee. She was rubbing at the sides of the stove with steel wool. That girl used the *littlest* scraps of steel wool! She moved faster than her mother, but she missed a lot of corners too. You had to keep after her more. Not that it helped; it was better to be still about it. She was temperamental. Jane favored Izola, favored that generation. The last of its kind, that's sure. But she had to admire Ruby. The girl wasn't *about* to saddle herself down with a pack of babies and clean out everybody's stove in town for the rest of her life. She'd done well in high school, and now she was takin' courses at the university. She planned on bein' a nurse, Izola said, or maybe a medical technologist. And she wouldn't stay down South, most probably.

"What happened to your mother?" If Izola had come, now, she'd have remembered to pick up a morning paper for her.

"She's at church. At the services."

"Oh, Ruby, I'm sorry. Did you have a death in the family?"

"Nome. Not exactly."

"Whatever do you mean, 'not exactly'?"

Ruby had her head all the way inside the stove, so her voice came back muffled:

"They're havin' services over what happened yestidday. Leastwise, *our* church is. Maybe some others, I don't know."

"Oh, you mean the assassination. You mean they're havin' services for President Kennedy."

"Yes'm. Guess that's it."

"So she sent you."

"Well, she don't like to let people down. She sent me yestidday evenin' to serve over at the LeBlancs, they had a party before the high-school game last night. And I'm to stop over at one more place after I finish here. *If* I get everythin' done right, she says."

"Don't you worry about that, Ruby. You get done what you can by twelve-thirty, one, then you go on ahead. Your mother likes to meet her obligations, I know. And anyway, there's not enough to keep you goin' on much past that. I want you to vacuum and dust, and clean up the bathroom when you finish out here. That's about all. Oh, and make up a batch of tuna salad for you and me for lunch, will you? I want to bring mine to the beauty parlor. You lock up on your way out, you'll be through long before I get back."

Thank the Lord for coffee. She'd watched TV half the evenin' last night, and now she looked forward to the papers. There'd be a lot said, a lot to read about. Bloodstains on her stockings and her new suit. She didn't even change her suit for the swearin'-in. Not that you could blame her. With everything else she was feelin', she must have wanted, some part of her, to show those bloodstains. To have all that you love taken away just like that. One shot out of a rifle, and it's over. Too soon to feel it yet, to know what happened. In Washington, she wouldn't even leave his casket long enough to come down from the presidential plane by the passenger ramp, they showed you that. She stayed with him on the cargo lift, and then jumped on down after it. And when she went to open the Navy ambulance door, she couldn't get it right, and the Attorney General had to open it for her. So young and fashionable and rich and smart, with all that glory, look what it gets you. She'll have two orphans to raise now. Well, it happens to the poor, too; it happened to that officer Tippitt; he was a father too. And was it Marina Oswald's fault that she had a crazy Communist for a husband, that he had to go and assassinate the President? Three women without their men now in one day.

Just as well not to read the papers. Besides, there wasn't time. She had to get that laundry goin'. If Mother had called *up*, now, instead of writing that long, tormented letter, she'd never be off the phone in time for her shampoo-and-set. Anyway, having to write, she'd be able to choose her words, though she couldn't for *life* think now what to say to her.

It wasn't any help to have the dryer full on so you didn't have to listen to all the racket. Place was busy today, probably because of the game tonight. State U only played Hampton once a year, and you *know* that Castle Hill Drive will be lined from here to Bayou Fourche with cars full o' whiskey-wavin' fans. *Goin' to the game*? Tristan was askin' everybody. *Folks goin' to the game tonight*? He was *just* full of it today, you could tell the way he shampooed you.

"*Tris*tan! I asked for a shampoo, not a scalpin'!"

"Come on, Miss Jane, you're not feelin' that tender today for me, are y'? All you girls act the same. It's shameless. Not even Elizabeth Taylor'd melt down for ol' Tris, without all this fussin'."

"Not if she knew what you do to a lady's scalp, she wouldn't. Leave me some hair there for Ada to work on, hear?"

"See she don't turn you into a lollipop again. Had you so teased out last time, you in your toreador pants that day, I almost put a cellophane wrapper around your head."

"Fresh. Careful I don't put one around your *mouth*."

While Ada did her with the big rollers, she put words together for her letter. Ada never did put much stock in talkin'. She had her troubles, you had yours, why run on and on about it. You just tell her what was on for the evenin', and how you'd need it for the week, maybe even say somethin' about your dress, the woman had a genius for matchin' a hair style to an occasion. Tris dancin' all over the shop, runnin' at the mouth but never droppin' a stitch, gettin' the shampoos and manicures done, sweepin' up the hair, pickin' up a comb-out. Ada all crisp and starchy, movin' the customers right along; between the two of them they turned over a good business.

Dear Momma, of *course* you know B.J. and I will be up there for Thanksgiving, I don't know why you even *asked*. School's out by noon Wednesday, and we'll be up there that night. I want to help you stuff the turkey, and set up all the fixin's Thursday morning, just like always. I can just taste that oyster stuffing! You distress yourself too much over Will. You know there isn't anything new about it. He and Daddy have been at one another for as long as I can remember. Sometimes I think they couldn't do without raising up such a storm. It sounds worse than it really is. I wish you wouldn't think of yourself in the middle of it. It's two different temperaments, is all, and that's not a woman's fault. I know you miss me, I miss you too, but you know there aren't that many miles between us. They didn't drive me out of the house with all their fighting, you mustn't think that, no more than they drove out Lee. He had to get out on his own is all, just like I did. We grew up, Momma, it wasn't anything anyone could *help*.

Lord, God, it was goin' to be different for her and B.J., it just *had* to be. Thank you, Momma, thank you for teachin' me by your own sufferin' what comes first, the man and his woman. Children can tear you apart, if you let them. I'm resolved to *keep* all that laughin' and good cookin' and good times, just takin' off when it pleases you, to go fishin' or bicyclin' together, or to a movie, or over to New Orleans to see an opera. I'm resolved to never,

never let it die, this feelin' between him and me. Oh, that crazy man! Does what*ever* he takes into his head. He'd get up at three in the mornin' and start makin' crêpes, if he had a mind to it. Last week-end, said he had to do somethin', and just painted my apartment door flamingo. Playin' his records so loud you could hear the music in the next parish. They'll be throwin' me out on the street if he doesn't behave. Not that I care. When I'm with him, there's nothin' in the world that's beyond my power. Other people say they can feel that thing between us, like electricity cracklin' in the room. And I believe it. Used to be like that between Momma and Daddy, *she* said so. Why would she make it up? She let Will do it, she let life do it, poor Momma, she's never been very strong. You can have it all, if you just put a mind to it, all that lovin' and the pretty babies too, if you set your mind to it. Saw a picture of her, holdin' baby Caroline by the window, teachin' her something, *Kennedys don't cry*, I think it was. Then came the little boy. Read that they had their suppers together in the White House, with a sheet of plastic under his high chair, the four of 'em havin' supper like any ordinary family. Came as close to havin' everything as anyone could *come* on this green earth. Wealth and position, power and love, good looks and charm and good times sailin' and horseback ridin' and playin' ball. She said she was determined to do it right, the family part. They were married ten years, but you could see there was still that thing between them.

I'm gonna make me a life, Momma, as good as it can get. Honey, I don't know what to tell you, what's done is done, you just didn't reach high enough. *I want you to be happy, Missy*, she'd say, and she meant it, and it hurts, because daughters think that about their mothers too. It's not easy to go off knowin' you can't change it for them, and they can't change it for themselves. Not natural to worry over this too much, if you don't take the chance when it presents itself, you can just say good-*bye* to any future. Even when he was four, five years old, you could see it was bad between him and Daddy. They're both so stubborn, so much alike, when you think of it, well, what *do* you *do*? Give him a good spankin' every time, until he learns it doesn't pay to be a mule. But Momma was never much for punishment. Poor Momma, she didn't see back then, when there was still time to change it, where it was all goin'. If *that* dies, what's between you, what's left to *live* for, what means *any*thing? Wouldn't stay in the same house with a man, never mind the same *bed*, with that feelin' dead. B.J., I told him, I don't know where it came from, I don't know how we found it, but I'll die before I'll let it die, I'll kill you and myself before I'll let that happen! *I'll have to pass up the pleasure*, he said. And I asked him, What *do* you mean? And he said, *Seein' you all murderous bright, in a long white gown maybe, with a big dagger in this fair hand, all lighted up with fury, your eyes turnin'* *into orange flames, and all your yellow hair tumblin' down your shoulders, you'd be splendid, Lady Jane, I'd have to put your mind to somethin' quick.* And I asked him, Like what, B.J.? B.J., can't you ever be serious? So what does he say to me, but *like this and this and* this, *this is* no *time to be serious*!

Time was up. Tris took the rollers out. Ada was combing a woman with frost streaks through the sides of her black hair, and the woman was speaking so distinctly that even Tris kept still, to listen.

"Doubt they'll cancel so late, but you never know."

"Haven't heard a word," Ada said. She flipped the shoulder-length hair up, Jackie Kennedy style. You had to be young, younger than that woman was, to carry that length really well.

"All I read in the paper today is cancellations. Harvard-Yale game called off, right after they heard about it. Air Force Academy against Colorado cancelled. Princeton against Dartmouth, Duke against North Carolina. Nothin' goin' on at West Point or Annapolis today, either. Wyoming against Texas Western cancelled. Maybe even Michigan State against Illinois. More. Boston U against Boston College. None of those that'll play will be seen on TV, either. Be all news from here on, through Monday."

Must be one of the university people's wives. Maybe related to one of the coaches.

If they cancelled now, she'd have enough gumbo for two weeks to dispose of. Would've told them by now, probably. Game or no game, B.J.'d be there, and that's what counted. Fact, she hadn't had him to herself for a long time now. Had that mania to perform, loved to have a crowd around him, just ate it up the way they laughed at his stories, all that drinkin' and screamin' and talkin', might be good to have just the two of them left alone tonight, curled up on the sofa.

"Be a big funeral to watch Monday," Ada said. "We'd be closed, anyway. Your school open, Miss Jane?"

"No. They closed the parochial schools right away. Maybe *that* decided it, I guess. We heard about it just after early dismissal, that Monday's off. What about the store?"

"Stores'll all be open, far as I know."

"I'm sleepin' all day," Tristan announced. "Not even no big TV state funeral's gonna get *this* boy out of bed on his day off!"

"Now, look who went and painted her door bright pink since I was last here!"

"Momma! Momma, how long you *been* here?"

"Careful, don't let me mess that beautiful hair-do. Oh, Missy, it's good, good, *good* to see you!"

They hugged and hugged, and Jane was so flustered she dropped her key ring. Finally, and clumsily, arms still around one another like school chums, they got inside.

"Look at you!" they both called out together, and then her mother held her arms out wide, and took Jane inside.

"Wait, wait, let me look. My, you're trim and lovely, as always!" Jane stood back to admire the pert little grey felt hat, the small gold earrings, the grey checked wool suit and shiny black pumps. Intoxication cologne misted the air that was just now thickening with the aroma of her gumbo.

"You haven't been cryin'!" But she could see that her mother *had* been, though it was necessary for her just then to pretend she had not heard mention of the fact. Jane just let her go about plumpin' the pillows on the couch and settin' a picture straight on the wall. She followed her when she wandered out to the kitchen, finally, to lift the lid off the pot and study the gumbo. Then she set her down, and busied herself getting ice out, fixing a Coke for them both. When she sat down across from her at the table, her Mother reached out and ran her hand over the hair smoothed back from her temple, and then stroked her cheek. Her eyes were very soft. And her voice.

"I do owe you an apology for that letter. I should never indulge myself so."

"Momma, if you don't have *me* to listen to you, who do you have?

Don't worry yourself over it. I just wish I could make it right, you know? Are they speakin'?"

"Just barely." Her Mother looked for words in her Coke glass, and reached in with her fourth finger to give the ice cubes floating at the top a good stirring. She sighed, very lightly. Very lightly.

"It's such a conso*la*tion to me to know you're settled in, doin' what you want to do. I think of that while your father's holdin' forth, while Will's tearin' up the house with his rages. It gives me such pure pleasure. 'Nuff of that now. What're you doin' this week-end?"

"We're goin' to the game tonight. And I have a mess of papers to grade. We'll be gettin' Monday off, what with the assassination, so I'll have a little time to catch up. I was about to write you this afternoon. Truly, I was."

"Sweet Missy. I know it, know you were."

"How was the drive down?"

"Barely noticed. What with my own thoughts."

"That fog, I mean. It was miserable yesterday. But the sun's about to break through."

"The air seems so strange this week-end, Missy! Not that people say much about it one way or the other. What do you think? I don't know *what* to think. It's an ugly thing. Ugly. Your Daddy says he's not surprised, says he had it comin'. Nobody's about to mourn, you know? But it's so *bru*tal, don't you think? What are people sayin' down here? They were always so much more tolerant than up in our part of the state, you know that."

"Hadn't *thought* of that, you're right, they are. But not all *that* tolerant. Why, I had two or three clappin' their hands when the news was announced. Heard it happened in the other classes too. But my little third graders, Momma? Little eight-year-olds? It's just not right. I told them so, too."

"Hard tellin' *what* will happen next. Your Daddy says things won't change all that much. You know how he hates Johnson, says he's a traitor, that that's worse than Kennedy, because you could never expect more from *him* than what we got. But one of our *own*?"

"Oh, Momma, it's all so far off. You know? I mean, what does all this have to do with *us*? With *anybody*?"

"I know it. I've never been anything for politics. Still, it stays in your mind. I didn't even cook supper last night, what with your Daddy and Will out late. Just made myself a sandwich, fixed me a Coke, and sat there watchin' that television. Can't say why, just watched it until it was bedtime. *Past* bedtime."

"I did, too. Didn't talk to a soul, and nobody called me, either. I tried to reach B.J. But Fridays he's hardly ever in, anyway. Last night was no different. Can't imagine *what* he'll say. Some crazy thing. You know B.J., he can't be serious for long." She laughed and hugged herself. Her Mother laughed too, those three little notes she sang, high to low, when she was enjoyin' something with you. She reached across the table and took Jane's hand and opened it, studied each and every finger, then closed it again. And clasped it.

"Missy, I just want you to be happy."

"I know. And I *am*, more than I ever dreamed a girl could be! Oh, Momma, that man has me *goin'*! You know?"

"I know. Make it so you keep it that way, hear? Lord, I don't know what's got into me lately!"

"Oh, Momma. Honey."

A big tear was rolling down her Mother's face, making a path down from the corner of her eye to her chin. Her eyes were brimming, and it embarrassed her so. Jane went into the living room, quick, to fetch her pocketbook, and her Mother hugged her waist with one hand when she brought it back, and reached in with the other for a handkerchief.

"Wait." She patted her face dry, patted her eyes, and then took a big drink of her Coke. "I'll be all right now. Honestly. Time in your life you'd cry over steppin' on a bug."

Jane kissed her Mother's cheek, then sat down across from her and waited.

"I know it's gonna be different for you, I just know it. You'd be amazed at what a comfort that is. When you really love someone, their happiness brings you yours. Ridiculous. You comin' with B.J. for Thanksgivin', yet somehow I couldn't wait."

"I'm glad you didn't. Stay, Momma, stay the night. You like our friends. It'd do you good. I don't like to think of you drivin' back this afternoon in a state."

"No. No indeed, I'll be all right. Your father and I have some place to go tonight, a big party that was planned back a while ago. I don't dare to miss it. Really. Just seein' you is the best cure ever."

"Wish I could persuade you."

"Not this week, darlin' girl, thanks anyways. I must admit your gumbo's startin' to smell mighty temptin'."

"Make you a sandwich? Ruby came today, can't you tell? Otherwise, you'd find me all over this apartment! She made me up a batch of tuna salad."

Her Mother shook her head. "Couldn't get anything *down* me at this time. What happened to Izola, she sick again?"

"They had some service at her church today. Because of yesterday."

"I suppose the colored really feel they lost somebody big. Indeed, iI suppose they did. Up home the whites hate him for the very same reasons the colored love him."

I suppose they did. Up home, the whites hate him for the very same reasons the colored love him."

"I suppose."

"Hard to believe he's dead. He had real vitality. Hard to believe you can cut all that life down so sudden."

"Whatever you think of them, of the whole bunch of them, they really had a good time, didn't they? She knew how to dress *up*, didn't she? They had the best of everything, you know? Parties and dancin' and laughin' and all, and at the same time the most important people in the world comin' there, to play concerts and all. Not just musicians, but painters, writers, all the important artists goin' in and out, feelin' at home up there in that big house."

"Pool parties. Pushin' each other in the water. I felt two ways about it, that it was just a bit disgraceful, given their position. But all the same, they were young, and good-lookin', and they knew how to have good times. You have to admire that in people, Missy. Government doesn't have to be so *dull*."

"She'll have to move out now. I don't know what's comin', but, oh, my, it will be different!"

"Yes. Never mind what she was, what she believed in and all, she's a woman first. A wife and a mother. She has to raise those two babies by herself now. Look what little difference it makes, to have all that money and influence! What good's it do her?"

"Wasn't too long ago she lost a baby, too. Why, just this past summer they buried him, didn't they? And her first-born died too, a little girl, never even did *have* a name."

"She must be very strong. Some say they didn't care much about each other. But I don't believe it. You know how people like to talk."

"I don't believe it either. Why, Momma, anyone could see how de*vo*ted they were! Did you see that look on her face at the swearin'-in? So *lost*. Like a woman just is, when the man she loves is taken away from her. How can she stand it, however will she stand it? Poor thing. I feel for her."

Even as she said this, Jane felt taken by surprise by the force of her feelings. She saw with wonder how her own hands were shaking, and she was gratified that her Mother was the one she was talking to about it just then. And not someone else. Not *any*one else.

"That time in your life is pure glory. Pure, pure glory. I feel for her, too. It's so unfair, Missy. For whatever reason, so unfair. Every human *being* deserves to live that time through."

"Oh, Momma, I just look forward to it *so* much. I'm so eager for it, I could just taste it! Just thinkin' ahead, to marriage, and always bein' together, and our own child, his and mine, and bein' a little family together, I could just die of it, it's so beautiful!"

"It *is*, Missy. It will be for you, it's got to be. I won't have anything else for my little girl."

"Sweet, sweet Momma. Just think, I'm givin' you another son to love, too! Not like the others. This one's fun, real fun, he'll flirt with you 'till you won't know *what* to do with him! No one can be serious for long with B.J. around, no one could grieve for anythin' very long!"

"I know." They laughed together, thinking about him, about his long legs, the way he straddled chairs and looked straight through your eyes into your very soul when you talked to him, as if you were alone in the universe, nothing, no one else mattered when you were talkin' to him. He knew how to make you feel a real woman, a true lady, all at the same time. He had that callin', you could not resist him, no, you could *not*, nor imagine your very person livin', really livin', with him not around, once you knew him.

"Havin' his baby picture framed, insistin' you hang it up on your livin' room wall, his fancy bare bottom up there on your wall!"

"Paintin' my front door flamingo."

"Layin' back on the couch with his big ol' long legs draggin' halfway across the room, directin' the whole opera playin' on the hi fi, every note--"

"And when your neighbor complained, he sat her down across from him, and in half an hour he had her so involved in that music, she burned her supper!"

"Takin' off, drivin' across the river after two in the mornin', just because he decided he had to hear that trumpet or clarinet or whatever it was, gettin' you out of your bed and into your dancin' clothes at two a.m., just because he took it in his head that he had to hear it--"

"Oh, Momma, what was I like before him? I can't even remember. Tell me, what was I like?"

"Just as beautiful, Missy, you were always beautiful. I know you don't believe me. But you were. Finished school, finished college, got yourself a job, set yourself up in this apartment, I'm so proud of you! Never think, sugar, that you couldn't be independent if you *need* be!"

"Oh, Momma, don't talk like that *now*! I never want to be again!"

"No, let me finish. I know how you feel, but you mustn't, you mustn't give yourself up like that, not to him, not to me, not to anyone, hear? Once you've found your way, you mustn't ever forget that you can do it! Lord knows, nothin' will ever happen, you and B.J., you've got only joy ahead, nothin' but, Lord knows what I hope for you, what a mother hopes for her one and only lovin' daughter. All the same, Missy, never put out of your *mind* what you accomplished by yourself. Be proud of it, like I am proud of you!"

"Never know, do we, what might happen. But, Momma, I won't think about that now, won't let anything spoil what there is *now*, will I?"

"No. Not anythin'."

Jane knew there was more she was supposed to hear, knew it well because she knew her Mother well. Momma had told her before how she used to carry her from room to room, just tellin' her, *Precious baby, you are so beautiful, oh, how I love you, love you*! Every birthday she had, Momma said, *I declare I don't know how it happened, how I got to be this age*, every birthday she declared surprise and disbelief. Once, only once, she had allowed herself to ask, in anguish, *Wasn't it all just a dream*? It was beyond Jane's capacity to bear. And her mother had given her to know that she would never forgive herself this indulgence. Never. It was the *fearin'* for her that her Mother meant to express now. But she loved her Missy more than her own need. Jane wondered at it, at this selfless love. Like all great gifts, it had been unasked for; and where it would lead was impossible to foretell.

"Well, now." Her Mother got up from the table and replaced her chair. "Time I got going. Your gumbo will be the talk of the evenin'. It's all in the *roux*, isn't it? *Did* make a good cook out of you, didn't I?"

Jane followed her into the living room. "Wish I could persuade you to stay on."

"Only a matter of days before Thanksgivin'. Got to get me dressed and ready for that party. Talk, talk, talk is what we'll hear tonight. They all say Goldwater is on his way to the top now, did you know that? Oh, Lord, but there'll be an earful of politics tonight!"

"And him not in his grave yet. He was so *young*, Momma, and so handsome, so strong, it seemed! Him and dyin' weren't in the same thought, were they?"

"No, indeed." Her Mother opened the door, and then burst out laughing at the mad, bright color of it. "That man, that *man*! See to it he behaves drivin' on up next week, want you both in one piece at the weddin'. Come, give old Mother a hug."

"Gladly. Gladly."

They hugged and kissed, and hugged again. Her Mother shooed her back inside; it was winter-cold out there in the hallway. As she had done since she was a child, Jane peeped out from the curtains to watch her Mother go, and waved at the car until it disappeared. Then, when she turned away from the window, she caught the time. Four-thirty! Lord, she had better scurry. B.J. would be over in no time, no time at all.

Blue Sunday

F*uneral-time in the First Baptist Aunt Sally up in the choir, all in pale blue chiffon. Soft blue silk ribbon looped around her waist Rolling bosom puffing in, puffing out And all the congregation gathered around that shiny coffin Daddy looked up, looked straight at him, straight through him Stained-glass windows Bearded men in bright robes with bare feet curling Women in long white gowns with golden hair flying in back of them Panes of every blue, midnight and early morning blue, bluefish and bluegrass blue And an organ sounding a chord, a bright blue chord tearing through the dusty in-church air They were all around him, the Catholics were all around him He lay there, stretched out on the blue wood, with his arms all wide Like he'd been crucified They were mourning their President And then he started to moan, first soft Then loud moans Louder And he was trying to get up, to lift himself up And they said, Lie back down. You're dead. You're dead. But he kept trying to get up, fighting that deathweight on him, fighting it They whispered and they sang, Don't y'all know you're dead Stand up for Jesus, Oh rise, all rise All ye sons and daughters of the Lord Ringing around the body, looking down on him And that blue chord swelling That blue siren His head was tearing in two Started at the widow's peak and went on down Split his face in half Kept going Blue, burning scream*

His eyes flew open. *Don't move, don't move yet, see where it starts hurting first, so you know which way to go*. TV still on. His chair all warmed up from his sleeping there, how long, fifteen minutes? An hour? Two hours?

There was Chief Justice and Mrs. Earl Warren, crying, coming down the steps of the White House.

"Lois? LO?" Gol damn, where was that woman? "Lo! LO, what time's it, what you all up to?" His voice was muffled from sleep, and the velvet drapes were still drawn, and he was furious at how he sounded to himself. He wouldn't call her again, wouldn't give her the satisfaction. He listened,

listened to the kitchen and heard its silence, even heard the dishes waiting to be washed stacked on the drain board. She can't keep to nothing more 'n' fifteen minutes. Couldn't even stay in the apartment of a Sunday. *He* knew where she was, always running off up to that cotton-head friend of hers upstairs with that fat turtle of a husband of hers, that Virginia and her *Bob*bie-boy, *that's* where she was. Virginia giving her a sewing lesson, then fussing around that machine, their mouths going sixty about this material and that. And that dumb turtle chewing gum, laying back on the couch, flipping the pages of his outdoorsman magazines, playing the big Sportsman. And all the while favoring the end of the couch--gave him the best view of Lois' bottom when she bent down to look over Virginia's shoulder.

"You're always imagining things! I don't have to listen to this!"

"Imagining, huh. Maybe my legs are busted, there ain't nothing wrong with my eyes. I can see where he keeps *his*!"

And her slamming drawers closed, packing up again, throwing her clothes all in a heap across the bed. Doing her weekly act of leaving him.

"What do I get out of this, anyway? Tell me, what's in it for *me*? No love, no joy, no laughing, not since I can remember! Nothing to look forward to but more o' the same. And me not getting any younger. Twenty-seven years old already. And you. You're almost thirty. Thirty!"

"So, if you're not getting any younger, just where do you think you're going? Who's gonna take *you* in?"

"Didn't it ever occur to you, Joe Osborne, that I don't need no taking in, that I can take right good care o' myself, have been doing just that for several years out of high school, now?"

Taking dresses off the hangers, throwing the hangers in one pile and the dresses in another. She was gonna have *some* mess to straighten up when this was over. Didn't she ever get tired of this? Must be some other way to conduct a battle.

"I mean, who's gonna take *real* care of you? Like, legs 'n' all, you know that I can do?"

She sits down on the edge of the bed, shoulders dragging down, all ready to cry. "Sometimes I think you have no feeling left in you at all. That those drugs took out your heart with all that pain."

Now she starts in about babies. Babies. He didn't believe in all that for a minute. And she knew it. Poor Lo, she couldn't keep an *apartment*, a little three-room apartment running so's you could find two socks that match in the morning, poor Lo with six, seven different balls o' ol' brown lettuce wrapped up in wax paper in the refrigerator. And some egg salad so old it'd kill a mule if you fed it to her. Bath-tub with another ring every six inches up from the bottom. And the insides of her dresser drawers with everything from pieces of broken earrings to gum wrappers rolled up with the chewed gum still inside 'em, what in creation would she do with a baby? Who'd kill who first, her the baby, or the baby her?

Now he stands in the doorway, leaning on his crutches, waiting until she gets herself all cried out, until she cleans the closet out so her clothes are spread out all over the bed, dresses and sweaters and her long blue dress, and her underthings in a little pile half-hid under the pillow, so shy still, even after their being married going on five years, still so shy about his seeing such things. And she was his girl, she was *his* girl, and that was one way that she didn't change. That revved him up, and he even thought she knew it somehow.

"Those two years before the accident I took care o' you."

"Huh. That's a good while ago."

"And you know when I finish my schooling, you can quit your job and lay around and eat chocolates all the day. If that's what you want."

"Don't want no silly chocolates."

Coming over slowly, working one crutch and then the other, taking his time, putting them up by the dresser, then, and clearing a place for himself on the bed beside her, and forcing her to look at him, lifting up her face and holding her eyes with his, though she'd fight him, she'd always fight him then. And then kissing her, kissing her most hurtfully, not letting her mouth go, no matter how hard she pleads. And they fall back together, like into water, right from the edge of the pool, easy, and he takes her then.

Jesus a'mighty! Right there on TV! Murder, right on TV for everybody from the Ubangis to the Rooskeys to watch. A live show on TV. There he was. They brought him out of the jail, and you see that man in the coat come right out from the line of people, just come out, and point a gun at him, and pull the trigger. And Oswald makes a face, grabs at his side, and falls down real slowly, like the kids do when they play cops and robbers. It wasn't even a too convincing piece of acting, but it's for real. There was Oswald, flanked by policemen, stepping out of an elevator and onto a ramp, down in the basement of the jail. He takes no more than a step or two. And a figure darts out of the small group on the left there, the viewer's left, just while Oswald is walking toward the armored truck. And, CRACK! One shot, and he clutches at his side, and he starts going down. Right away, people start gathering around the one who did the shooting. No question who it is, you could see him for yourself right on TV. Short, stout, middle-aged. You don't need a trial. You wouldn't believe how little time it took before a news reporter could tell us who it was. A night club operator, name of Jack Ruby. Anyway, there's this confusion on the screen. An ambulance pulls up. They bring out a stretcher and they put Oswald on it. You don't know how bad his condition is, but you have this feeling about it, it's only just beginning. Anybody who saw that film of what happened on Friday in Dallas, and thought that would be all the show for now, he better think again.

And just like you're switching channels, the scene shifts, and you're looking at the portico of the White House. They put the casket on the caisson. It's drawn by seven white horses, three of 'em without riders. And you see all the black limousines filling up the driveway. The camera moves over the whole thing, like the picture's shot from a helicopter, and then it moves in on up to the flag at half-mast. They really know how to do that, they know how to make you feel it. You see her and the two children coming down the steps, following the casket, and they bring it to the Capitol rotunda. And you think, *Well, he's leaving the White House for the very last time*.

Meanwhile, back there in Dallas, they show you that shooting scene again. In case you missed it, you can see Ruby shooting Oswald all over again. Or in case you were in church. Which is where Lois was, Sunday morning she *had* to be in church, even *this* Sunday morning. And when he saw it, he yelled out, he really did, just like you do at a game, and he grabbed for his crutches and got up out of his chair, and hopped around the room like a jack-rabbit gone berserk. You have to have *some*body to talk to about it. When he was so sure there wasn't nothing going to happen right away again, he tried calling Mary Lou. First, her line was busy. Then, when they *did* answer it, it was only little Fred at home. They were out over to the neighbors'.

"Freddy? Freddy, this is your Uncle Joe. Your Momma or Daddy home?"

"No, I don't think so."

"Have a look around, will you, Freddie, but don't take too long, remember this is long distance."

Well, hell, it was a stupid waste to call like that, they really *weren't* around. And Freddie, well, you'd expect a little more 'n' that of a boy of eleven, Christ, he hardly knew the President'd been shot, you had to remind him, and then he said, "Yeah. Oh, yeah." Like you were reminding him that next week was Thanksgiving. Well, maybe he oughtn't to've lit into him like that, but, Christ a'mighty, all that excitement going on.

"Now, listen, Freddie. You just go on in and turn on your TV, and you are going to see yourself a murder right there on the screen, a man shooting down the man who shot the President. And I say murder, because Oswald will soon be dead, I'm positive of that. And *stay* by that TV, because the whole thing is just beginning, you hear me? You just remember it was your ol' Uncle Joe told you that, because history is being made right now, and there's a lot more to come, I can feel it, I can *feel* it, hear me?"

And just saying that got him all hot and excited, he didn't even know he could feel the violence coming until he told Freddie. And now there he was, yelling over the long distance phone, plain yelling from Louisiana into Alabama, that Kennedy was the fourth President of the United States to be killed by an assassin. First, he told him, there was Lincoln, just ninety-nine years ago, yes sir, Freddie, back on April 14, 1864. And in 1881, President Garfield. And in 1901, President McKinley. Except Garfield and McKinley didn't die right away. Just Lincoln and Kennedy died that same day. And on and on he went, giving his only nephew a lesson in American history over the long distance phone, hearing nothing but the boy's breathing at the other end. Then telling him about the things that were bound to happen next, that Kennedy's shot, then Tippitt, then Oswald, now you just watch somebody shoot Jack Ruby, and then somebody shoot *him*; but that's nothing, *nothin'* compared to what's gonna happen at that funeral tomorrow. On and on, until he realized the boy thought he had gone crazy.

Mary Lou had no more sense than Lois. Even when she was little. Always screaming and making a fuss over nothing. Always had her head turned the opposite way from where life was happening. They shoot the President of the United States, never *mind* how you feel about him personally, they shoot him down, right there in broad daylight, in Dallas, Texas, while he's riding in that car, waving at people, and BANG! Shot down dead. A war veteran, too. Lois goes upstairs to see Virginia, and to shake her bottom in front of turtle-head, that's how impressed she is. And not two days after, the one who shot the President is shot himself. And Mary Lou is over at the neighbors'. Doing some fool thing, they could spend five hours in a row transplanting a boxwood, and end by putting it back right where it was in the first place. Up all night the night before playing canasta and drinking beer. He knew them.

Well, we'll see what they'll all do when it all blows up.

You could feel it, outside and inside. Calm. The spell of calm. It was calm as death. It deceives a lot of people. A blue, blue quiet.

Mud, thicker 'n' thicker as he went down to the bayou, feeling his way along with the third leg, then the fourth. Right crutch down, SQUISH. Left crutch down, SQUASH. Following them as best a cripple could. Slow, deep heat working him through, bleeding his body. That vampire heat, sweet and deep as a woman, reaching all through him. The air breathing honeysuckle and pine and verbena, and all the thick rot, like hot metal, down there. The ground giving way under him, where the water hyacinths covered the marsh, that pretty lavender menace looking innocent as a meadow down at the bottom of the slope. That decaying sweetness down in all that duckweed muck of cattail and alligator weeds, flower-bloom mixed with dead fish, dead pond weeds, dead plants of every kind, choked by the hyacinths. *Deadly things*, Jay had said. *Look delicate as any hothouse flower. Once they get in the bayou, you can't blast 'em out, you can't burn 'em out, you can't run 'em down. No poison strong enough to kill 'em. You try ripping 'em out by the roots, by next spring they'll be back in again, doubling their numbers, covering the bayou, so you think it's solid land down there, a purple 'n' green prairie. But it's a moving prairie. You put your foot down in it, you feel yourself starting to sink. Earth melts down into water, everywhere you take a step, you go in deeper 'n' thicker, till you're not walking, you're wading, then maybe swimming along with all the catfish and bluegill and shrimp and sac-à-lait and crab, the alligators and snakes.*

He could just barely hear their voices. He was soaked through, his shirt, his britches sticking to him, so he'd have to pull 'em off like an extra layer of skin. Mud midway up his calves, now, creeping up to the top of his new boots. Crutches dripping with it. Sweat running down both sides of his face, the inside of his head a mess of jelly. The air so heavy-blue with swampscent it couldn't carry their words back anymore. Just the muffled sounds, so he knew they were down there ahead of him, he didn't lose them, not yet. Though he sure could. He told 'em to go on without him, that he'd wait up on the ridge, and that's where they thought he was now, up there maybe a quarter mile back, where the ground was wet but still solid. Thought they'd have a look down there, didn't have nets or even the *intention* to see what they could catch, just took a notion to pull up and get out and have a look around. He wasn't one to hold 'em back nor to say he'd go with them like an ordinary person would, because he'd be in the way. They'd deny it. They were good friends. They'd lift back the curtain of Virginia creeper and Spanish moss, make out a path for him while he worked his way down. Uh-*uh*, he wasn't having any of it. Let 'em go. Keep far enough back, they'll never suspect you're coming part way down. Far enough back so you can turn around and get out before they start up again.

They'd be back sure, if they saw anything worth coming back to, they'd take a canoe down there and get in some fishing. Jay took him out on the bayous so long ago he forgot most of the names he taught him, of the birds and bugs. Didn't forget that heat, though, and that whispering, haunted feeling you got down there.

He couldn't hardly breathe. It felt like he was drowned, down in the bottom of a creek, everything closing over him. Good place to stop. He was standing like in the heart of a circle of trees, their branches all locked together, the willows and oaks and cypresses, the tupelo-gum and hackberries. He could tell one from the other all right, Jay taught him well about the trees. But they were all reaching *in*to one another, the branches and leaves tangled up together, all fanning out into one another, willow withes snaking through the hackberries, so you couldn't tell where the red fruit was growing from. And the oak leaves like a mass of green hands lacing right into the arms of the cypresses all hung with their darkgreen leaves and gray, misty webs of Spanish moss. And that moss wound right into the tupelo-gum. The sky was moving down just as he stood there. Up on the levee, it was pure Louisiana blue sky, with schools of white fish clouds moving in it. But blue and shining, except where the sun was smoldering, a yellow-white eye burning in all that blue. But now it was darkening, moving on down, and the trees were still, and he felt like they were coming to life, like they drew him in here, and they were all around him, giants in green cloaks with hidden eyes, sitting in judgment on him. And the sky closing over them all.

It was so still. Lord, but the birds must have been noisy. He hadn't even noticed them, but now, in this stillness, he felt their waiting with him. Not one thing stirred. The wind was gone. The trees brooded around him, spread all around him, darkening and quiet as death, shadowing all around him. The thick mud held down all the four feet of him, not sucking him in any deeper, but maybe it would if he stirred. You could smell the air, all rotten and sweet and swollen up. You could feel the birds waiting, and the trees all shrouding with a kind of silvery gray-rose haze. And the dark green judges turning ghosts, and all of them a still life under the lowering sky.

Jay'd been looking down at the bayou, poking his head between a clump of resurrection fern and the trunk of a cypress tree, studying the water down there, all dark like tea, but shining, and telling him this bayou wasn't there last spring, it was made since he was last down here, and probably wouldn't be here next spring, that they came and went, *whereas*--and he smacked the tree trunk--*this creature will live almost as long as God. Nothing can rot this wood, Joe, if it can live down here in the swamp, it can live anywhere. Which is why you and I will lie in it some day. Nothing makes a better coffin than a cypress-*

Move. Move. If he could only move. It was like the will was drunk clear out of him. Cussed legs. Cussed, cussed legs. Riding along, cruising along, thinking you're free and you've got it all set, feeling young and strong and able, and *free*, oh Lord, *free*, free to move. To *go*. And then that crash. And that long, long night. And coming awake, wishing to *God* you could stay down there in the dark and the cold, not having to open your eyes ever no more to find yourself on your back, down there, more dead than ever alive again. If he could only *move*!

It was coming down, closing over him. And there he was, leaning on four legs, each one deeper 'n' the other in mud, just waiting while it turned blacker 'n' blacker. Hot and shivering, soaked so his clothes stuck to his body. And then a blade of yellow and white flashed. And there was that sound in all the leaves at once, like pods busting open, that soft popping faster 'n' faster, he could feel the big drops of rain-water, warm as tears, splash on his head, on his shoulders. Then it came rushing down, like that blade tore the belly of the sky wide open, and down she poured, and the sky was thick--a moving, churning mass of smoky blue with those inlets of white light floating in it. Trees weren't judging him nor *no*body any more, even those huge, deep willows were humbled now, like they were huddling together while they took their punishment, and forgot about him standing in dead center of 'em, alone like no tree could never be alone, not able any more than they were to move from where he was. Him nothing much more than a dumb animal who had a little bit more bad luck than some but knew enough when a force was bigger 'n' him, knew well enough that there was violence out there, just like inside, it broke in its *own* time. And when it broke, you *took* it is all, you just *took* it. Not even murmuring. You want to cry out, to yell till all the graves open up. No yell in you, no cry big enough.

They showed the 21-gun salute, and then them playing "Hail To the Chief." They were talking like real orators today. You could almost cry, just from listening to them. Senator Mansfield almost singing, "In a moment, it was no more. And so she took a ring from her finger and placed it in his hands." Never had much use for the man, nobody around that he knew *did*, all that talking about what you could do for your country and there he was, doing like any politician does, doing for himself, no, any fool'd know what all that high talk was about, still, you listened, you had some respect. "Gave of his love that we, too, in turn might give. He gave that we might give of ourselves, that we might give to one another until there would be no room, no room at all, for the bigotry, the hatred, the prejudice and the arrogance which converged in that moment of horror to strike him down."

Think we're all like Bobbie Miller, think we're all a mess o' turtleheads down here, think we're all dumb and mean like him, hardly civilized full. Bobbie's *Nigra* this and *Nigra* that. *Virginia*, he says, *did you get the Nigra to clean up around here? Virginia, where's my socks, did the Nigra take 'em?* Bobbie Miller, he's got Nigras in his bathtub and in his salt shaker, his britches are crawling with 'em, he shakes Nigras out of his shoes every morning before he puts them on. The Nigras're responsible for the fact that he can't keep a job more'n six months, says he couldn't sell a dime of insurance, it was all due somehow to the Nigras, says those Nigras're sucking the country dry, it's because of the Nigras Russia beat us in space, and what with them 'n' the Jews and the Catholics, we'll soon be in World

War Three, and we'll get blown up. Yessir, nobody can tell you better 'n' Bobbie Miller about how the Nigras are ruining the economy, the whole South. He sits there on his big, fat ass in the chair, sending his wife out to work every morning at that dumb job in the laundromat, he'd be out on the streets here without Virginia's job, and all he can do is tell how the *Nigras*'re lazy and shiftless. And they're hot for the white women, too, he'll start you in on *that*, all the while peering out from behind his magazine with both those dead turtle-eyes right square on my wife's bottom, he tells how the Nigras are after our women. And let me tell you, Senator Mansfield, where this Nigra-baiter hails from. You think he's from Mississippi. Or Alabama, maybe. Or that he learned to talk like that right over here in Louisiana. Well, sir, can you believe it, this Bobbie Miller, he was born and raised in no other place than a little town in the Midwest. Yes sir, I hear he wasn't here two weeks before he was asking if he could sign up with the Klan and looking into the White Citizens Council. Senator, this boy was born with a white sheet over his head! We're gonna have to make him an honorary Southerner, yes sir, we're gonna have to baptize Bobbie Miller Southern, 'cause he can talk a *storm* on Nigras, whereas I was born 'n' raised right here in Belle Ville, Louisiana, and I never even knew one for the first ten years of my life!

Now ol' Impeach-Earl-Warren's talking again: "What moved some misguided wretch to do this horrible deed may never be known to us, but we do know that such acts are commonly stimulated by forces of hatred and malevolence such as today, and are eating their way into the blood-stream of American life."

Freedom riders 'n' boycotters 'n' civil rights agitators coming down here, preaching 'n' marching 'n' demonstrating. And you know what's waiting for 'em. You know there's a Bobbie Miller in every woodpile. 'N' when they catch him, what do they do? Put him on TV is what, make him into a movie star. Like that Byron de la Beckwith. Like they'd do with Oswald, if he didn't get it from Ruby. You could see the killer in Oswald's face. Those snake-cold eyes. His whole face was one big snarl. Well, he got his. Right before God 'n' everybody, he got his.

"If we really love this country, if we truly love justice and mercy, if we fervently want to make this nation better for those who are to follow us, we can at least abjure the hatred that consumes people, the false accusations that divide us and the bitterness that begets violence....Is it too much to hope that the martyrdom of our beloved President might even soften the hearts of those who would themselves recoil from assassination, but who do not shrink from spreading the venom which kindles thoughts of it in others?"

Yessir, he could've told Freddie, it was just under one hundred years ago that the body of Abraham Lincoln was laying on that same catafalque.

Now John McCormack spoke of the grief of the Kennedy family, a grief that, he said, was shared "by countless millions of persons throughout the world, considered a personal tragedy, as if one had lost a loved member of his own immediate family."

They showed you Robert Kennedy's face, now, all drawn and pale.

"Thank God," McCormack said, "that we were privileged, however briefly, to have had this great man for our President. For he has now taken his place among the great figures of world history."

Well, one thing sure, if they shoot you down like that you'll be remembered. That's *one* way sure.

They showed you Lyndon Johnson walking up to the catafalque. Then a soldier placed a wreath there for him. Then *she* came forward, holding Caroline's hand, and she knelt down at the side of the coffin. She kissed the flag draped over it, and then Caroline did the same.

The whole Kennedy family was leaving the rotunda now. And the first of that long line of mourners started walking past the catafalque.

Hungry. He sure was getting hungry. Some wife he had, some girl he picked out, she was some pickings, that Lois. Girl'd mess up a peanut butter sandwich, never mind no Sunday dinner. She'd be back down after five, *six*, maybe, she'd come drooping in, all wore out from doing nothing up there, and get herself a beer, and when he'd mention something about supper, she'd look at him like she was the normal one, she never did believe in eating anything. Skinnier every year, lucky if she'd weigh ninety-five pounds with her apron full o' stones, even Mary Lou said she was cheating him, he wasn't getting his money's worth, she'd look at him like *he* was the one who was crazy because he wanted Sunday dinner. By the time they'd work *that* out, he might as well get in the car and go on out and get them some burgers to go, or maybe fried chicken. Better stop off at the grocery store, too. Nothing in the fridge except a few beers. And those balls of lettuce scattered around. And maybe some week-old egg salad you wouldn't give to a dying cat.

Where'd they all come from, all those people colored and white, old men and young boys, nuns and old women and people holding little children by the hand, filing past the catafalque.

He groaned out loud, heaved himself up, reached for his crutches. Damned if the room wasn't closing in on him. TV was driving him crazy. Had him hypnotized. Enough's enough. The old pain creaked in his hip when he pulled himself up out of the chair.

Heard them at the door just as he flicked the TV off. Swiveled around on his crutches, to see that party of three come in. Laughing, Lois holding herself, her face all red and twisted up from laughing, actual *tears* in her eyes, saying, *Bobbie, stop, have mercy!* and that loud voice, too high for a man's, going on about some nonsense in a drawl so thick you'd swear he had a mouthful of Alabama clay, and after him comes Virginia with a big swatch of bright blue cloth in one hand, and a cigarette going in the other--

"Whew! Stuffy in here! What you been *doing* this afternoon, Joe Osborne, cooped up in here?" She looked at him and tried to keep on laughing, but it didn't work, what with him glaring at her, hard as he could, asking *Where you been?* and leaning on his crutches, not moving, his eyes travelling first over her blouse, then her toreador pants, her sandals, taking her clothes off and putting 'em back on with that accusation in his eyes, deliberate. She stopped full in front of him and looked down, and felt that her blouse was coming out of her pants, and started to tuck it back in, her face paling.

Bobbie leaned over the back of the easy chair, locking his hands together, and letting 'em dangle down, his big back porch jutting out in back. He worked his gum from one side of the mouth to the other, smiling like a crocodile.

"Watching that show in Washington, and sleeping between times, most likely. Right, Joe?"

Virginia busied herself looking for an ashtray. Maybe because she was smarter than the rest of them, or maybe because she was so dumb she never had nothing to say, you couldn't get two words out of Virginia. Either she laughed at everything you said, or she looked from one face to the other, waiting for somebody to speak. She'd wait for an *hour* if she had to; she'd wait for *ten*, if need be. Virginia was all right for what she was, she just wasn't much. Kind of dumpy, you could just see what her mother must look like, brown eyes big and watchful in that round face, taking in everything slow, real slow, her mouth hanging open all the time, surprised at everything. Virginia was kind of sad, you could just see how she'd be taken in by the first cheating person to come around. She didn't ask for nothing from life, and nothing's just what she got. *Worse* 'n' nothing, married to Bobbie Miller. Lord, couldn't you just see the brood they'd have when they started breeding, fat little turtles with little stumps for arms and legs, and those staring, chocolate-drop eyes. Virginia deserved better 'n' that. *Any*body did.

"Joe? *Joe*?"

"I ain't deaf."

"Come on, honey, we was just gonna pin this up with my light blue dress, you know, the one you like so much, that I wore to Cynthia's wedding. Virginia's gonna help me make a chemise out of it, and I came down so we could try it on and pin it up. And Bobbie said, Whyn't we all go out and get some spaghetti tonight, over to Tony's Place? Come on, honey, do you good to get out of here."

"*You* left those drapes closed."

"Didn't want to disturb you. Why, when I left, you had dropped off to sleep in your chair with the papers. You looked so peaceful there, I didn't want to disturb you, is all. You were up last night with that TV, Lord, I don't know till *what* time!"

Bobbie grinning, working his gum from one end of that smile to the other. "Not much show last night. But I caught *today's*. They sure took care o' him, didn't they? Bet they didn't have to pay that fella. Bet he did it for *free*. That Oswald, now, I'd like to go possum-hunting with him. Sure wish I had his aim."

"Tell you what." He kept staring at Lois while Bobbie was talking, and he kept staring now. So far as he was concerned, nobody had said nothing. That's what Bobbie's talk was worth. "You and Virginia, you two go on back there and get your pinning done. Then we'll just let them go out and get their spaghetti."

"Oh!"

Sounded just like a five-year-old that you told her she couldn't have candy because it was too close to supper-time. What *was* all this? What did the three of them have going, anyway? He was about to ask her, but, no, not in front of *him*.

"That's it, Lo. You heard me. Now go on back there."

She pouted, so that when she went past him he reached out, before he knew what he was about, and grabbed her arm just above the elbow. She winced like he hurt her, and he pinched tighter.

"Got something to say about it?"

"Joey! Come on, hon, let go o' me, that hurts!"

When he did let go, he pushed her a little first, so that she stumbled, or *made* herself stumble. She started to cry.

"Come on, Virginia, let's get on out o' here."

Virginia never lifted her head up, just followed her to the back bedroom.

"Now, what did you go and do all *that* for?" Bobbie had straightened up, and folded his arms. Half that sick smile was still on his face. His jaws never stopped working that gum.

"Way I see it, that's none o' your affair."

"Wow-ee." Bobbie whistled through his teeth, shook his head. "Something's got you mighty worked up this afternoon."

"Where'd you hear that kind of talk?"

"*What* talk? What're you referring to?"

"That talk about Oswald's aim. I know you well enough to know you're too stupid to think that up by yourself."

"What's got *in*to you? I don't know if I should leave Lois down here, with you like that."

A bolt of heat shot through him, right through his chest, and shook him so bad that he wondered at it even as he lifted up his right crutch and drove the heel of it straight into Bobbie's chest. His gum near shot out of his mouth, he was so surprised.

"Nobody looks after my wife except me. Hear?"

"Joe, put that down. Put that down now, somebody's bound to get hurt."

He turned the handle, just like you were turning a big old key. And he drove it deeper in.

"I can take care of my own wife, see. Nothing you or anybody has to say about it."

"Now, just put that *down*!" Bobbie pushed at it with both hands. He *had* to step back, that gives you satisfaction. He kept it raised at him.

"You are positively crazy. You know that? *Crazy!* Don't need to have no truck with you. Virginia! Hey, *Virginia!*"

"That's right, you call Virginia. And you get the two of you on out of here. See that you *stay* out, too."

"What's going *on* in here?" Lois came running out, wrapped around in that blue material like a mummy, her eyes scared. One of her shoulders was bare. The sight of that heated his blood. Virginia still had pins in her mouth. One look at Bobbie, another look at him, and she took out those pins and headed for the door.

"You're sure some friend, sure some neighbor, Osborne. Goll-lee, *some* neighbor!" Come on, Virginia."

"Yeah, go on, Virginia."

"Joe Osborne, these're my *friends*. You can't treat friends like that!"

"Lois Osborne, this is my house. Nobody tells me what I can do in my own house, not you, not anybody."

"Your house, huh. Who pays the rent around here, huh?" She was crying, now. Really crying and yelling. "Who'd pay for our spaghetti tonight, huh? Can't treat my friends like that, just can't. I won't allow for it." All choked up and crying, she went back to the bedroom.

Bobbie was still at the door, standing there for the longest time, just shaking his head.

"Pity that poor girl. I just pity her."

"Go on, *go!*" He lifted up his crutch again, waved it at him.

Bobbie looked at it, then at him. *I wouldn't fight no cripple*, his eyes said.

"Get *out!*"

Bobbie lifted up his hand, a sign that he was leaving anyway. He even shut the door behind him.

"Lois! LO!" But he knew she wouldn't come, knew that if he wanted her, he'd have to go after her, him and his four legs. He couldn't understand why it was so, he was shaking all over, and crying, too. He was so hungry he didn't want to eat anymore, he was past it. He could hear her sobs in there, and his own retching up from deep in his throat, from some place in him that had been savaged without his knowing it, and it sounded so funny if you'd think about it, her in there and him out here, both wailing like they were at a funeral. Part of him wanted to laugh at it, but the sides of his face hurt from being stretched out so far, and every time he started to laugh it turned into another sob, so that it wasn't anything in his power to stop, it *had* him. Couldn't comfort her, she couldn't comfort him, he just let go. And it got worse and worse, he cussed a little to himself between times. And then it was played out, it was just about over. And now, it was over.

Cried out, he went and opened up the drapes. It was evening, well into evening, fine time to be opening them. That twilight blue outside, all up and down the street, that haze. They'd be coming all night, walking past that raised bier. Nothing to see, it was closed and the flag draped over it, but they'd be coming anyway. Into the morning. Here he'd been feeling this powerful feeling all day, that welled up so inside him he wanted to run out in the street and shout it so they'd all have to listen, that the whole thing was going to blow up tomorrow, you could feel it in the air, that nobody'd seen nothing yet, that most likely it would be tomorrow. They'd have all the heads of state gathered together in one place, that was the plan. Get them all together, and then blow it up.

It was bound to happen, you could feel it in the still, blue air this very evening. Him not in the ground yet, nor the other one. Wouldn't even be time left to bury the three of them, Kennedy and Oswald and Tippitt, wouldn't have time to put the spade in the ground for either of them before they'd touch off that fuse, and they'd all go. All the heads of state, and all those buildings flying up in the air and raining back down, pieces of stone and glass and human bodies all broken up and mixed together. The day of judgment tomorrow, tomorrow, and none of 'em prepared, none of 'em feeling it coming. Not Lois with her balls of wilted lettuce scattered around in the empty refrigerator, and her blue mummy cloths. Not Virginia with her cigarettes and her cow's eyes looking around at everything, confused at it all. Not Bobbie with his chewing gum, nor Freddie with his racing cars and his ignorant parents shuffling that deck of cards, not any of 'em prepared for it, thinking the beginning was the end. Oh, a few knew. Jay, wherever he was, now, Jay would know.

Nothing to do but wait it out, might as well everybody be a cripple like him, there wasn't any place to hurry to, *it* was hurrying to them all. Not even a day away. If he'd kept his own head on him, he wouldn't've bothered to get violent with Bobbie, it was pure waste. Couldn't *account* for what got into him, except that whatever there was in Dallas, he must've caught some of it. Like fall-out.

Those dugout shelters wouldn't do much good, either; how long could supplies last? And they'll be at one another, sure, for whatever goods they've hoarded.

He crutched himself to the back bedroom. She was sitting on the edge of the bed, her back to him, sitting there in her slip, her head twisted to one side, still sobbing, but slow now, and hopeless, like something was broken in her. He saw with pity how her shoulder blades stuck out under the slip straps. There was a little arc of pimples across the middle of her back.

"Lo?"

She shook her head, not turning.

"Lo? Come on, now. We both had enough."

She moved her head a little, so that one side of her face came around, looking down, first, like a wupped puppy, and then on up to his face. There was fear in her eyes, and he felt shame, and then something a lot worse than that. *I don't want you*, he thought, with amazement, *come on, I won't touch you, I won't do nothing to you. I don't even want you.*

"What the heck, Lo, we're both hungry 'n' tired, what say you and me, we'll go out and have ourselves some chicken. Come on, now, you get dressed, and we'll go out for some supper. Just you get some clothes on here, come on, and we'll both have some supper, and we'll feel better."

He kept on talking like that, not moving from the doorway, just sing-songing at her like she was a little child you had to convince it would be all right. Talking until she started to move. She gave one long, shuddering sigh, knowing that the fight was over for now, and she got herself up off the bed and over to the closet, still sniffling a little, and moved the hangers around, looking for something to put on. He saw the little round depression in the bed where she'd been sitting hunched over, and beyond that, through the curtains, the blue light deepening, the cold blue November light at dusk, coming in through the white fiberglass like a growing shadow. All quiet and mournful, now, the light that comes after a storm, that kind it was, so deep and quiet you wouldn't believe the skies would ever change from what they were just now.

A Time To Be Far From Embraces

He rode the white bird to the stately sweet gum, deep crimson it glowed and he saw far, far down she seemed to unfurl from its strong trunk he saw her pale green gown floating around her she was smiling, beckoning and the perfume of jasmine was drifting in the ether and the scent of fresh mint, and the apricot musk of sweet olive and the heavy sweetness of ligustrum Slowly his great bird circled over her head, over her bright hair and he called her name, *Natalie! Natalie!* He saw magnolia blossoms opening as hands open

His eyelids fluttered; he lifted his hand from his side and drew his fingers across them to keep them still and took comfort from the mist gathered under them, dampening his cheeks, as he felt himself cast up on the shores. The soft closing of the kitchen cabinet bade him a kindly good morning. Greta was about his coffee, bless her good soul, she had let herself into the house quiet as a whisper. And any moment, the pungent aroma of his dark roast with chicory would come wafting in here, tempting him to rise and greet the day. She would slip outside to put up the laundry and see to the yard at his very first rustle in here, there was no more considerate woman under heaven. Natalie had never had to instruct her that he wasn't to be spoken to until he'd showered and dressed and breakfasted, that everyone had to be made presentable all around before making talk. From the very day Greta had come to them, both of them had seen how she had the instincts of the nobility. How often had Natalie confided to him that if Renée grew up to equal Greta's mannerliness, she'd count herself a truly accomplished mother.

The brilliant red of the leaves of the sweet gum that was a sign from her, surely. It told him that in the autumn still, she was beckoning to him. And the redeeming brightness of her hair. The mingling of fragrances, flowers and her perfume. The vividness of her beauty, the radiance of her youth, her health. The offerings from the blossoms of her hands. *For I have loved thee with an everlasting love*

She had returned to him for this birthday this Friday, bringing him this most perfect gift.

How he would tease her, tease them both, in the afterglow of the special breakfast always spread for him on his day. The snowy linen, the sparkling china and their best silver. The frothy yellow of his eggs scrambled just so. Butter biscuits that *had* to have been made in heaven. Yellow chrysanthemums in the aquamarine bowl. The gleam of the morning sun in the Wedgwood jasper, it always put him in mind of Tennyson. *So flashed and fell the brand Excalibur*. Everything so tastefully arranged. Mother and daughter giggling out there on the sun porch, waiting for gift-presentation time. "November twenty-second," he would announce, that would be their summons to come on in, now. "Anniversary of an historic day. The first of Sagittarius, the last of Scorpio. At eleven-O-seven let us commemorate the advent of the young prince, Gordon Stephens!" Then she would laugh, "You Arsh, you do go *on* so!" And Renée would climb up on his lap and fuss and fidget because he was so particular about the way he unwrapped his presents. And Natalie would say what a wonder it was that he'd been born and raised on a big ol' farm, way, way up North, up in the big, wide Midwestern cornfields, his ways were so Southern, and a person would have to listen very hard to catch the foreign traces in his accent.

Very, very faintly he could hear Greta humming. She would be setting out his breakfast things the instant she heard him stirring. He lifted back the sheet and light blanket and reached down over the side of the bed to set his slippers out so he could step right into them. Renée's package had arrived yesterday from Princeton. She could trust him not to open it early. He decided he'd wait until after he'd had his supper, that way he'd have her surprise to look forward to all this day. Since she'd gone off to college, it promised to be one of the longest yet. Never mind, he was to see her in less than a week now, they were going to have a grand Thanksgiving holiday together in the nation's Capital. Plus she'd be sure to call him tonight, and what could buoy his spirits more than the prospect of hearing her voice this very evening?

"See you bid Miz Renée trot herself back here come Christmas!"

Greta pat-patted his arm and withdrew her hand and stepped back from the car.

"I'll do that, dear."

"You'll find some particular treats in that box lunch I fixed you, ol' Greta knows what you like."

"Bless you." He started up the motor and settled himself in. "Thought you wouldn't allow rain on my birthday!" he called, and shook his finger at her. She lifted the hem of her apron and flapped it to scold at the weather. Then she pointed to the wash line strung with laundry all the way to the Chinese elm in the middle of the yard that was to show him proof ol' Greta hadn't been daunted by any overcast. He shook his head at her, laughing, wanting to get out and come around the car to give her an extra hug.

If she guessed how she held it all together for him, she would keep it her secret forevermore, that's how fine she was. Friend to him, grandmother to Renée to the very pale, Grandma Landry and Grandma Stephens put together couldn't go beyond it. They were jealous, and they had good cause to be jealous. He sat there for a long moment, cherishing her, cherishing the proud lift of her head, the all-knowingness in her warm, brown eyes, the pure affection of her smile. He loved her, loved the look of her, and her crisp, bustling ways, and her composure through it *all*, through it all, and the sprightliness of her humor. It seemed to him he had known her all his life.

As he backed slowly down the driveway, she stopped her waving to point, and he nodded vigorously. She was reminding him she'd made up her mind that morning to collect all the drupes from the sweet gum and scoop them up once for all. "Give you a blowout yet, those prickly things." To thank her a second time, he blew her a kiss.

Birthday or no, Friday was his day to teach class at the Law School he'd graduated from, never mind how long ago; in his last letter he'd confided to Renée that Grandpa Stephens believed you ought to start counting backwards the day you threaten to turn thirty-five. "To his way of thinking, thirty-five's a right dangerous age. I'm not there, of course, honeybee, so I'm in no position to testify as to the truth of *that* particular superstition." She'd be sure to have a first-rate tease for that one on the phone tonight, times she almost came up to Natalie's mark this past year or so in the Tease Department.

In the pale light of this morning, the pyracantha berries looked burning red, they drew his attention the minute he stepped out the back door for his morning inspection. He'd remarked to Greta he couldn't recall seeing *any*thing so glowing red this side of sleep. "Never seen such myself," she'd murmured doubtfully.

A *red* red, it put him in mind of their apple orchards at harvesting time. Just like that he could see his father sitting in the maple rocker the November before his going, Great Grandma Stephens's afghan spread over his legs. The violent orange and purple and blue of the squares on that afghan, Dad used to remark they'd put out the eye of God Himself, no blasphemy intended. Those faces he made while he was reading. Pushing his lower lip way, way out. Raising the one eyebrow and then the other, and then both of them together. Making a big round O with his mouth. Frowning until his eyes were so squinched, they all but disappeared.

Right up to when Dad died, Mother would carry on so about their birthdays, August's, then his, August's on the fifteenth, his on the twenty-second, two years and one week apart, exactly, and she never once permitted August's to take the luster from his, she just made the very same fuss all over again. Biggest sin a parent could commit was favoritism, that was gospel to her, she said if you couldn't live up to it, you'd best have an only child. Dad had lived by it too, he'd been fairness itself all through their growing up, he'd never once shown any preference for August, though they'd both known from the beginning that August would be the one to stay. That it was to be their second-born who would keep the farm in the family.

The big celebrations in November. Mother would bake for days for August, and then she would bake for days all over again for him. Indoors, the goodly warm air of the kitchen. Cinnamon and nutmeg and cloves. Out on the porch, you could sniff the bitters in the nip-in-the-air. The hoarfrost on the grass crunched under your feet by late autumn. November came in with the dead souls of Purgatory wailing on the wind, as how Mother saw it. Dad would remark that she was haunted, far as he'd go in *that* regard would be to confess there were November nights when the moon looked like a big lighted pumpkin swinging above the bare elms.

Here he was, on the campus. This time, he'd got himself here by pure animal reflex, no question about it.

He drove up into the lot back of Brooke Hall and parked, and crossed the boulevard and walked the entire length of the Parade Ground to the Law building. He saw that the flag was at half-mast. So much dying on the campus, this must be the third time since September, if he remembered correctly.

The bells in the campanile of Memorial Tower chimed. Three quarters past eight. The little light they'd had was fading fast. There was a rain-heaviness riding in on the air. And the wind was carrying in all those noxious fumes. "Never remember it bein' like this when I grew up," Natalie had claimed. "Those were the days, Gordon. That beautiful time before Progress came." Her doctor would hold forth for *hours*, if you'd let him, on all the poisoning, on the dead fish washed up on the beaches, on the exhalations from the oil refineries and the gas fields, on the burning of wastes, and the clouds of effluvia from the open sewers. He'd thunder that God meant humanity to farm, to *till* the soil, not *defile* it. Poor old Doctor Delaroderie, he'd have been so much more at home if he'd been born in Iowa. Among the Amish. "What we ought to do is issue gas masks all around," he'd grumble, "or at least antibiotic popsicles people could lick while they go about their business."

He was almost at the top of the steps when he felt the first raindrops sprinkling his hair. Half a dozen days from now, he and Renée would be climbing the steps of the gleaming marble building that had served so beautifully as the model for this one. He had promised her that, after her four years up North, she could come home to attend his alma mater, if she still insisted on it, if she was still so sure this was her true vocation.

He had just finished his lunch at his desk, and was about to start work on the codicil to Riché's will when Jo Anne buzzed him and asked him had he heard the news, that President Kennedy had just been assassinated in Dallas.

* * *

He drove, drove with nowhere to go, drove around the high school and then out to the television station, and then on out to the oil refineries. And then he turned around and drove back downtown and then onto Dubonnet Drive and out to the campus, thinking he might see people milling around. But there were only a few stray figures scurrying to get out of the rain. He drove into the lot back of Brooke Hall and sat there with the motor running and the rain running down in big wide ribbons splashing on the windshield. Beat, beat, beat, it was drumming the roof of his car. He started up the motor again and switched on the radio. A man was talking and sobbing outside Parkland Memorial Hospital. He switched it off. In Dallas the sun had been shining brightly, otherwise they never would have had him in that open limousine.

He found himself on Morning Glory, only a block from the old home. He pulled up in front of the big house up at the corner and sent himself out around it and past the long hedgerows and down the old driveway and into the garden. He saw that the leaves of the oak tree were like stars that had been dipped in pale blood, he saw how the branches of the pines curved upward, as if in supplication. He saw her hands moving through the bridal wreath, slender and fluttering, her fair hands. He saw her rock back on her heels and push the sunhat back on her head, the sunhat with the Garbo slouch and the lemon yellow ribbon she tied under her chin. He saw the flash of sunlight on the blades of the pruning shears open on the grass. He saw the dark mole burrowing deeper into her back. He saw himself, a drink in his hand, watching her, his earthly treasure, his prize, his kingdom, his

Natalie. He was reclining in the chaise lounge on the patio, in the shade of the Japanese plum tree.

He heard a low, choking cry whirr in the back of his throat and then hush itself. As though words had fluttered their wings, and now folded them under.

He switched the radio on. The Presidential plane had just landed at Andrews Air Force Base. They had lowered the casket and carried it to the waiting ambulance. Robert Kennedy was there to meet it, and to embrace the widow, to give her the embrace of consolation. Lyndon Johnson was saying, "This is a sad time for all people."

On the morning Dad was to be buried, August had sent him up to see to Mother. Early as it still was, neither of them had liked the sound of that quiet when they'd come into the old house. She had been so obstinate the night before about wanting to stay there by herself that last night before the funeral.

If he had only called out to her. But how could he rightly remember? He had gone over this ground so many times, yet there was still so much tilling he had to do, grief makes you hallucinate as powerfully as love does.

She had left the door open. In a time of mourning, we're all so trusting.

It was August's doing that he'd been up there at all, he oughtn't to have listened to August, he ought to have obeyed his instinct once he saw that open door, he ought to have turned himself around and marched back down those stairs. If it hadn't been for August fretting like an old woman, he never would have violated her privacy like that, never, he was too well-bred for that, she had brought him up too well for him to have trespassed. It was on his wedding day he'd heard her say it herself to Grandma Landry, that she'd have to claim a smidgen of credit for the way he'd turned out, she'd done her very best to teach both her boys the traditions of her birthplace. "I transplanted well's I could," she'd laughed. "But I can't help but think all this was destined...that Gordon was meant to come back to stay. To fill out the life I might have lived if *my* parents had stayed."

She must have just swung her feet down onto the floor. Her pink nightgown was clinging to her, as though she'd just been swimming.

But it was her hair. Tumbling down everywhichway around her face, bewitching her into looking haggard, old, everything she despised. She never made her appearance in the morning until she'd braided it and wound it around her head. My coronet, she called it, proudly.

She was staring ahead into widowhood. She was murmuring aloud, "This is the day we must put him in the ground."

To civilize memory. That must be the highest art, surely, to learn how to cultivate memory. Left to its own workings, it grows wild, in no time at all everything lapses into a jungle. The gift of memory. To return it in good coin, that was the covenant we made with the Giver. Memory must be tamed if we're not to slide back into the state we began life in, if we're not to undo all the long, hard, loving labor of those who went before us, who brought us here. The living must teach themselves how to remember before crossing the bar. We must make memory compassionate. We the living must do unto the dead as we would have the living do unto us after we've taken our leave.

He turned the key in the ignition. St. Anne's was less than a mile from here. It seemed the place to go, the church where they'd been married, where Renée had been baptized, where they had said the Funeral Mass for Natalie.

He had overheard Coutant remarking to Jo Anne, "This can't help but make a martyr out of him." No one else in the firm would talk like that. And Coutant had *meant* for him to overhear it, he'd stood directly in front of his office door and he'd spoken quite distinctly. Coutant's all-innocence look when the remark had produced the effect he surely intended it to, the amazed look on both Jo Anne's *and* Coutant's faces when he'd brushed past them and called out he was leaving for the afternoon and wasn't to be disturbed at home for anything. Natalie had never cared for the man, she had seen right through his falseness. That last big party she'd been well enough to attend, when there'd been a frank and open discussion of the freedom movement and what the Citizens Councils were doing, she had reminded Coutant that the word "government" wasn't coterminous with the people ensconced in the Capitol of their state. She had had him to know his was not the voice of any South *she* knew about.

The strength and courage in her own sweet voice. The play of candlelight on her hands, on the necklace around her throat, in the hair curling at her temples, *real as my own*, she had marveled, she had made him promise she would not be without it when her time came. "Promise?" The tears standing in her eyes when she asked him. He had sworn on his own eyes he would see to it. He had kept his word.

* * *

Senator Mansfield had been reading: "In a moment, it was no more. And so she took a ring from her finger and placed it in his hands."

This late in November, there would be snow. Snow falling on the old farmhouse, and on the highway winding through the fields. And the bare branches of the elms would be a dark fishnet flung out under the horizon. He used to draw on his boots and button up his overcoat and pull down his ear flaps and wind a muffler around his throat.

"And so she took a ring from her finger and placed it in his hands and kissed him, and closed the lid of the coffin."

His breath was a white scroll unrolling on the air. He and August would take turns pulling one another on the sled. They would climb up on the roof and knock the icicles down. Dad would help them make their first snowman of the year.

"The gods are jealous," Mother used to say. Friday night he'd heard himself saying it to Renée when she'd asked him, "Why, Dad, *why*?"

The shock and disbelief of Friday. And for the past two days, the same reel played over and over again, beginning with his quick, light steps down the ramp... To be torn from life like that. The very air must have throbbed with the hurt and the astonishment of it. The scenes shifting back and forth these past days, the jumble of it, Oswald and Ruby and the White House with the flag at half-mast, and the Presidential portrait with the singing of the hymn in the background, "Eternal Father, strong to save. . . ."

The pinkgold light of Sunday evening was falling. He closed his eyes and sent himself into the garden again. It was early evening. He imagined the bouquet of apricots, as though the sweet olive were blooming. He imagined her singing in the lemon and lime twilight. His lips strummed with the remembrance of her. He thought of her running under the cypresses, her hair on fire with the sunset, and the Spanish moss lifting and falling. They were young, still, then. The dream of it was still living. He saw dusk spilling down through the Japanese plum tree, he saw little Renée drowsing on her tricycle, he saw her lipstick-red wagon, and her first big teddy bear sitting up in it, pert and smiling.

The Southern sun was always a long time dying, the Louisiana sky was a field of flowers, of roses and asters and violets and forget-me-nots. There was a Gregorian chanting in his head. Passionale. Good Friday. The immaculate, dry host was melting on his tongue, he could taste it now. And the priest shook the bell three times, and the light, silvery syllables of the handbell shivered in the quiet. He genuflected, made the Sign of the Cross. The fragrance of sandalwood, of the melting wax of the candles, and lily-of-the-valley. *Agnus Dei/Qui tollis peccata mundi*. He thought his very soul might take leave of his body.

The lyric diving and floating of the birds at sunset. The sweetness of the ligustrum and the sweet olive and her perfume. They say he had cried out, "My God, I am hit." *And I, the last, go forth companionless,/And the days darken round me, and the years* How could it be, that one so living, warm and breathing in the one moment, is in the moment that follows so utterly gone?

Those last weeks he would carry her out to the patio in the evenings. She had felt lighter and more fragile in his arms than Renée ever had been, even when she was still a little bit of a girl.

Her sewing basket would be up there on the white pedestal table. "Person's got to keep *some* kind of busy work in her hands." Next to the sewing basket, the aquamarine bowl with chrysanthemums, Greta saw to it there'd be freshly cut flowers for her to look at.

Yellow chrysanthemums. Flowers of autumn. Flowers of farewell.

Towards evening, Miss Summerfield would wander among her fig trees and pecan trees in her big yard next door. "Good evening, Miss Summerfield," Natalie would call, bright and neighborly, "your palmettos seem to have done right nicely this year." Those last weeks, Miss Summerfield had taken particular care not to admonish Natalie about the Japanese plum tree they'd lost that summer. There wasn't one I-told-you-so, though Miss Summerfield had loved that tree as if it'd been her own, and she'd pleaded with Natalie to allow her to send Houston over to burn out the caterpillars attacking it so viciously. Natalie simply wouldn't *hear* of it. She said she couldn't bear the thought of his doing that, soaking those old rags in gasoline and wrapping them around big, long poles and plunging those burning torches into the branches. *Incinerating* the little things. "A tree is life, too, Mrs. Stephens," Miss Summerfield would proclaim, "and a sight more splendid than those nasty things." He'd sided with Miss Summerfield, but Natalie's will had prevailed. She'd said there had to be another way than to take one form of life for the sake of sparing another form of it. He was so thankful now he'd let her decide.

Thanksgiving holiday or no, that trip to Washington next week was part business, the Law Institute was convening, and he had some preparing to do. People in Coutant's camp were already busy at work drawing up a statement endorsing states' rights and another one censuring the Civil Rights Bill. He'd best get himself stirring, if that other voice of the South that Natalie had told Coutant about was to be heard. He'd take a drive on out to the lakes to refresh himself first. They were always so beautiful this time of year, this time of day, too, just to *see* them was bound to inspire him.

Late November or no, it was a sultry evening. He parked and got out and went on down to the edge of the water. Three white ducks were paddling right on by him. They preened themselves, fluffed out their feathers and scudded away. Farther on out, the water glittered like a bed of rhinestones. Over on the other side, the trees made a vestibule of dark green foliage, branches of the cypress and the tupelo gum forming a kind of passageway to a place beyond them he was too far away to feature. A light, moist wind came up, he heard the dogwood back of him rustling with it. In the spring, the dogwood was like nothing so much as a belle of the old South in her crinoline skirts, Mother used to remark that so wistfully.

August had it right, it was better that she stay up there with him and his family, there was so much stirring down here, so much uncertainty about what might be coming, at her age it was best Mother stay with what was lasting, with what would never change so long as the country lasted. “Let’s not have the war-between-the-states all over again over me,” Mother had laughed. “I know both my boys love me the same. Mind, I’m depending on both of you to make me your very best, most sensible recommendation.” Dad would have wanted it that way too, surely, that she stay near the farm.

How Mother would *remark* that the assassination happened on his birthday!

He would be buried tomorrow. On his little boy’s third birthday, how very cruel life could be.

Country won’t see his like again.

“Deifyin’,” Natalie would’ve teased. You Arsh have that habit of deifyin’.”

whither shall I go?/ Where shall I hide my forehead and my eyes?

The lake was swallowing up the sun, the night insects were beginning their music, the air was turning that soft blue, the cypresses seemed to be sorrowing into the water.

He thought he caught the scent of fresh mint.

It could not be.

The light breeze came again, faintly tinged with jasmine.

The deep crimson glow was mirroring itself on the water, spreading a bright red, wavering path strewn with leafy shadows across the mere. He saw her, saw her dark and merry eyes, her tender smile. He saw her waltzing. Waltzing in a great marbled hall, on floors that shone. Waltzing in her gown of pale green. Waltzing with him, with Kennedy. They were dancing, her face looking up into his, and his looking down into hers.

He rode the white bird, the great white heron circling above them, he moving clockwise, they moving counter-clockwise on the water. Shadowless, he turned above them, and shadowless they turned on the glowing crimson surface of the lake.

Sowing In the Shadows

Sowing in the morning, sowing seeds of kindness,
Sowing in the noontide and the dewy eves;
Waiting for the harvest, and the time of reaping,
We shall come rejoicing, bringing in the sheaves!

Never knew how long that road would be. Mama, you warned me. You spoke of it when I was happiest, I never knew why it was then. There I was, delightin' in the purest of things at the time, the wet cool grass workin' its way up through my toes, the fat-bodied bees drinkin' nearby, and me dreamin'. Dreamin' about nothin', just bein' *happy* is all. Just happy *bein'*. And your back all stiff and angry-lookin', though you never truly was, standin' at the stove most often then, sayin' how long the road is. Mama, if you knew how I need you, miss you. Worse than then, it's worse now, when I'm too big, too old to be comforted by anyone, too big and too old for anybody to bother about if I cry, here's when I need you. Lord, that old longing fills me, and it's like I'm turnin' to salt myself, a whole pillar of it, a tremblin' pillar of salt is what I am. Just to hear you say *Honey*, just to hear you say *Chile* that way.

I know what you felt for me. I didn't know then, but now, with my own daughters, how could I not know. They're *you*, anyways. One of you and another of you, a little different here, a little different there, but all the same, the same. You grieve for a girl. And it makes you hard, that grievin', because it goes hard. I understand you now, Mama, wherever you be, I know you hear me, and you know I understand you now. It'll be the same for my girls. They don't need no forgivin' from me. Think I don't remember what it was, to be a girl. But I remember.

If the Lord hears my prayer, they'll only have girls themselves. Only have girls. No, Mama, I don't pray for him no more, I don't pray no more for Will. You do still, I feel that you do, but I'm not out that far yet. Anyways, it's no use. Your boys, Mama, they had the world come on down on them and ride right over them. They stayed where you put 'em, and you prayed it would pass over them, pass over their heads. And your prayin' was heard. What would you do if they came to you and said they were goin' out to *meet* it, what would you do then, I'd still like to know. Cause if I knew, I would know what *I* should have done. And what to do with the livin' hours of every livin' day, now. Not knowin'. Not wantin' to know no more. They bring me their tales, tales of catchin' 'em and hurtin' 'em and killin' 'em , oh, Mama, spare me those tales, keep those story-tellers from my cabin door! If I heard nothin' more in my days than the whippoorwill sang the night he come, I'd have bad dreams enough to keep me tossin' the rest of my life. Comes up from inside of you, Mama, you know, has nothin' to do with all that goes on out there. Besides, that don't change. I told Will that. But, Will, he don't hear nothin'. Never did. Except those freedom songs.

I saw pictures of the Reverend King, Mama, he's such a fine lookin' man! His face is kind, and knowin'. They say when he preaches, a common stone would run blood out, and I believe it. Heard him on the television when the Simmons left the house to me that week. Wouldn't that be all, if they knew I watched me that show! He's a brave man, Mama, I can see, surely, why Will answered to his call. He'll walk right into the fire, I know it, with Jesus on his lips. And his eyes are good eyes. They beat him and they walk over him, and they turn dogs on him and send him crazy letters, but that don't stop him none. He's not gonna be stopped. Never saw such a man before, one of ours.

Mama, they're afraid of him, they wouldn't dare to harm him. Surely, in the beginning, surely, when he was in all manner of danger, that's when Jesus save him, as only Jesus could. Now they can't touch him no more, and they know they can't. That's what makes 'em all the madder, that's what puts in their eyes that crazy look, like they want to kill every last one of us, yes, Mama, they won't rest until they get back at us, you can feel it in the way they look at you. And that wasn't before. That's what I tried to tell Will. Will, he's got no protection, he's nothin' but just another one of us. They can set their dogs on him, they can catch him and string him up, or throw one of their bombs where he be stayin' the night, they can blow him up, nobody'd do nothin' about it, oh, Lord Jesus, who would pay it mind? And they fixin' to do it all now. Yes, Mama, they fixin' to really do it up to us. Cause they feel like nobody's gonna stop 'em anymore. Not since last Friday, since they took that own President's life away.

Saw her, saw her picture in the paper. O' course, they showed the widow most, and those two poor orphaned babies. But they showed her, too, at the church, day they buried him. Had one of those black veils over her face, just like the widow did. But you could see somethin' of her, all the same. How can she take it, Mama, how we all supposed to take it?

Look at Him up there, look at Jesus layin' in her lap, is this what Mamas get? Look, His eyes all rolled back in His head, the thorns still stuck in Him, His hands and feet all bloody. They cut Him down, and they gave Him over to her. Now she can have Him, now He's dead! So she can give Him a proper burial.

No, Mama, I don't talk blasphemy, and you know it. You know I was always the most believin' of your children, you said so yourself, that I was the truest Christian of all, no, I don't talk blasphemy. You know I love Jesus as I do, that don't change my feeling about His Mother. I look at her face, I try to see what's in there, in that grievin'. Is there forgiveness? How can they speak for her, how can they say that she forgives? They say *Jesus* do, but they don't say nothin' about her, nobody talks about that. Maybe they're afraid to think about it, maybe the preachers don't want to pay mind to it, it's just too worrisome, it's just too deep.

Will she forgive? Lord, Mama, will she forgive? He was so high, the highest of all this country. So young and so strong and so proud! Not a man, not a woman in this parish would deny that greatness, no matter what they thought about him otherwise. Big. A big man. He'd fill up all the space around him. Same as Reverend King. Giants, one Negro, one white. Look into all the cabins down this road, see if you don't see 'em both on every wall, see if you don't. People know a great man when they see one.

Didn't stop 'em. No, Mama, they weren't afraid. Who could do such a thing, put an end to that life, kill like that, tell me, Mama, who could do such a thing? Nothin' human, I know that. No one human. But what difference it gonna make to her? Now he's gone, now her son's gone, what difference it gonna make?

Tell me, Mama, what is this life, where we be goin', why is it we lay down like we do, spread out our bodies, and I don't mean to blaspheme, you know I wouldn't blaspheme, just like on the cross, to deliver up our babies? What's it all for, Mama, do you know now? Can you tell me, just a little? Big tears comin' down again, I was always so emotional, you mustn't pay it no mind, you mustn't grieve for me, you just rest, you just rest easy, Lord knows you deserve to.

She's got two more sons. Lost two, got two left. Must be some comfort. Oh, I know what you taught us, you said if you had a hundred, each'd be like the only one to you. You said makes no difference, when you lost one, you lose that one, ain't no other one to take its place. Maybe a new one, but never that same one. But, Mama, forgive me, maybe it do make a difference. Believe me, if I had just one more boy, even a little one, to start all over again now, oh, I know I'd ache, but I wouldn't ache like this, like now, when there's only Will. Only just Will. All I'll ever have of a boy. And I just know it. Too old now to have any more. And tell me, Mama, why would anyone except a crazy person want any at all, never mind wantin' more? Don't last no more time than it takes a zinnia to bloom and fade, that early time. When they so small and stick to you like they was grafted on. You sing to 'em, you talk to 'em. And they look at you like you was straight from God. Oh, Lord, Mama, is it all for just that feelin' we can get then? Lord love you and keep you, Mama, I know what you felt for me, I know what you passed on to me. We all feel it. I look at that woman. She so rich and famous, she had a son he became President, it ain't no different for her. We all the same.

Like to go on over to her. Like to put these big dark arms around her, like to hold her like you hold your own kin, and comfort her. And I just know she'd allow it. I know what she lost. What we all lost. Maybe like he was my son or my brother, maybe that close I felt him to be. For you know what good people is, you know what they made out of. You look just once in his brother's eyes, in Robert's eyes, there's somethin' in that face almost too pure and hurtful for this old earth. Well, she's got him, and she's got that younger one. All she's got left now. Now they taken the others away.

Took him, Mama, took him away! War's wicked enough, Lord knows I know it's wicked. But *this* one! Wasn't even fightin' with anyone. Just ridin' in that fine car. Just laughin' and wavin' at folks, and the wind blowin' the hair in his eyes, such a fine and strappin' man. And they cut him down. Yes, they cut him down. Enough to break you, enough to break your heart in two. Here comes those tears again. Who can help it? Nobody human can help it.

Sowing in the sunshine, sowing in the shadows,
Fearing neither clouds nor winter's chilling breeze;
By and by the harvest, and the labour ended,
We shall come rejoicing, bringing in the sheaves!

Mama, Lord help me, Mama, I feel that doom all around. Don't know no more if it's outside or inside. That terrible doom. Like it's all about to just be startin' now. Like this was just the beginnin' of it. And I think of Will until I can't think no more. Until when my eyes is closed, all I see is a dark red river. That's what our insides is.

A woman knows too much. A woman remembers too much. No use to speak of such things to men, Mama. No use to speak of it to them! I knew

Will was comin'. Before there was any sign of *any*body comin' anywhere, I felt him on his way. Like he came to *me*. Came to my door and walked right in, like it was just me he was lookin' for. He appeared to me, Mama, that chile appeared to me most a year before he got himself born. Like it was me he was choosin'. Don't ask me why. You can go up and down this road and find a likelier body anywhere than this poor one, so heavy and so slow. You felt me, too. You felt all of us. And I felt the others, too. But it was more 'n' feel. And Lord knows it was early, maybe he had been no more 'n' a wick of a candle, not even movin'. Like to tear me apart, just rememberin' that feelin', knowin' he come to me. Mama, forgive me, you earned your rest, but who can I tell my fear? Forgive me, Mama, I never told no one, and I never did intend to, it's just all this dyin', all this killin', so I can't keep it to me no more. I saw him, Mama, yes, I saw *him*. Just like he be now. That straight way he stands. That easy smile. His quick temper, too, the fire in him. And you know what I said, Mama? Mama, is it a sin, please, let me confess to you, I said to his appearance, *Go, go away, go into somebody else's body, go*. 'Cause I knew he'd be more of a human bein' than I could rightly raise, he'd be too much for me

Maybe it was all because of that weakness, then, I had so bad, that weakness after Virginia was born, that child was just in the wrong place, you remember, and it took all I had to bring her out right. And I was played out, for a long time, you remember. Maybe it was *that* got into me, I didn't think I could do with another one so soon, I had to get my strength back. But, Mama, I could lie to Jesus even, may the Lord forgive me, before I could lie to you. That's how true I'll always be to you, that's how much I want to be the kind of person you always wanted me to be. It was more than just bein' weary over Virginia's birthin'. It was that I knew he was in there. And I didn't think I had what a woman needs, to bring him up like a man has to be brought up. If it was a girl, Mama, I would never have made no prayer to her like I did to Will, you just got to believe me. It was because it was *Will*. I knew who he was, and I knew he made up his mind on comin'. And it wasn't patience I was needin' so much as pure blood and bone, pure *spirit* to meet all that fire in his. And so, and Lord forgive me, Mama, I said, *Go. Go.* I tried to spirit him out of me into some other woman's body. Some woman that was stronger. That could meet him like he needed to be met up with. And he looked at me. He looked at me, and his eyes were sayin' to me, It's *you, woman, it's you I picked, and I am here to stay. I came in* this *door. I came in* this *cabin*.

Was it that way for her too? Did she see him comin' too? Know someplace inside herself that he'd rise up to the highest place in all this whole world, and then get himself killed like that? Mama, Mama, did she know it too?

Don't need no papers, Mama. Don't need no television to tell me what's goin' on all over. Just like in slavery. A boy ran away. Everybody waited. His Mama, she did more than wait. A part of her was followin' him, runnin' and breathin' fast and hidin' and thirstin' with him. And she was prayin', *Catch me first, before you catch up with him, Come, Lord, send me a sickness, somethin' that catches up with me, and take me in his place. Just let him go on, let him be free, now he made up his mind he has to have his freedom.* And then they bring him back. And she gives a cry when she sees them bringin' him in. To be whipped, to be branded, maybe even to be killed right off. She gives a cry that you could tear open the Lord's own heaven with it. 'Cause she can't save him, cause the Lord didn't want her in his place. 'Cause she couldn't *take* his place. Cause nobody asks no old mother what to do, what's right to do. They ask the boss, they ask the *chickens* before they ask the mother. Lord, Lord, what wickedness did we do, that they made us women? Don't need no tales to tear me all in pieces. They tell me anyways, but I hear my own. They come from inside my head, inside of me, whatever's there, I know. Part of you follows. Part of you is there with him. When they come after you and take you away, when they do violence to your body, when they lift up that big rifle like that crazy man lifted it up on Friday and just tore out his life, she knew. I know she knew. Maybe long, long ago. Like I know about Will.

Here I am, snufflin' again, Mama, I just can't help it. Never knew such sadness before. Like I was eatin' ashes. You remember what Cousin Rosemarie told us. They found the body of that poor, unsuspectin' boy in the Tallahatchie. They drug it and they found young Emmett Till. And there they was, takin' up collections to defend his murderers. And she went with more 'n' half the town of Negroes to that trial. And there they was, standin' right in front of the Confederate statue, where they had the words about "the cause that never failed." They all stood there in that witherin' sun and looked and looked at that courthouse, knowin' what kind of justice was in there. And there they was, after the verdict, settin' out those little jars on the store counters, collectin' again. Collectin', this time, to keep Tallahatchie County separate but equal. Thought Will would go clean outen his mind, listenin' to Cousin Rosemarie. Lord, Mama, what made Will think it's gonna change?

Mama, Mama, did I make it come to be this way? Don't spare me, I need to know, I got to know the truth now. Can't walk no more, this road's too long, I got to know. Got to know if it was my sayin' that, was that what made him so all-fire burnin', so aimed straight at riskin' his life, like he's doin' at this very moment? If I didn't say *Go*, like that, if I just pretended I didn't see him, and stayed on peaceful, if I said to myself it's just one of those dreams you get when everythin's kind of a sick yellow in front of your eyes and you're all fevered and dizzy and it was all from Virginia's birth, maybe it wasn't Will at all in there, maybe, oh Lord, *maybe I dreamed him into me*, and made him so stubborn and fightin' and darin'. Mama, Mama, is it our sins that makes our children, is it our sins they have to pay for? Didn't *mean* to, Mama, didn't mean that dream, I didn't mean to try to whisk him away. But I can't go back on it. I said to him, *Go*. And everything you say, it happens when you don't want it to happen anymore. Remember you warned me never to make a wish, cause it might come back on you, you said, it might come true.

Couldn't see her face for that black veil. Maybe just like folks can't see us rightly, for all this dark skin over us. Couldn't see her face. Couldn't look into her eyes. If I could, I'd know. I'd know what she be feelin'. And if I was there, she'd know. And *she"d* be comforted. High or low, makes no difference when there's grievin' over a child. Women, we all suffer the same. You and me, and my girls, and her, her, Mother Rose, we all feel the same things inside, no matter if we wearin' the finest silk or an old cornmeal sackin' dress, no matter if one's got a son in the White House and the other's got a son in a cabin, a boy tellin' folks older than his own parents that they got to go reddish, that after all these years, here he is, promisin' them that gate to freedom's suddenly got to swing wide open. Is that why they killed that fine man, Mama? Because he was gonna help us *reddish* to vote? Did he die for *us*, Mama, did he die for *us*? Is *that* what's doin', they're takin' that high life for our misery, is it Jesus on the cross all over again?

But she's got those two others. I got no other boy, only my girls. Girls that'll lay down like you and me, and bring forth more girls to do the same, and boys like my Will. So's they can grow 'em up and watch 'em go off down that dark, lonesome road. Head high, proud and strong and believin', to their death. Yes, Mama, to their death, to all our death. 'Cause if he had to die, what's to spare Will now?

Mama, Mama, did I make it so? You know, if I could call him back inside me, I'd melt him on down, smaller 'n' smaller, where no one could touch him or see him, see him in all his brown glory, I'd put him back inside me. Back where *you* are now, Mama, back where God stays. You know, I shouldn't prayed he'd go on into no other body, I should've prayed he'd melt on back down like that. 'Cause in another body, he'd still be born, and grow up and claim what's his, and be hurt for it. Maybe, oh Mama, maybe have to die for it.

And if I had those others. What she be thinkin' now? Lost the first one. Saw a picture of him, he was as fine as the President looked to me. Lost him too. Now this one. What she gonna tell the others? I look at him, I look at Mister Robert. Never saw eyes like that before in no livin' bein'. You saw him, Mama? You know what I speak about. There is such a hungerin' in those eyes of his. And such a goodness. Hurts me to think about it, never mind to see it in a picture. Like to burn me far down inside, that look of his.

The Reverend King, he's got a Mama too. A fine good woman she is. Think I could draw a Bible lesson from her. She plays in that church. While they all stand there, just like me standin' here now, singin' hymns, drawin' strength and comfort from all around me. She plays in that church. And you know that he's in her head, all mixed up with the singin', just like it be for me now, the words of the hymn, and Will. She thinks about her boy with all them comin' at him, and him keepin' on walkin' right into them. And she *knows* what they fix to do to him if they think they can get away with it. And she knows now they'll think they can. 'Cause look what they did to the *President*. Lord, God, Mama, when I think how they shot him down. Him slumpin' over. That great big beautiful head tore into like that. It like to tear me in two. I want to go back to that time and save him. Yes, Mama, I wish I could warn him, I could say, *Don't go this way*. If that sun wasn't shinin', if it was rainin' in Dallas that day, it couldn't happen, they'd have that top rolled up right over him, and we'd still have him now. So young, Mama, so young he was. So young and so fine spoken and so strong!

Here I be. Weepin' 'n' singin' 'n' talkin' to you, not lookin' at this one or that one, just feelin' all their company all around me, feelin' the warm feelin' of that, and smellin' the old wood in here like it's the most familiar smell in the world to me. Never once lookin' at my preacher husband up there. First time I been to church that I didn't look over to him. I don't know why. We don't speak much, not since Will left us. I know he's grievin', but he didn't try to hold Will back. He didn't believe it was his place. And I did, I tried. So when he went off, he had to go off lookin' at me in that sorrowin' way. Like he won't forgive me. Though he *know* I wish him all the world, he *knows* it! Lord, Mama, he's my only son, how can't he know what all I wish for him, I wish him anythin' left in these old bones and blood he could draw somethin' from. Let them take me, Mama, let them take me, so I can go home to you. Spare Will. Let my boy have his time on earth.

Go then ever, weeping, sowing for the Master,
Tho' the loss sustained our spirit often grieves:
When our weeping's over, He will bid us welcome,,
We shall come rejoicing, bringing in the sheaves!

They didn't let our President have his rightful time on this earth. They took it away from him. Just like that, they took it. So it's too late to pray, now, about that. But it's not too late for Will, no more 'n' it's too late for those two brothers he left behind him, nor for the Reverend King, they still got a chance, oh, let them have their life! Mama, all the mothers prayin'. You'd think all heaven'd just melt on down, listenin' to us all. You'd think it be enough to make the Lord Himself go weepin'.

I know my preacher husband's grievin' up there. You like to see a ghost when he heard about the President. He come after me out in the garden, and he bow down his head, his old gray head. And he fall right down on his knees, and he start that terrible sobbin', and he tell me they killed him there in Dallas. Didn't believe it, he said, didn't want to believe it. Nor neither did I. Thought he like to gone crazy from all that's goin' on around us, from Will bein' in danger 'n' all, that he dreamed a bad, bad dream. Wisht it was so, wisht it was a bad dream.

Mama. Mama? Don't tell me nothin' no more. I don't know nothin' only 'cept this one thing. We lay down, we deliver 'em up to this hard world. We got no power, not even to save 'em from all that's waitin' for 'em. It's a curse to be a woman, though you never said so, I know you knew it too. But one thing. One thing I'll tell you surely. Wouldn't be no woman to shoot that rifle Friday. No woman do that. Wouldn't be no woman to set police dogs on people peacefully marchin', no woman to go clubbin' people in the head, no woman to throw no bombs in no churches, no woman to catch my Will 'n' hurt him. No woman, that creature who'd do any of those things. And if it look like a woman, it ain't no woman that laid down and brought forth a child would do it.

Only they do it. Only them. Makes no difference the color, they all be men. *That's* what the races are, Mama, only them two, just men and women, that's what the races be! Lord, God, what they do to each other, they seem to be just itchin', just *achin'* to go at each other, with words, with rifles, with whips, with every manner of ways to hurt 'n' to kill, they goin' at each other. And we bring 'em forth. Yes, and we lay 'em back in the earth. We stand dumb 'n' grievin', and they just go on and on, no end to it, Mama, no end to it. Highest and lowest, we got to give 'em up for that, for *that*!

Don't know what it be inside of 'em, Mama. You take the saintliest. You take that preacher husband o' mine, you take Reverend King, you take the President, it's in 'em all. They do it to each other. They do it to *us*. Call it wantin' freedom. Call it wantin' power. Don't make a difference, it's all the same. And when I come home, Mama, when I come home to you and to the Lord, I'm gonna ask. Me, your old Annie, who never asked for nothin' 'cept that mornin' I took it in my head that I had to have that patterned piece o' cloth they sent us on down. You remember that? How I cried 'n' cried for it? Had those tiny blue flowers on it, you'd think that it was all the world! Well, I'm about to ask, I am. Ask the Lord Himself. 'Cause only He can know.

What it was they done, to make 'em all like that. What it was *we* done, to make us stand dumb 'n' grievin' just to be witness. In your time, in my time, Mama, in all time, oh, Lord, it keeps on goin' that way.

Bringing in the sheaves! Bringing in the sheaves!
We shall come rejoicing, bringing in the sheaves!

Mama, rest now. Rest, Mama. Now I prayed myself clean, be a long time before I'd raise you from your sleep out of such need. You know what, Mama? From all you taught me, from all you give to me out of your goodness, comes my voice here. Strong as you'll ever hear it, strong for all my fearin'. You'll hear it sweepin' right along with all the rest. For you, Mama, and for Will, and for the girls, and for my man, all my kin and neighbors, and for all those in every place that lost that good man with us, and got a Will out there, Lord keep them all. Lord hear us, hear us in our faith.

Bringing in the sheaves! Bringing in the sheaves!
We shall come rejoicing, bringing in the sheaves!

Flight From a Phantom

A house lays claim to its inhabitants after a while. I don't know how long people have to live in a place before this possessiveness begins to show its hand. But if I lived in any house for longer than a year, I'd find little ways of asking for pardon as soon as I began thinking of moving away, I'd begin making apologies. The god or spirit of the place has an animal sense of it when the people who live in it decide to leave. I know that's an oxymoron, but that doesn't trouble an animist, which is what I've discovered my religion is.

We left Louisiana during the summer of 1964. I thought at the time that we'd be going back home up north to stay. I still had the notion there *is* such a place, home, and that home lay in a certain direction, in a certain region of this country. Since then we've moved from one place to another in Central and South America, moved more times than I care to count; it's made our three children into true citizens of the world. But that's another story. The one I want to tell here is a little cautionary tale that taught me that a house feels scorned by people when they decide to move out of it. It's apt to chase after them, to try to pull them back--especially if they've been so careless that they haven't performed some little ceremony of leave-taking on Moving Day. If you discover this too far out on the road to turn back and make amends, your only chance of escape is to hoodwink the Thing into believing that's what you intend to do.

I'll tell you how I happened to realize this, and I promise you I'll make no commentaries. It's said that a word to the wise is sufficient--an adage I hope for your sake is a workable truth.

I left our car in the driveway with the motor running and my husband Bob and our two little sons inside. I'd suddenly remembered my mother's superstition about asking the empty house for its blessing before departing for good; it made me think I might have left something, although we'd stripped the place bare. In fact, that very morning I'd dropped off a carton of last things in the collection receptacle provided by a local charity, dust-wreathed things deep inside cabinets, things in the corners of closet shelves.

Although it was early evening, the air was still sultry. I went from one empty room to the next, and then came back to stand in front of the big glass doors opening to the postage-stamp-sized patio. I'd left the drapes half-open as the realtor had advised me to do. The neighbors' children were playing in their driveway across from our yard. Donnie sent the ball through the basket with his lazy, easy grace. His younger brother was rolling on the grass with their dog. And their sister was in her accustomed place, on the hood of the family's station wagon, and in her customary uniform, shorts and a halter. I had the thought they might have agreed beforehand to make this tableau for me, for my last look. I can see it still, very vividly too, as I write this.

Beyond their home, the cypresses seemed to yearn toward the sky, their braids of Spanish moss curling sinuously in the shimmering air. Birds were cawing and diving through the trees. A swarm of white fly lay like pollen over the yellowing leaves of the ligustrum in our yard. That morning I'd seen a blue lizard gleaming on the flagstones. Blue! I thought I was dreaming, but it was real. One of Hughie's sand pails lay in the banana plant in the corner of our yard. I'd made that plant's leaves into dragons' tongues in a story I made up for the boys once when they were ailing from the flu.

The lidless eyes of the windows bored into my back; the house was stifling. I felt pity for it, as if we'd forsaken it; then I laughed the feeling away. We had a long trip ahead, and I'd used up so much of my strength already that I'd have to give all my attention to the task before us.

Bob gave me a quizzical look after I got myself back into the car and slammed the door, but he didn't ask me why I'd gone back. Joel piped up, "Mommy, are we really going now?"

I looked back at the boys. Joel was kneeling at the window, looking for the last time at the only home he'd ever known. Hughie was leaning against the bolster pillow. He seemed sleepy and contented enough. I'd asked his doctor to prescribe a mild sedative so he could weather the long trip.

"Yep. And only about a thousand miles to go, Joel. Hughie, how is my little fellow?"

The child burrowed deeper into his pillow, and lifted a chubby hand to say it was all right.

"He'll never have to suffer like this again," I told Bob as I backed the car out of the driveway. "I'm convinced his asthma comes from living down here."

Bob leaned back and stretched out his right leg, grimacing from the pain it gave him to do that. He grinned and made his old joke, "Damnyankee foreigners, outsiders, trouble-makers, agitators, serves you right, his asthma and my leg."

I didn't smile back. I didn't want to tell him, but I'd made up my mind we'd cover two-hundred miles that first night before stopping at a motel. While I waited for the traffic to clear so I could turn at the first corner, I realized my hands were clenching the wheel, my neck was aching with tension. He said something about taking it easy, that we had a long way to go. I made the turn, and our car moved smoothly past buildings I'd never see again, on a route I'd never follow again. He asked if we should take a last look at the campus. I could hear the weariness in his voice. This was only the fifth week after his laminectomy, and the surgeon had refused to commit himself about the effect this car trip might have on his back and leg. It would be a long, slow recovery was all he'd say.

I told Bob we'd seen the campus enough times to last us the rest of our lives. I was saying Goodbye inside my head, *Goodbye bayous, the egrets on your waters. And the hawks in the rainbow sky. And the chipping sparrows and the mockingbbirds and the woodpeckers, and the aching sweetness of the fragrance of the azaleas and pittisporum and sweet olive. Goodbye hackberries and canes and palmettos and live oaks and cypresses, and jewelweed with your crimson-gold bells, and spiderwort with your purple velvet, Goodbye mimosas with your lacy leaves, your delicate pinks. Goodbye morning sun exploding in the sky, scorching the soil, searing the skin, parching sweet reason, Goodbye dark brothers and sisters trudging down these dusty roads with your parcels wrapped in newspaper, Goodbye--*

Bob's voice broke in upon my valedictory to remind me to make the turn at the airport. I told him impatiently I knew that. We were driving through the oldest part of town, past gray tumbledown shacks and stores. It had taken ten years, our disenchantment; I'd almost despaired we'd ever leave. But the November before, just after the assassination in Dallas, Bob had said we were getting out. I gave in then to my homesickness for the north, for home. Even as Bob was talking about starting all over again, with our eyes open this time because we could never be young and whole as we'd been when we first came down here, I felt my heart soar with the memory of snow. Snow. I could almost taste the cold whiteness of melting snow.

Then I heard that terrible cry inside my head. One of our neighbors had died the week before, and the night after the funeral I'd been up rocking Hughie long past midnight. Our little one had been wheezing and coughing, fighting for his breath until I thought my own throat would close with the grief of my powerlessness to help him. At long last, he'd dropped off to sleep. I'd stayed there, holding him a while longer to be sure he wouldn't wake up again, when I heard that cry, a high-pitched, inhuman wailing, and then the words, *Ah, God, what's happened to your face?* Bob had hurried into Hughie's room, stumbling over stacks of packed cartons. He'd almost fallen. That would have been our undoing, if he'd fallen. He'd told me the cry was from the Lewis's, that one of the youngsters must have had a bad dream. Miraculously, Hughie had gone on sleeping.

I sensed a swirling as of mist, but finer than mist. I felt it with that sixth sense, a blend of hearing and touch that puts every nerve in the body on alert. Anything could happen. I might miscarry. Or Hughie might have an acute attack. Or Bob might have some kind of seizure. Or something might happen to Joel, just because we imagined he was the least vulnerable of the four of us. In April, Bob's best friend had died. In July, with no warning, no history of back trouble, Bob had suffered a ruptured disc. Just before his surgery, the doctor had said he did not know if Bob would ever walk again. And we hadn't been able to sell our house, even though at least forty people had come to look at it. The house was still in our name.

The photograph of the three slain civil rights workers flashed on the windshield. Bob was shouting that I'd missed the turn. I slammed on the brakes. Joel cried out; Bob shouted something; and I put my foot down hard on the accelerator again.

"What in the name of God's gotten into you?" Bob yelled. "This damned leg....I wish I could take that wheel!"

"For the good God's sake!" I was shouting, trembling. "Can't you all be quiet? Can't you see what a strain this is?" I turned into a dead-end street and parked the car and leaned my forehead on the wheel.

We all sat motionless, I couldn't say for how long. At last I said I was sorry, I didn't know what had come over me. Bob murmured *it's okay,* but it wasn't. I backed the car into a private driveway, narrowly missing the garbage can, and pulled out onto the street, turning the wheel with unnecessary force.

Somehow we got back on our way. We'd talked about getting a new car with air conditioning, but there had been Hughie's asthma attacks, my pregnancy, Bob's surgery, the move. The heat was intolerable, it bled the strength from one's body. Although I'd taken a shower just before we left, my armpits were soaked, my skirt was sticky, beads of sweat were trickling down the backs of my legs. I tried not to think about the life I was carrying inside me.

When we reached the airport at last, and drove around it up onto the main highway, Bob laughed and said, "An auspicious beginning." I know he was sorry he'd lost his temper.

I also knew why I'd missed the turn.

We'd been on the highway for less than an hour. Joel had settled down with his books, Hughie was sleeping, Bob was studying the map, I was becoming aware of a change in the sky. We were entering the swamps, and the live oaks and cypresses along the road stirred with a moist, sweetly scented wind. A storm was brewing. Bob looked up and asked was I thinking what he was thinking, that maybe the whole idea of taking off at this time of day was crazy, that once we started through the swamps there wouldn't be any place to stop for at least an hour. I asked him in anger if he wanted to take a motel room *now,* he answered with the question what else would I suggest, I asked him how his leg was, he said no better, no worse and that his leg had nothing to do with it.

"Then we're going on," I said. "We're getting out of here."

I knew he was furious at my stubbornness, that he was raging at his enforced dependency. I turned on the radio, and there was our all-time favorite testimonial delivered in the Cajun staccato he loved to mimic, *Good ol' Doctah Tichenah's! Bes' an-a-sep-tik in town!* Then came the news that two men in the Parish had broken out of jail and were being pursued in the bayous by a posse with police dogs.

It was too late to turn back. And I knew that if I still had to decide, I'd have gone on.

I felt the swamps close over us. I thought of the savaged shapes of the live oaks, and of the sac-à-lait and snapping turtles and snakes and alligators in the shadows all around us, readying themselves for the storm.

Very, very slowly the phosphorescent light began dimming. Then a few drops of rain struck the roof of our car. Under the smoldering blue of the sky, the trees began swaying. The air was oppressive, sickly-sweet. At last we heard thunder rumbling low and menacing. I felt Bob's accusing eyes on my face.

When we entered the swamps, the sky had been mauve and rose and flaming orange and a silken, pale blue. I had thought of the swamps as an isthmus between two worlds, one we *would* cross. *Must* cross.

I sensed the swirling again. This time it was a dervish encircling me. It felt...brooding.

Halfway through, we were stopped by a roadblock. A short, stocky man in a policeman's uniform took his time getting to our car, walking with his thumbs thrust into his gun belt. He ducked his head and peered in my window at me, giving me a good long look. And then did a study of Bob, and then of the children.

"Your driver's license please, Ma'am."

I handed him my wallet without speaking, without even breathing.

"Heading north, eh?" His florid, smiling face was inscrutable.

"We're going on a little trip." I hated the tightness in my voice.

His eyes flicked over my face and came to rest on Bob's again. "You lettin' the little lady drive in this?"

"My husband had back surgery very recently, Officer. He's not supposed to drive yet. What's happening?"

"Well, folks, I don't want to scare you none, but there's two escapees in the area, that's why we're stoppin' all the cars. Those are two mean fellows, one of 'em may be armed. Like as not, they'd do just about anythin' to get out of the Parish. Now, you folks just roll up your windows far as you can stand, and don't stop for a thing 'til you get to your first town up ahead. Still Creek. You can get some gas there and look around, see if you ought to go on tonight."

He glanced up to read the sky. I waited, my hands folded in my lap.

"Just sprinklin'. But might start pourin' any minute now. Sir, I hope you won't let the little lady here do anythin' foolish, that's a mightly lonely stretch o' road ahead. See you keep her goin' 'til Still Creek."

"I will, Officer. And thank you."

He took another look at the children. I caught the sweat and strength of the man as his shoulder brushed mine. *Cute little fellows,* he said, and told us we could go on.

I must have driven at least ten minutes before saying, *I know, you told me so.* It was then that the generator light flashed on, a bright red glow, an eye of DANGER suddenly opening. I could taste the panic I felt as I asked Bob what it meant, what in hell should we do now. He ordered me to stop the car, he said there's something seriously wrong when that button flashes on, he had to have a look. *Stop the car!* I echoed, and wanted to know if he thought I was crazy to stop the car out on this road, with those two men loose. He shouted we had no choice, that the car would stop by itself soon enough. *Are you sure?* I asked, once, twice. *STOP THE CAR!* he roared.

I pulled over to the side of the road, three, maybe four feet away from the swamp, and shut off the motor. He punched the glove compartment open, grabbed the flashlight and was out of the car in seconds, limping and cursing. Miracle of miracles, Hughie was still asleep. Joel whispered *Mommy, what is it?* and I whispered back *Let's ask God to please help Daddy while I go see if I can help him too.*

I felt the Presence swirling, swirling. It meant us harm. I felt its cruelty. I opened the car door. The rain began rushing down just as I went around the hood to his side and stood, humble and shaking with chill and terror. Waiting. He handed me the flashlight in silence, and I held it for him, listening to the rain punishing the trees. My defiance was gone. All I could think of was, Had I time to repent? The trees were rustling and murmuring their lamentations in the deepening of that dark. Bob kept prowling around in the wires under the hood, his poor leg twisted, the back of his shirt soaked. Joel began bawling and knocking on the back window, crying for me; soon, Hughie joined in. I stood paralyzed with dread for that eternity, waiting for the violence to break upon us.

When we got back in the car, Bob and I were beyond any exchange of words. I turned around and promised the boys it would all be all right.

The red light glowed steadily until we arrived at Still Creek. By then we'd moved out of the storm into a radiant sunset. I asked directions and followed them and located the garage. It was closed, of course. I went into the phone booth and called the number posted on the door, and the manager answered, and I persuaded him to come out and look at the generator.

It took him less than ten minutes to get to the garage, and Bob and I talked to him, I with that slight drawl that had come into my speech by the late '50s and that returns with every encounter I have with someone Southern-born. He grunted and frowned and scratched his head and poked around under the hood. Then he announced that we needed a new armature, and he went into his garage to see if he happened to have one.

"Of course he'll find just the right one," Bob muttered. "Just the right model, just the right year." I think he muttered that ten times over to me. All the while he was repeating this, I came to an understanding about what I'd have to do.

The man *did* have the right armature. It had taken some looking, he said, he didn't even know he had it; there was only the one, of course. While he installed it, Bob and I took the boys to a roadside restaurant not fifteen minutes' walk from there. Bob said he needed to shake his leg a bit; he took up his cane. He'd carved it not long after his surgery. From an enormous cutting from a tree that had turned up on our property. We'd never solved the mystery of how it happened to be there the day he came home from the hospital.

I was very careful to eat only bread and cooked vegetables, and I ordered the same for the boys. Bob had a steak, so that was all right.

After we'd paid the manager--and he absolutely refused to let us pay him extra for saving us as he had--Bob announced we were going on to the next town where the man had said there was a motel, and we were going to take a room there.

I agreed at once.

That night, arms aching, the blood drumming in my ears, I sat up with Hughie until dawn. It was then that his crisis passed, and I put him down in the bed next to his brother and crawled into bed beside Bob, taking care not to awaken him. I prayed, prayed *hard* a prayer of thanksgiving for the Providence that the house was still in our name, that Bob had not yet been replaced at the press. I prayed gladness for how *simple* it would be to resume. For how bright and *lovely* the swamp roads would be in the morning sunlight on our way back. *We belong,* I prayed, *We belong, we belong*. So would my prayer continue all that day now dawning, and all the day after that, as I would go on driving northward, homeward.

"All of us are creatures of a day;
the rememberer and the remembered"
--Marcus Aurelius, *Meditations*

Creatures of a Day

The azaleas blossoming in early spring, red and white and yellow and purple and pink, the whole of Belle Ville a garden of azaleas And the trees, the trees The sweet gum, the oak, the cypresses The mimosas with ferns like green lace, their delicate pink flowers

The perfume of sweet olive and ligustrum

The sun-spangled blond stone of the campus buildings, their brick-red shingled roofs. "Comic-opera buildings" Arturo said they were "A set they trot out every mornin' and erect--one of my most cherished *verbs, cher And they put a li'l ol' palmetto here, an' a li'l ol' palmetto there And voilà! An instant banana republic!"*

The unending skies of Louisiana Forget-me-not blue "After nightfall, cher, that's when they-all come creepin' back And fold up all those buildings again And stack them on flat cars And take them on back out to the sugah farms"

Cougar Alley lies on the other side of the spearmint-green parade grounds "My most fray-vo-rite *eatery is The Sugar Bowl. Mine!" M'sieur did declare And the movie-house was* his *movie-house and the Laundromat was* his *Laundromat For he lay claim to every one of his haunts, the bookstore was his, the drugstore was his The drugstore where the Latin American students hung out Making* piropos *in honor of those dark and ravishing Southern beauties They met there after their classes in sugar engineering And after their classes in English-for-foreign-students One section of which was presided over by Arturo Who delighted in translating the* piropos *for M'sieur and Company And English-for-foreign-students class was where Arturo met Jacques Whose family had escaped from the Nazis and were living in Venezuela And they had sent Jacques to the university down there To prepare himself to preside over his father's estate But Jacques had become a worshipper in some kind of cult That had him kneeling on the floor and rapping out messages to the Other Side In the wee hours So he was thrown out of one apartment after the other in Cougar Alley And Jacques wrote science fiction stories under the pen-name Abraxas And Jacques fell in love with buxom Camille Who was studying to become a diva And who could not be torn from the side of her beloved Peerer Who was instructing her in Italian and French in exchange for voice lessons For Peerer aspired To become a member of the chorus of the New Orleans Opera Because then he would* nevah, evah *Have to conduct language choirs In the steaming classrooms of Brooke Hall, no,* nevah again

When Tess arrived with Michou, both of them still known then by their given, *foreign* names of Moira and Mark Michael Fishbein, they went to the address that Mark's Chairman, Quint Gilbert, had given them, the place in Cougar Alley just down the street from where M'sieur lived. The landlady gave them a consummate look of suspicion, Mark said he *marked* that look well. And she led them through her drawin' room into a hallway, and then up a winding staircase. The wallpaper was all-over cabbage roses, and there was a portrait of Douglas MacArthur up there on the wall at the landing. And MacArthur was looking straight down into their atheist Communist souls as they made their ascent towards him.

And the landlady led Moira and Mark Michael into an attic, that was what was known as *the apartment,* and there was a young couple there, wan and wilted, packing up to move out. And the landlady recited her Thou Shalts and Thou Shalt Nots, making mention of drinkin' and smokin' both bein' prohibited on the premises. Michou did some embroidery work on this part of the tale: "and lights out at nine-thirty." And O'Hara said, "Don't forget, bananas out at ten." And M'sieur said, "Mark didn't take that apartment, because Mark doesn't like Douglas MacArthur." M'sieur commented that in all the pictures *he* had seen of Douglas MacArthur riding in triumph up the downtown streets of Chicago with ticker tape laurels on his brow and all those Midwesterners cheering, there was no sign of either Mark or Moira, which went to prove they were two people who ought rightly to be put under suspicion of subversive intent, what with their birthplace and that Fishbein and all.

After the commandments were recited, Mark and Moira thanked the landlady and went to the drugstore in Cougar Alley and called up Quint Gilbert to ask if there were any other prospects for living-places. And Quint Gilbert suggested, "Y'all might ring up Tom O'Hara." O'Hara lived over in the barracks, Quint Gilbert said, and the O'Haras had a passel of kids and cats and dogs, and while he didn't know how much O'Hara could tell them about rentals in Belle Ville, he was their Yeats Man and Fishbein was their

James Joyce man, so, "y'all ought to be gettin' to know one another right soon, anyway."

O'Hara came on down, and the three of them roamed Cougar Alley and they found an upstairs apartment-to-let in a frame house two blocks from campus. And O'Hara helped them empty out their car and carry their worldly goods up the stairs.

Cockroaches big as butterflies were flying around what they supposed was the living room. In the kitchen Moira found a mean-looking spider more alive than dead in the kitchen sink, and a whole battalion of ants marching across the counter, "genuine home-grown Louisiana red fire-ants," O'Hara guessed. In the bathroom, silverfish and centipedes were making heavy traffic in the tub. And she cried, but she was careful not to faint for fear of what might be lurking in the floorboards that might come up and crawl on her while she lay dying. O'Hara promised she'd get used to the bugs and beasties of Louisiana in no time, that he too had once been a Yankee, lest they-all forget, and so had his wife, who now went calmly down the road stepping over a cottonmouth once without turning a hair while she was on her way to show the bairn the Cougar in his lair; and on the way home they stopped at the place where a neighbor reported sighting an alligator one morning.

After they finished unpacking, O'Hara went out to fetch M'sieur, and they all sat around and took turns telling the story of how each of them happened to end up in Belle Ville, Louisiana that September of 1954. Moira wanted to be last; and when her turn came, she said since she was a camp-follower, she'd tell them about their adventures on the road. It was near Canton, she said, that a sheriff had stopped their car, their old Ford with the green bug deflector and the Illinois license plates; and he had shone his flashlight over their earthly possessions piled up in the back seat, their books and frying pan and shoes and useless winter-wear. "First thing you do tomorrow," O'Hara interrupted, "is get yourself some Southern license plates. Since Black Monday, they see NAACP-CIO-FEPC-Communist-tools-of-the-Rooskies-government in every car with a Yankee license plate." M'Sieur wanted to know if the police found fugitives smuggled in the trunk, a pinko or two, because the Fishbeins looked like the kind who'll take in spies. She told them Mark had been trembling so much that *she* had to be the one to speak up to the sheriff and that she explained they were just now moving South. And she offered to let him search their car even though it had taken her and Mark halfway to forever to pack it up. And the sheriff said, "No, Ma'am, don't b'lieve that's necessary. But you-all roll up youah windows, hear, roll 'em up taght. Theah's two desper-ay-does loose in this territory, escaped from the prison. And you folks better mind who you see on the road, don't let nobody flag you down, those two are mean. Yes, Ma'am, those two are mighty mean." A few miles from there, they had a blowout. M'sieur put in that decent people didn't have such things, or if they did, they certainly didn't have them in *public,* but that she could go on with her story, he'd overlook her indelicacy because after all she'd only been in civilized country for one little day. Mark Michael knelt under the car cursing and sweating, she went on, and she herself paced the highway, scared out of her wits. "Cha," M'sieur chided, "you can talk more clearly than *that!"* Well, Moira said, she was wared out of her skits, and so she stuffed the book of Travelers' checks into her private place. O'Hara remarked that the story was just only now getting interesting.

"I could hear twigs snapping in that pitch-blackness," she told them. "Both sides of the highway sloped down into woods, and I just knew those woods were full of robbers and murderers and what-all. And then a hearse slowed down and pulled right alongside us, I swear, a *hearse,* and the driver asked Mark if he needed any help, and Mark said, No, thanks, and I was screaming softly to myself. We stayed in a motel in Canton--"

"You screamed all the way to that motel, of course," M'sieur reminded her.

"So I did. And all through the night. And the next morning, while we were having coffee and doughnuts in the café across the road, we heard a news broadcast over the radio. And we found that those two desperadoes had held up the drive-in movie theatre the night before, *the one right next to our motel--"*

"Undaunted by yon screams," M'sieur put in.

"Undaunted and unabashed. And they'd stolen a car. Not *ours* of course, even desperadoes aren't desperate enough to steal *ours."*

"We hate cars." M'sieur flicked the ashes of his cigarette into the lid of the Mason jar that was his very own portable ashtray. "Whenever we see a car, we stand still on the sidewalk, and we point to it--" He lifted a bony index finger, screwed up his French blue Cajun eyes, and pulled the trigger. "And we utter the magic words, and *voilà!* The car melts away, and the driver is sitting on the street."

"May all drivers of cars land on their arses in a pool of broken glass," O'Hara proposed.

"Except for our Mark here," M'sieur said softly. "And his lovely Moira."

M'sieur was M'sieur Marc, and there could not be two Marks in our *grupo familiar,* we agreed, one of them would have to be re-christened or re-*brissed.* M'sieur said Mark looked like a Michou to him. O'Hara seconded the motion, and since he had once been a seminary student he conducted the naming ceremony. They poured a libation of Coke on the floor, drowning two cockroaches, and then sprinkled a few drops on Mark Michael's head, and he was twice-born as Michou.

Moira wanted to be twice-born too. M'sieur asked what her middle name was.

"Theresa. Ugh."

"Named after the saint herself, no doubt," O'Hara said. "Wasn't she the one who could make roses sprout between her alabaster toes?"

"Let us pray," M'sieur whispered, "they sprouted only in such chaste places. What about Terry, as in Terry and the Pirates?"

"Never. Nevernevernever."

"Tessa? Tess?"

"As in Tess of the d'Urbervilles?" But she still was doubtful.

"And as in Tess-tosterone," M'sieur reminded her.

"And don't forget Tess-tickles" was O'Hara's contribution.

"Not to mention Tess-taments, Old and New," Michou mused. "And Tess-timony. And--" He whistled. "Tess-tellation. And Tess-tate, as in the word *intestate?"*

"For years I thought when they said someone died intestate that meant they cut the poor guy's balls off," O'Hara confided.

It was the Tess-tate that convinced her, Moira said. "Call me Tess."

After O'Hara's repeat ministerial performance, they talked, smoking endlessly, and it was then they discovered they were all fine singers. M'sieur offered to sing the Sextet from *Lucia* in all six voices himself: "Cha-cha-cha-cha-cha-cha-*cha*-cha-cha, Chachacha."

"Bravo!" Tess applauded. "You have a loverly voice, M'sieur."

"That's because I used to sing High Holy Mass."

"I too, M'sieur."

"Three apostates in Louisiana," O'Hara sang, stuffing the extra syllables into the notes of the first line of the melody to "Three Coins In the Fountain." Tess and M'sieur sang the rest of the song in syllables of *Cha.* Michou conducted with a curtain rod.

After O'Hara and M'sieur went off into the night, Tess told Michou she thought that with his tonsure and his raspberry cheeks and his French blue Cajun eyes, M'sieur looked like a dear little monk. One with a delightfully depraved soul, she added, maybe that went along with his being a professor of Classics. Michou said the climate might have something to do with it, he had been in Belle Ville less than forty-eight hours and he was already feeling somewhat depraved.

The following Sunday, which was the day before Registration for the Fall semester, they waited their turn in the receiving line at the President's house. And Mark Michael Fishbein and Moira Fishbein were presented to the Dean. The Dean was at the front door, and he asked you where you were from, and they said Illinois, so the Dean told an Illinois story. The person directly in back of them in the procession of new faculty called out cheerily that he too was from Illinois; and the Dean had used up the one Illinois story he knew, and he looked at Mark and Moira as if they were responsible. After that, Michou in his one good dress suit, and Tess in her one good summer dress, walked straight through the President's house and out into his garden, and then crossed the street and went back to the parade ground. And here they met people from all over the country, and even from other countries; and they called one another immigrants and refugees and they laughed about it. And Michou took off his jacket and loosened his tie, and Tess took her earrings out of her ears. And she and Michou held hands and strolled over to the Greek Theatre and went down the stone steps in that melting sunlight, and around the stage and into the grove where there is the little pond with water-lilies floating on water green as limes. And it was cool there, and sweet. And Michou was going to spend the next one hundred years reading and writing, studying and teaching all the books he loved. And Tess was going to live the life of the poet with him at her side.

Although they had married the same year Martin Luther King and Coretta King had married, the same year that John and Jacqueline Kennedy had married, the year Julius and Ethel Rosenberg were executed, they would begin telling time by another measure, so they pledged that September afternoon. The year of 1953 was in another region, a region they had exiled themselves from forevermore, the region where SEATO was formed, and the Supreme Court ruled that segregation in the public schools on the basis of race was unconstitutional, and the United States Senate at long last censured Joseph McCarthy. "You mustn't pay attention to newsprint," M'sieur had warned them, "or the angels will weep for you." The angels' tears were for those for whom it mattered that Eisenhower held a summit conference at Geneva with world leaders from Great Britain and France and the U.S.S.R., that the A.F. of L. merged with the C.I.O., that the first atomic-powered electricity for public use was produced in a plant in Idaho, that millions of Americans were vaccinated with Salk vaccine, that Eisenhower suffered a heart attack, that in Montgomery, Alabama, Martin Luther King led a boycott of buses to protest the segregation of Negro passengers, that Autherine Lucy became the first Negro to enroll in a public school in Alabama. "You must spread your wings and soar above all that," M'sieur had counseled, "you must pay no more heed to such than you'd pay to the mares who come riding on the night as it slouches toward morning," nights when the rain pours down, filling the bayous and the ditches and overflowing the canals and flooding the streets of Belle Ville. "So that if you want to get yourself around, you'll have to go by pirogue--"

"Where are we going?" she asked him. They were lying across the two beds they had tied together to make a double bed, she was whispering into his hair while small silver knives of light twisted their threads in the mirror on the bureau. And the air wove sweetness with decay, scents of jasmine and ligustrum with the detritus of what their neighbors threw into the creek beyond their bedroom window. Lurid, green patches of flesh-like scum encrusted the water that gleamed like tar by grace of the milky moonlight bleeding through the membranes of sky. In the dry grasses of his hair were southern perfumes now, and animal sweat, and weariness, a markmichael musk. Pleasuring was in bright rings, ever-widening circles of light. Down from the bones in her skull she was dissolving, the skin over her face, her neck, her shoulders, her taffyapple breasts melting away. Down, down to the center of her being, the burning, shadowed islet, down to the humus hidden in pale rushes, *"J'ai perdu ma force et ma vie,"* he was sighing, and her legs were gone entirely, she was a wick wasting, languishing in the dreaming and the dying, and now a coldburning root; she cradled his head, and the heat drew them down, he would die of it, he said, die of the Perfect Joys, "That's the way to go, Tess-girl, just when you're finishing, have an elephant step on your back." The sun was eating its way through her Celt-fair skin, she said, it gnawed her moles, set her hair on fire; rashes braceleted her wrists and her ankles; her freckles increased and multiplied, "If we stay down here, one day I'll have skin cancer, Michou." He suffered more, he told her, for he was sheathed in the down of his rust-brown hair, her cinnamon teddy bear, he shed in the bathtub and on the bed sheets and along the insides of his undershirts and shorts. His hand cupping the mossbed, he demanded, "How would you like to have this covering over every inch of yourself?" For an answer, she asked, "Where are we going?" Tonight she wanted to conceive their child, she longed to conceive their child. Last week, they had said to one another what did it matter if they never had a child. But that was seven whole nights ago, tonight the child-hunger had returned.

"Where are we going?" she bedeviled him, full knowing he would answer, *"No one* is going, people don't *go* anywhere except to their death." On Monday she said she could not live anymore without a child. On Tuesday she said it again. And now it was Wednesday, and she was still saying it. She would go to the doctor again. And the doctor would prescribe hormones for her, big orange biscuits to swallow with milk. And small grey pebbles too, thyroid pills.

He brought her a little booklet he made, his own drawings and the words of a simple story by James Thurber, a story that there was a man and a woman and a flower. But she wanted there to be a man and a woman and a child. And he asked her, "Where is the free spirit I married, where has she gone?"

The justice of the peace who'd married them had given her the license for safe-keeping. He had said, "Never trust the man with that piece of paper, always give it to the ladies." The entire ceremony felt like it was over before it began, it felt quicker even than the Mass said by her father's favorite priest, Speedy McIntyre, the man could whisk through the whole business in nineteen minutes flat. The edges of the papers on the J.P.'s desk curled and uncurled with the rhythmic whirring of the fan, he had turned down the radio, there was a baseball game on that afternoon, they swore to be faithful to one another in sickness and in health, in the Iron Curtain and the Red Menace, in the Korean War and the Witch Hunts, in the postwar boom and the postwar baby boom, *until death do us part*

He was going away, her Mark Michael had gone into her Michou, who was going away. For half a year now, he had been taking leave of her.

That first time, they had taken him to the same hospital where Huey Long was taken after he was shot.

She had come home from her seminar and found him sitting in the butterfly chair, staring out the window, staring at the apartment building across the street where The-Fat-Lady-Who-Beat-Her-Kids lived, and she had asked him, "Where does it hurt?" and for an answer he had covered his eyes with his hands. And she had pried his fingers away from his eyes, thinking that so long as she could see his eyes she might keep him there still, keep him whole. But he was closed, he would not let her in.

The boy, Micah. The *bar mitzvah bucher.* "Today I am a man." The young man, Mark Michael, the tall thin ghost who stalked her in the stacks of the library with a humor and a sadness in his eyes. Silver eyes inside the tortoise-shell frames of his glasses. A smile wistful and wry. Words: "Be generous, Moira. Come with me." He said he had seen Joyce's Nora in her. And then Joyce himself, in his yachting cap and with a patch over the other eye, so he knew she was the mirror image. And then Yeats's Maud Gonne. And then Constance Markiewicz. And the others, all the mythic lads and lasses of his *très riches heures* gathered in one, in her image, in the creature who now held her soul hostage.

She pulled down the venetian blinds. She made his favorite meal, roasted chicken. But he would not touch it. She drew a chair up to his and tried to feed him salad. He would not chew, he sat there with the lettuce leaves sticking out of his mouth, he reminded her of that daft canary she had bought as a gift for her parents when she was in high school, her last anniversary gift to them, the year she tried to keep them from divorcing. She filled a bowl with cold water and brought it to him and sponged his face and hands, she helped him undress, she put him to bed. All the while she was saying to him they were in a strange land, they had no family here, it would be cruel of him to abandon her here, their friends were too new to help them, they had only one another, he was terrifying her, you do not do this to someone you say you love. He lay beside her, he was mute, all his words had left him. She kissed his salt eyelids, his dry lips, she spoke his names over and over, Micah, Mark, Mark Michael, Michou, but he responded to none of them.

When morning came, she made dark roast coffee with chicory and pretended none of this had happened, and called to him, but he would not answer. She stood over him and pleaded and threatened, and finally she left the apartment. When she returned, he seemed not to have stirred. She went back to the campus, looking for M'sieur. And as he came toward her outside the Library, he was saying, "Tess-girl, we missed you at our lirrel luncheon!" She told him Michou was having a spell, and that she was beside herself. And M'sieur brought her to his office, and closed the door, and had her sit down and tell him everything.

Arthur kept vigil with her in the Solarium of the hospital. And the next morning, Mark opened his eyes and smiled and told them to go and get some breakfast for themselves. She came undone at the end of the corridor, where there was a vase filled with pink and purple azaleas in front of a statue of Our Lady of the Immaculate Conception. "Look, Tess," Arturo said, "Tosca has been here this morning." And she said, "I don't understand what's happening." And Arturo promised, "It will be all right, *cher*, it will be all right."

She would say to him, when he was looking so deeply into that savage, exotic country he had come to inhabit for a time, "My name is Moira." But he would reply, "No, your name is Tess." And then she would argue, "My name is Moira, and it might be best if we leave this place, Mark." She blamed the jasmine, she blamed the sun, she blamed the dark roast coffee with chicory. But he insisted she was Tess and he was Michou and they had no other home but here, and in one another.

Dr. Guy was young and blond and handsome. And she did not trust him. And this was the first thing he remarked to her, that it was obvious to him she did not trust him. He spoke laconically, and with the voice of omniscience, the voice of one in the loathsome habit of reading others' minds. "Naturally, you will resent me. By definition, you would not be able to trust me." He gave her some pills for Mark, and said she ought to be grateful they had happened to choose him for Mark's physician. Because others were *putting people like Mark away.* And still others were slicing out what they supposed were the offending parts of the brain. But he, Dr. Guy, knew that, although excision might take away the misery, it would take away James Joyce as well. And he wanted her to know that it was Mark's suffering, and not he, Dr. Guy, who was coming between them. His clear grey eyes were innocent of both accusation and compassion; they contemplated her in her peasant blouse and cotton skirt, her bare legs and her white ballerina slippers, and the spider bite on her ankle; they studied the white worm of terror gnawing her breastbone. And then he told her to call his office and make a series of appointments. Because after releasing Mark from the hospital, he would be seeing him for quite a long time to come.

During that long wait she lost her poet's voice. And she told Mark when Dr. Guy said Mark was healing, that she no longer could write poetry, that she was in search of other work to do. He was reading Yeats's poetry to her at the time. The words took shape in the corners of the room, and spoke in his eyes, and rebuked her. And in their shimmer she saw their figures wandering in the enchanted forest of the library where they first had met, hansel and gretel hand in hand, following the crumbs they had scattered on the way they had so willfully lost. They had made themselves up in one another's image, they had transposed ancestries, they had played the owl and the pussycat, the orphans-of-the-storm, the luminaries of their age. They had nibbled at the windows of the candy cottage, and then the door swung wide and admitted them. If they were to be childless, she told him, she must find a new life for herself, away from the campus.

"Cha." M'sieur was shaking pepper into his shrimp gumbo. "Our Tessa-girl's going out into the wicked world. She's departing from our Realms of Gold, she's going to become a newspaperwoman, cha." He turned to her and took her arm and tucked it tightly under his own. It had been snowing cracker crumbs on his one good suit, his blue Teaching Suit. "Tessa Starr, Reporter. Cha. O, I *like* that, cha."

"You're holding my writing hand," she accused him. "As if I'd ever betray our little secrets! Those I love are in my poems. But you'd never find them in any newspaper articles I'd write, I swear it."

"I'm afraid for you," Arturo said. "You're so *lirrel!* And there are all those awful, snoopy people in Journalism. And somebody might hang one of those big black cameras around your *lirrel* neck and send you off to some dangerous place to take pictures. With none of us around to protect you."

"Had a wife and couldn't keep her," Michou chanted. "I wooed her in the library, and I wooed her in the classroom. I wooed her under the cypresses, and in the evening wooed her in the shadow of our own Cleopatra's Needle, yon Memorial Tower piercing yonder sky. Amid the musk of the camellias and sweet olive, to the music of the bards I wooed her--"

M'sieur's hand pressed her arm, held her still. "Look at Peerer," he said. "Hush all your mouths and look at Peerer. Peerer loves beans."

Peerer looked up, blinked at them, and then went on putting away his red beans and rice.

"All together now!" M'Sieur waved the baton of his butter knife.

"Peerer loves beans," they chorused.

"Beans," Arturo rhapsodized. Arturo could say "Beans" just like James Dean says it in *East of Eden.*

M'sieur pointed a trembling finger at Arturo. "Say it one more time," he commanded. "Just as it should be said."

"Beans."

They all sighed, in a communal coming.

Then M'sieur bade them all look into Michou's eyes. "Michou has eyes. Look at Michou's eyes. We all *love* Michou's eyes."

Peerer loved beans, and Michou had eyes, and after lunch they went their separate ways, then, Michou and his company into their long reverie in *a world I never made--*

When they spoke to you, they did not look directly at you. "Yassuh," they said, or "Yas'm," and then "sho is a lovely day." They kept to the back and to the side, and spoke to you only when spoken to; and they came and went in all the back doors, they *kept their place*

"Cha, Tess-girl, beware. Lest the angels weep for you."

Small brush fires were burning everywhere she looked and listened. In the department store, and at the bus stop, and in most every conversation. Many were the tales of *old wounds opening.* "Because of the NAACP," she heard some say. "The N-double-C-P-A," the gendarmes of the Old Order fancied up the spelling, "however you say it, they're Communist agitators." "It's *past* the time to get the U.S. out of the U.N." "It's *past* the time to impeach Earl Warren." "It's *past* the time to cut foreign aid." "Got to keep the Nigra-loving Communist CIO out of the South." "Betcha the N-double-C-P-A's got its central headquarters in Russia, and Krushchev says he's got in mind to bury us-all." "Had no trouble with them, no trouble at all, until these outsiders came in. Stirrin' things up, lookin' to agitate. Just like they did before, makin' the South into their scapegoat all over again. And them with their rats and their Harlem, them with their big money and their big talk. Goes back a good while, this meddlin'." "Yes. My Daddy told me all about the FEPC and the New Deal and Mrs. Roosevelt and now all these social scientists."

"Tess-girl, you don't want to bother your head with all that ugliness. You and Michou, you live so beautifully, cha."

M'sieur's father was a shrimper in Bayou Bleu. And M'sieur *put in residence* Christmas and Easter and summers, that was when he ate his fill of oysters and crayfish and chicken and wild rabbit, *every manner* of gumbo, and listened in on all the grievance talk about the oil companies, that was when he went out in the pirogue with his father and brother, and caught up on the news of their neighbors, that was when he *let the good times roll.* Arturo's father was a minister. And he had taught Arturo to be gentle in the face of all the evil of this world. And Peerer's mother was a social reformer since her widowhood, she was up to her yellow-and-white coronet of braids in the doings of the Forgotten Man Committee, *all whipped up about the prisons.* Peerer's father had smoked himself to death, Lord only *knows* what his mother would say if she saw how they-all puffed away at this lunch-table. O'Hara liked to keep two cigarettes going at the same time, his fingers were always prowling around in the breast pocket of his shirt, checking to make sure the pack hadn't walked off between belly-deep drags. Now, *he'd* had one of those standard-issue Midwestern boyhoods, when he was nine his mother threw a butcher knife at him, almost did a van Gogh on him; it knocked his metabolism all to hell, but it gave him his Moment of Truth, it was O'Hara's recommendation that people screw more often, then they'd have less time and inclination to worry about *putting in residence,* or turning the other cheek, or doing good in the prisons or preaching against smoking, or carrying on about separate-but-equal, for that matter; now that he was mentioning it, O'Hara said, he thought the size of the member and the number of balls of guys who carry on about skin color could use some looking into.

"Where are we going?" she asked him. Here it was, he said, that he would *gladly lerne and gladly teche,* here in Louisiana, with the green and gold radiance of the swamps after the rains cleared, here with the trees stronger than human presences, the pecan trees, the sweet gum and tupelo gum, the oak and the mimosa, and the pines in the piney groves. And the water hyacinths ghostly white in winter, then purpling again in the spring. And the knees of the cypresses rising from the swamps. *And the fierce hot yellow mouth of the sun on your face. And the roads winding. And all along the roads the low, earth-colored cabins, and the figures in the doorways. And the oil refineries at the edge of Belle Ville.* And the savage beauty of the skies filling with the great egrets coming home in spring, here it was he would *gladly teche* of the beauty that was truth, and of the truth that was beauty, of *all ye need to know*

In 1957 Russia launched its Sputnik, and Congress passed the first federal civil rights law since Reconstruction. The Civil Rights Act of 1957 established the Commission on Civil Rights and instructed its members to investigate charges of denial and of violation. And a Civil Rights Division was opened in the Department of Justice, to enforce laws and regulations. And Governor Orval Faubus defied the Supreme Court order of Black Monday. He sent the Arkansas National Guard to bar Negro students from entering Central High School, and he warned there would be riots if Negroes were admitted. And President Eisenhower placed the National Guard under Federal control, and sent troops to Little Rock--

"Both sides mean business," Jimmy Landry told her. "Thing is, though, we sure could use some *leadership* on both sides. The Supreme Court is way ahead of Ike. And down here, our *alligators* are on higher ground than the critters who're crawling out to take their stand on defending what they're pleased to call The Southern Way of Life. Watch out, cher, there's some mean times ahead."

He had scratched at his head with the eraser on his pencil and given her a look of calm measuring that first morning she was on assignment as his assistant, on loan from the university. She had told him her name was Moira Fishbein, but that she answered best to "Tess." He had scratched at his head with his eraser and studied her, and then drawled, "Mrs. Fishbein, yes Ma'am, Miss Tess." And they both had burst out laughing then. Direct and personal with one another from the very first, she knew that could only happen down South.

He took her out to lunch, and she told him about the frogs in the creek croaking and croaking night after night, wonkwonkWONK, *old men at a summit meeting,* wonkwonkWONK, until Mark said he couldn't *take* it anymore, he wouldn't put *up* with it anymore, and so Mark called the police, Mark wanted to sign a warrant for the arrest of the *frogs,* they were disturbing his *peace.* Well, the police came to their apartment, and they sat down, and one of them asked Mark, "Where y'all *from?"* and when they both said, "Illinois," the police guessed they were city people, and they explained about frog giggin'. And they drank down their Cokes and they kept their notebooks open the whole time to be polite, with the dark cones of sweat spreading under their arms, and the disbelief in their eyes, and then they told Mark they used to swim in that very creek when they were boys, that was before people took to throwin' their rubbish in the water. By *that* time Mark had found his temper again, she told Jimmy Landry. The night before he was a sight to behold, standing in pitch-darkness at the edge of the creek, standing there in his pajama bottoms, throwing stones in the direction of the old wonkers, swearing at them in Yiddish, asking them things like, "Who *needs* you?" and, "Where are you crawling with your crooked feet?" And Jimmy Landry said there was *never* such, no, *never such,* and would she please have mercy, his cheeks felt so sore from laughing he felt he was comin' down with the *mumps.* And Jimmy Landry said he thought they would work together right well, that up to this very morning he thought *he* had claim on first prize for bein' the most peculiar person in the Parish, but that was before he heard about Mark Fishbein and the frogs.

Jimmy Landry favored Uncle Earl's word for rabid segregationists--*"Grass-eaters."*

"I do not idealize *any*one, mind, and that includes the Almighty, though He be my Judge, Tess. Fact is, I regard any insistence upon His innocence of a touch of meanness now and then as sure proof of what the *true believers* call atheistic materialism. However that be the case, Uncle Earl *does* call 'em as he sees 'em. Do you know, he asked that old Neanderthaloid what he thought he was gonna do, now that the Feds have got the atomic bomb? Now *this* kind of man, our Uncle E, is dangerous to the *true believers,* this kind *thinks too much.* And he's all the more dangerous because he's so clever in concealing the fact that he thinks *at all.* Uncle E, you see, wants the Negroes to have their day at the polls. He is all-out opposed to the law that allows any two registered voters of a Parish to challenge any name on the voting list on the basis of alleged irregularity in the original application. Do you know, *cher*, that you can have your neighbor's name 'segregated' if, say, he has no document handy to prove whether he was born, say, on the 17th or the 18th of December? Now, once his name is segregated, your neighbor would be entitled to receive notification that he's been challenged. Not that he ought to *depend* upon receiving it. But let us say for the sake of the argument that he does receive such notification. He must then be able to read said communication. And I hesitate to hazard an estimate, Miss Tess, of the number of people in this Great State, black or white or jellybean green, sextoon or seventoon or octoroon, who--owing to the munificence, expansiveness and sheer and unabashed spendthriftism of the state funds for public education--how many preliterate, non literate and plain old *il*literate citizens we now may boast. Why, you have only to consider the appropriations for the educational institutions of this sovereign state, you have only to consider the condition of the buildings and the provision for the staffing of our public school system, to appreciate what the combination of poverty and the separate-but-equal doctrine have wrought for the future of our children, be those children what*ever* shade or hue. Well. Cher. Where was I? Your neighbor by some stroke of Providence is able to read the notification that the Registrar *is* bound by law to send him, to the effect that his registration has been challenged and that his name has subsequently been segregated. Now let us further say that your neighbor is a stubborn fellow, and that he made up his mind he's going to vote. He must then find three people who are willing and able to serve as witnesses to the legality of his registration. All this he must do under unremitting harassment, both of himself and of his family. *And* of the hapless lawyer who consents to represent him. Having fulfilled all these requirements, your neighbor then will request a hearing before the Registrar. And when this hearing is granted, your neighbor must demonstrate his fitness to vote by answering such questions as, Who was the Lieutenant Governor of this sovereign state in 1904 (his name escapes me, *cher*) or, What was the upper limit on the appropriation for the state university back in that same year? (It was $15,000 annually, and you may check me on this.) Or, What is the meaning of this passage in the Bible? (Said passage will be in the Greek language.) By the way, *cher*, the answer to this last question is that the passage means that no Negro is gonna get to register to vote in this Parish. Nor should this surprise you, nor should it appear to you to be a merely allegorical tale. It is a proven fact that, since 1956, two full years after that decision of the Supreme Court of these United States, at least thirty thousand names of as many Negro voters were dropped from the registration rolls. *Nor* should it surprise you, now that you have been living as a *bona fide* citizen of this sovereign state for some years and presumably have kept yourself informed about its internal divisions, that at least half these disenfranchised Negroes are from Parishes in the Northern reaches of the state. *Surely* you have apprised yourself of the fact that the French Catholics entertain, if that is the proper word, a far more tolerant attitude about the political participation of Negroes than do their Baptist brethren to the North?"

She pleaded for mercy. She said he made her head spin. "Give me time to *absorb* all this. No one I ever *met* talks like you."

"Indeed, if I may plead your indulgence to contradict you, *cher*, *all* the Landrys--which in this sovereign state of Louisiana embraces a goodly portion of the total population--speak like I do. We imbibed this propensity for running at the mouth with our mother's milk, if you can feature that one. Along with a healthy skepticism, by the way. Cher, it's not my flapping *tongue* that's makin' your head spin, it's the continuous assault on your thermodynamical system from trotting back and forth between air conditioning and the Great Outdoors. In other words, Progress."

Jacques wanted to know if Uncle Earl was really *fou* or if he was being victimized by his wife.

"Her name is Blanche," O'Hara reminded him. "Ask Tennessee Williams what you can expect from a Blanche."

Tess reported that the consensus at the *Herald* was that Blanche would rather see Uncle E in his grave than see him in the Governor's chair.

Jacques announced they were all hiding their heads in the hot sands of the local political circus, and were forgetting that the two camps on this fragile planet were busily arming themselves for Armageddon. He said there were those deeply concerned about the American Sputnik being a Spätnik, and that these persons were merrily building missiles and pointing them in a certain direction. In Jacques's opinion everybody at this table ought to remember how to pray, since they might all soon be meeting their Maker.

"Meeting our Maker," M'sieur echoed. "Cha, I like that. Cha."

Arturo said he'd gotten all prayed-out in childhood.

Michou remarked that if they-all were about to die they'd best polish off their lunch meetings with read-alouds from the Stoics.

"Watch John Kennedy," Jacques advised. O'Hara commented that it was obvious Jacques hadn't been in the country for very long, else he'd know better than to think Americans north *or* south were about to elect an Irish Catholic to the High Throne. Talk of thrones, Michou said, reminded him of scatological matters. M'sieur was pleased to encourage the change of subject. O'Hara brought out his punch-line paper and told one from the Toidy Department. "It's wicked to use such language at the table," Tess scolded after her laughing fit subsided, "Peerer hasn't finished his lunch." "Peerer loves beans," they chorused. Peerer said toidy jokes were preferable to cigarette smoke blown all over red beans and rice.

"A goodly number of people in this sovereign state are going to have to take their stand on which is more important to them, being a Catholic or being a Southerner," Jimmy Landry told her. "There's north *versus* south in *Louisiana*-country, too."

Early enough in the morning that the sun still was gentle and the air soft-stirring, when all the humans you could see along the roads were Negroes going fishing, Negroes going to work, Negroes beginning the long day's living, Jimmy Landry came by for her in his Chevrolet with the flamboyant tail fins, his *hearse* Michou called it, petulant and jealous, "the hearse he *drives* too fast." Seated beside Jimmy Landry, she felt the speedspill of his words working their wizardry: her yesterdays vanishing, and then her todays and her sorrowing for her barrenness. He smoked and laughed and half the time drove with his elbows so he could talk with his hands. No matter how hot the day, he turned himself out in a dress shirt and tie. He had two suits, and two sports jackets, one of each blue and the other gray, she was sure it was deliberate. His shirts were crisp, and his smile. And as the passing hours steamed through his body, through the jimmy-landry musk of soap and sweat and Chesterfield cigarettes and last night's bourbon-and-branch, she thought of his blond wife with her bouffant coiffure and her pastel linen suits, and then of the heat, and of Michou's thighs upon her own, and of his slow joyful lifting over her, and of their pleasuring. And she stared at Jimmy Landry's wrists, at Jimmy Landry's hands, and then at his salt-and-pepper hair, the sweat beads on his temple, his frank smile, big, taking all of her in it. And when he came around to open the car door for her, she gathered up her things and looked up, straight up into his keen blue eyes. And she knew that he knew.

She was at his side now and again and again, his small companion, taking notes and listening and taking more notes while the social workers presented their grim statistics and the Negro doctors spoke of the needs of the community and the representatives of the white medical society spoke about the declining numbers of tuberculosis cases in the Parish during the past thirty years. "This Parish is not an island of want in a sea of plenty," one or the other would say every now and then. And while she scribbled notes about Hill-Burton funds, she thought of the condition of the back of her skirt from the heat, she thought it might well be soaked through because she had forgotten to hitch it up before sitting down, and she could feel the trickles of sweat running down her legs.

On the way home Jimmy Landry was telling the story of how Uncle E got Negroes jobs in Charity Hospital. "He'd say, 'Here we have white nurses servin' the colored men,' and next thing you know, cher, there was a whole passel of Negro nurses hired in Charity Hospital."

The roselight of the sky meandering towards dusk And the pale blue spinning white breathwings, spume on the horizon Where the blush was deepening And then the darkening of the trees And the feeling of the air Waiting for the sun to decide itself to fall The soft body of the sky pulsing, shadowing And little streams of milk running down the painted hills of *Loo-zee-annie evenin' sky*

And Jimmy Landry brought her home To Michou

O'Hara complained that one of his cats pissed on his one good suit. "And we gave this creature a royal name. Renenet. You'd think she'd have more respect."

"That's what you get for living with girls," M'sieur scolded. "You get your one good suit pissed on."

"I live with girls too," Michou reminded him. "And that didn't happen to *my* one good suit."

"Tess is different from other Girl People, cha."

They had gone over to Peerer's house to play Scrabble and listen to records. Michou and Tess had proposed the idea to O'Hara during their nocturnal wanderings in Brooke Hall, and they had packed him into the back seat of the old Ford. After they had driven around Cougar Alley and hunted down M'Sieur and Arturo, they went looking for Jacques and his new companion, who had said she liked best to be known as Olive Oil.

Peerer's mother had served them her ice cream, home-made-with-condensed-milk, and after she went upstairs because she was *an early retirer,* M'sieur warned them the stuff was going to give them all morning sickness, except of course for Tess and Olive Oil, who were virgins, but that they had to eat it all anyway, because Peerer's mother had made it, and she had made Peerer, and they-all loved Peerer.

They played Scrabble for a while, but Peerer kept making words like *Jo* which turned out to be legitimate, and that took all the fun out of it. So they decided to play Dirty Scrabble. Michou and O'Hara won, they tied for first place. After that, Peerer played his recording of Florence Foster Jenkins, and Olive Oil laughed until she near cried. And then Peerer played his recording of Saint-Saëns' Third.

Then O'Hara turned himself into Humphrey Bogart. He belted his imaginary trench coat, pulled the brim of his imaginary hat down over his eyes, and lisped out some smart remarks to Tess and Olive Oil. Then he shot them all dead. Then he stretched out on the floor and told them his favorite dream. "I'm screwing a purple woman wearing a purple dress in a room with purple drapes and purple velvet couches, all to the melody of *Deep Purple."*

"Our dream," M'sieur said, "is to be able to *watch* all that."

"Speak for yourself," Peerer told him. *"My* dream is that my mother reconciles herself to my aspirations to become a member of the chorus of the New Orleans Opera."

After a certain age, Jacques decreed, people ought to be entitled to file for a decree of divorce from mothers.

Arturo, who claimed he was an Authority on mothers, vowed he would keep his forever, if only she wouldn't stand in the bathroom doorway talking him to death when he was thinking of performing his Functions.

Olive Oil said they-all ought to be ashamed for not appreciating their mothers. "They make lovely hot lunches for you, and most of them have such sad, lovely eyes as they grow older."

That was Girl Person talk, M'sieur scoffed. "And besides, only Michou has eyes."

Arturo asked Peerer if they-all might hear "A Fors e Lui" by "Leaky" Albanese, and he promised he would come at the end of the aria, soon as he heard her sing the words "Crotch e delicieuse."

Speaking of coming, O'Hara said, put him in mind of a seminary story. He asked Peerer to hold the record a minute while he consulted his punch-line paper, and Peerer said he'd be happy to oblige. O'Hara found the punch-line and told his seminary story, and Jacques celebrated it by rolling around on the carpet and pounding his fists on his temples. Then Michou gave his offerings from the Toidy Department. And then Olive Oil told a joke about a woman-of-ill-repute. And Peerer remembered one about coon-ass octoroons. Curses, epithets, swear-words from seven languages flew around the room. Moths and giant roaches beat against the screen door. Peerer's mother went on sleeping upstairs.

She knew for certain the day she went to the polling place. There were posters planted in the grass every foot along the way inside; Jimmy Landry came by for her in his *hearse* after she voted; and on the way back to the office he recited for her what they said were the three steps to Mongrelization, "the blueprint for the destruction of our Christian and White American Civilization. Number One, bastardization of the white race by mixing in the schools. Number Two, teaching the propaganda of tolerance. And Number Three, integration of the churches." When they drove past the statue the W.C.T.U. had *erected* in downtown Belle Ville, he asked her for the hundredth time did she know who it was, it was Hebe, Wine-bearer of the gods. She knew for certain that day, and she thought she might tell him then, but he had gone on talking, saying he'd heard a rumor that a Professor of Classics intended to take down the sign on the campus that says Louisiana State University and Agricultural and Mechanical College and remove the word *university.* "Which goes to show you, cher, that our Classics professor is not far off the mark. A little learning is indeed a dangerous thing. Think what our good dry ladies would say if they knew the real identity of this idol they believe to be the noble symbol of abstemiousness! On the other hand, cher, if the people of this sovereign state, wets and drys alike, all had enjoyed a genuine education, we'd not *nearly* have the good times denied our dour neighbors to the north, our high-steppin' blowhards to the west, our grass-eatin' ones to the east. Now, don't you look all amazed at my castin' aspersions on the Magnolia State! There's a sayin' here, whenever someone migrates from the state of Mississippi to the state of Loo-zee-annie, the literacy rate in *both* states goes up!"

She thought she might tell him on their trip to the leprosarium later that week, but it did not happen. Then she thought she might tell him the day they went to interview the physician at the Clinic who was a One Man Crusade against the evils of cigarette smoking. Jimmy Landry took notes of that hellfire-and-damnation speech with his brown-and-yellow-stained fingers, and lighted up soon as they got back into his car. Somehow, she wasn't able to find the words to tell him that afternoon. She vowed she would tell him the next day, when they were to interview Peerer's mother about the Forgotten Man Committee.

She told him at lunch-time.

He had been talking sixty.

"Cher, the relationship between the races has not always been so tense as you find it to be now. And you may put that down to the decision of Brown vee Board of Education. There are whites who regard the Negroes as Untouchables, who make it a matter of public record that they will have no commerce with them if they can help it. At the other end of the spectrum there are whites who have taken the teachings of the Gospels and the words in the Bill of Rights to heart. And they will seize the first opportunity that presents itself to expose the injustices and cruelties all around us-all. You keep a sharp lookout for these folks, Tess. There are never very many of them. But the South never fails to deliver them up, these heroic and truly Christian souls. Now, in the vast gray bayou between these two minorities are timid or bitter or just plain ornery souls who scapegoat the Negroes because they need the back of *some*one on whom to heap the miseries and missed chances of their lives. All you need do, if you happen to be out for a night of evil, or to have political ambitions, which amounts to the very same thing, as you know, *cher*, is to stir up these folk. Appeal to the baseness, the meanness that's in every one of us. Lord knows, Tess, the conditions of poverty are as wretched for vast numbers of people in this Great State as they've always been. And a poor man who cannot feed his family properly, or hold up his head before his neighbors, needs to name *some*body as responsible. Now, cher, I am no historian. And I do not know if this is due to the so-called Black Monday decision or to the Reverend Martin Luther King's teachings about passive resistance, but there is change in the wind. And let me tell you, Tess-girl, when change comes in this country, change in *heart,* not just in the outward forms of things, it will be down here that you'll see it and feel it and know it's genuine. Not in that righteous, that rich and heartless and downright mercenary north of your past *lahfe*."

Lahfe This sweet and musical fall, after the bright rush of words. His eagerness to impart. Jimmy Landry was one of those who missed his vocation, she thought, but he would practice it no matter what hat he wore.

It was that separate-but-equal doctrine, he said, that made so much mischief, it was the draining away of limited resources that came from insisting on having two systems of education, both of them woefully inadequate, *that's* what kept the South in bondage. Young people of both races may learn something about their past in our schools, he said, but the system of education itself denies them their rightful future.

"All that's about to change, Tess. O, they will fight. And they will scream, *'Never!'* Louder and louder, those perfidious people who call themselves our political leaders will scream *'Never!'* And as long as the people of the cloth and the classroom keep silent, these witless, weasel-hearted white supremacists will have their way. But you watch, cher. One by one, the other voices will be raised. And that movement born in Montgomery will gather momentum. And it will sweep this region, and then it will sweep all of the United States of America."

It was not that he saw a future for her on the *Herald.* No, it was nothing that crass. He would have called it *atheistic materialism* just to think that. It was *this* that was unnatural, *this,* their comradeship. And they had made it natural. They were the *unlikeliest pair* on the whole *Herald* staff. And they had made it likely. It *wasn't fitten,* and they had made it fitten. They had *gone down a few roads together,* and this was the end of it. Just as it was beginning, this was the end of it. Because her old dream was coming true. Just when she had lost the sure feeling for it, her old dream was coming true.

"We are in for some troubled times, *cher*. Gird up your loins, as the Good Book says. Get ready to watch the show. It's gonna get uglier. All the snakes are comin' up out of their dark hidey-holes. And good people are weak, good people are afraid to speak their minds. And all the wicked and the ignorant can be heard from here to Sunday. And the Reverend King and his faithful are gonna shame a lot of nasty people by layin' down on courthouse steps and in front of church doors, and by sittin' at lunch counters and by boycottin' buses where they've been herded to the rear for too long. You know, *cher*, it never fails to amuse this ol' boy that our political evangelists exhort and rant and rave that we gotta de*fy* the laws of this country. And then, when *their* rags 'n' tatters of *local* laws are stuck together overnight with Scotch tape and rubber bands, to serve purposes I need no longer spell out for you, and then people defy *these,* why, then, they puff all up and preach against violatin' the *law,* and they put you away in jail for *criminal anarchy."*

The North, she told him for the hundredth time, was never this interesting.

He warned her, *Take care, cher.* She was choice quarry, he said, she was right fine quarry indeed for the KKK, her lawful name bein' Moira Fishbein, they'd get them two for the price of one.

She told him then.

He gave her a long, long look. And then he said, "That ol' libido. It's powerful stuff. A girl of your spirit...you'll be a right fine mother, Tess. But I'm gonna grieve to see you go."

Hot and still, the late night air The babies asleep The boy for her, the girl for him, the dream that had at long last come true Among the dark leaves And in the lace of the fern In every green thing growing you could feel the spiders spinning their delicate weirs She was become Woman now Mother of male and female She heard sighs before they were breathed, she saw through walls, through thickets of dreams, the small fists uncurling And the heads lifting and turning, looking for her presence And she listened For the calls of their need of her, part of her was perpetually awake now. So that even when deep-drowning In the bog of exhausted and dreamless sleep She could feel their small perfect bodies burdening her shoulder Their sweetness The round warmth of them heavy and filling upon her breast And their small cries sang through her marrow And their grave looks And their swift, wavering smiles Darted in and out Quicksilver needles stitching this new raiment for her soul

"You are magic," he whispered. "In the room on either side of ours there lies a child who came from your body. You are different now. New. And I'm almost afraid of your powers."

Without his glasses, he looked so vulnerable Perplexed She kissed his eyelids, the damp moss of them Softly, so as not to disturb him And left his side, and went into Teddy's room And saw his seven companions standing at attention Along the guard rail of his Big Boy Bed The yellow teddy bear Arturo had given him, "Blue Ted," Teddy named him And the Manx cat from Jacques and M'sieur's friendly dragon And the leopard and the roadrunner bird and the great white poodle, already graying a little And Peter Rabbit "The Guys," his entourage And the blanket he fiercely loved Now that Robin had irrupted into his small kingdom Was under his cheek And he was sweating into it And sleeping the sleep of young children Looking surprised and pleased

Tomorrow he would be asking, asking What the look of God was And why his sister made him feel mad and sorry at the same time And if he could marry them both, Mommy *and* Daddy And if once she was dead she would wait for him Until he could catch up with her And she would hum an old Irish melody, she no longer remembered the words And she would talk to him about his father's people The people their little family of four was part of And about the South that now was their home His pajamas were damp And his temples and his forehead damp but cool And his breathing easy

And then she went in to look at Robin Who would pluck at the sheet until she fell asleep Pulling on her thumb ever more urgently until the heaviness overtook her Lying just as she had been put down, never turning or moving Drawn up in the small conch of her secret self Here in the room that once was Mark's study That he said he would give up gladly for this plump and perfect creature Whose compelling gaze searched his very soul Robin, who had fallen into his life And made him whole And healed him As she could not, as Teddy could not As none but Robin could. "Drawn and quartered," he said. "Each of us born so, and only by a miracle finding the other quadrants one by one. We are halved like a sorbapple, the ancients said, they only knew the half of it. Four is a magic number, the most magic number there is."

Weak, she was weak, she could not resist the temptation Knowing she shouldn't, she lay her hand On the baby's back To feel the lifting and falling, to feel her life And weaker still She bent and nuzzled the moist neck Under the fall of feathery light hair Robin's ginger-ale hair, hers exactly

In her bare feet and thin shift she ghosted the hall And came into the darkened kitchen *"Cha, what a big house you have, my dear, what a new* life *you have now"* And lifted the latch of the back door And went out into the yard And the moon's silver glistened on the leaves of the pecan trees And in pools of smoking ash about the grasses And stained the swordleaves of the yucca Night-murmurings in the marshes beyond the fence The harshsweet incense of jasmine and ligustrum and swamprot Herself a stranger now she was a mother Who once was native to the soundful night

Her neighbor's eyes followed Charles Jackson into their kitchen. Her neighbor knew they-all sat down at the table together. "When in Rome, I always say, and I won't stand for it." Her neighbor's son stood on the other side of the hedge, chanting, "Nigger, nigger." And he tore out handfuls of spiraea and threw them at Charles Jackson. Charles went straight up to their door after that, and rang their bell, to speak to her neighbor about it. But her neighbor was afraid, and hid herself inside, and wouldn't answer the bell. The next day, Moira spoke to her neighbor about what her son had done, and her neighbor said, "Well, I don't b'lieve he'd do such a thing, but you know if it weren't for all this violence on the tee-vee and all this agitatin', stirrin' everythin' up...." And her neighbor's voice faded away, and her eyes said to Moira, "Go. Go on, just you go back where you belong."

One night, cars drove up on their front lawn. She and Mark were awakened by the lights flashing in their windows. And the car radios were blaring. Her heart raced, listening to the racket. There was running under their windows. And low, mean laughing. And she and Mark held one another.

And at long last, they heard car doors slamming and brakes screeching, they heard whoopie-ing and shouting, and then there was silence. And in the morning, they found their flower beds in ruins.

Teddy was mortally afraid of The Fog Man who came in the evening to spray the trees with insecticides. And Mark was nervous about carrying out the garbage at night. And when she took the babies for a stroll she was watchful for the dogs in the neighborhood. Because even the dogs were turning mean.

How had they come to be where they were, how had it all come about?

Out of sight, out of mind. That first year away, Jimmy Landry would call her up now and again. "To keep you informed, *cher*. And to assure you that the ol' *Herald* still serves as unholy witness." All through those summer months of her first mothering, Jimmy Landry was her line to The World. And Mark had been wrestling with his old demons again then, and she was thinking, "Lord, what'll I do, with this baby filling my life, needful of me as no one ever before was so needful of me? If Mark breaks again now, where will I go, what'll I do?"

But Mark grew strong again. And they took their savings out of the bank, seventeen hundred dollars, a down payment on their very first house. No one in Mark's family or in hers had ever lived in a house. It was *home,* they told one another, they were putting down roots in Belle Ville, Louisiana.

But they were putting their roots down in swampland. And the swampland was giving way. Absorbed in Ted, they pretended they were not sinking into the swampland. Mark was promoted and lunched and celebrated, and Quint Gilbert laughed, "Looks like we're fixin' to keep this ol' boy." And Mark turned thirty-three, and Mark turned political. He spoke often now of factions in the department, in the college, of the petty wars all around campus. And so it happened they came to have a new circle of friends, and when they went out they had a baby-sitter someone recommended, a sweet girl who turned out to be the daughter of one of Belle Ville's leading rabid segregationists. And they went to parties where the bourbon flowed and the talk was richer even than the food, where there was mixed political company. They were Mark and Moira Fishbein again, and she found she had a slight Southern accent. And she learned how you speak charmingly. And she had her ginger-ale hair teased into some kind of beehive bubble that Mark said made her look like a lemon lollipop. And then she met Hannah Mannheim, and Professor Felix Mannheim. And Hannah held both her hands when they talked, and looked straight into her eyes, and she and Hannah made womantalk, they told one another their stories, and that was how they became Family. Moira said she felt the Fishbeins were part of the

Mannheims' extended family, that she and Mark were an honorary daughter and son to the Mannheims. Hannah would hug her whenever they met, Hannah became as a mother to her. Many a morning she would put Ted in the stroller and walk over to Hannah's. So it was that she became part of that good house, of that good life.

Hannah lived her first-born's early childhood all over again in Ted's. Hannah came when Moira was ill, to take care of Ted, to feed him and tease him and grandmother him. And Teddy said he loved Mannyheimy. Hannah taught Moira how to make her own homemade yogurt, she taught her folk remedies, she taught Moira all the folk wisdoms she knew, including how to wean a baby and how to grow a busy-mother's garden.

Moira confided to Hannah that she wanted to convert to Judaism, and that Mark was fiercely opposed to this. Hannah said, "Perhaps it is possible to be a bit of everything." The Mannheims celebrated *all* the holydays and holidays, Hannah said, Christmas and Easter, Purim and Passover.

Mark said there would be no religion in his house, no Christmas, no Chanukah either, no Easter eggs and no Passover matzoh, *no nothing.* But Moira stood up to him time and again. And Moira's will prevailed.

Deeper and deeper the bog, deeper and deeper the swampland....the messages on the bumper stickers were ugly, one day someone wrote on the blackboard in Mark's classroom, *"Go home, Yankee Jew, and leave your money here."* Some people wore buttons that read NEVER, and other people wore buttons with a drawing of two clasped hands, one dark, one white. *"Criminal anarchists,"* those who wore these buttons were called, and they were shoved and kicked, some of them were beaten and put in jail, Jimmy Landry reported it all in the *Herald.* Then there came the moment when federal marshals escorted five little Negro children into the nearly-deserted grammar school. It was the first time since Reconstruction that Negroes had been inside schools white children attended. State police escorted the teachers inside *"for their own protection,"* they said. And hundreds of teen-agers rioted in a procession winding through the narrow streets of the French Quarter. And they beat a policeman *most savagely*

And the throng of women outside the schools chanted *"We're going to poison you till you choke to death"* And they jeered and laughed at the Methodist minister Because he had a black and white dog, because he even had an integrated dog. And Uncle E was dead, now And Jimmy Landry said, *"You just watch those ol' walls come tumblin' down"* And one candidate wore a tie with a Confederate flag on it And another played a guitar and sang "You Are My Sunshine" And all of them told the people It was their *obligation* to defy the law And the leaders vowed to take over the public schools And they shouted to the cheering public Who packed the House and

Senate chambers *"Segregation now, Segregation tomorrow, Segregation forever!"* And they took an oath before God and before all men That they would never allow mongrelization of the white race, no, never They would not *cotton* to the Communist-inspired *N double C-P-A, the N double P-A-C* They vowed they would *invoke interposition* That the sovereign power of the state would be as a shield Between the federal government and the people of the state of Louisiana They warned the banks they were not to honor checks Drawn by the elected school board of the Parish They introduced a grant-in-aid bill to provide state tuition For any student attending a private school And every day there were obscene phone calls made, every day crazy letters were sent To the parents of the children who walked to school Escorted by federal marshals And someone in the crowd of bystanders shouted, *"Jew bastard, nigger-lover, I hope you have a bunch of mulatto grandchildren!"*

And in Belle Ville they arrested Negro and white students For sitting down at the counter of the downtown drugstore together And they convicted them under a law That prohibits any act *"in such a manner as to unreasonably disturb or alarm the public"*

There came an evening when Michou and Tess went to Peerer's one last time, to eat Peerer's mother's homemade ice cream and to play Dirty Scrabble and to listen to Peerer's recording of Anna Russell singing *"My heart is red/My heart has dishpan hands,"* and to reminisce about their good times together. The occasion was a Farewell Party for Jacques, he was leaving the South, he was leaving the country, he was going home. And they laughed themselves sick about the time pore ol' Olive Oil got into the elevator in Brooke Hall, and it was empty, and it stopped on the next floor and was stuffed with The Three Musketeers, Miss Lark and Miss Horner, who weighed at least seven hundred pounds apiece, and old Professor Coutant who tipped the scales at half a ton, and Olive Oil just about went SPLAT! on the back wall. And in honor of Jacques, and in honor of all the evenings their little group had gone together to the *science friction picture shows* and watched giant grasshoppers lumber down Michigan Avenue in Chicago and spaceships touch down on the desert and a giant tarantula lop off the top of the Empire State Building in a rage, all the times they sat there in a row all a-tremble, holding hands, gasping with their buttered-popcorn breath, all goggly-eyed except for Arturo who all-out *cried* he was so terrified, in honor of all those evenings, when Tess brought along the toy kittycat Michou had bought for her twenty-fourth birthday, hiding it in her pocketbook so everybody could have a turn at asking where was Tessa's Pussy, in honor of all that, she wore a sun-dress to the party, and took off her shoes so that she was barefoot, and she sat at the feet of Arturo while he sang about *li'l Theresa in her camisa* to the melody of "Mona Lisa," and M'sieur said the words made him blush, they just weren't seemly now Tessa was a Mother-Person, and O'Hara remarked it was hot enough for him to wish he could take his pants off. And Peerer said O'Hara was a shameless man.

"Maybe he has something to show us," Jacques suggested. "An amazing proportion, perhaps. Or three, instead of the standard-issue two. Or perhaps one enormous pistachio."

Arturo reminded them there were ladies present. Olive Oil said hush, things were just getting downright amusing.

"Exposing oneself, abusing oneself," Michou pontificated, "these are only to be expected of one who in early childhood nearly had his ear sliced off by an outraged mother. A castration complex redirected farther to the north and somewhat to the west, perhaps the ol' boy needs to check it out every now and then so he can reassure himself it's still there."

"What I've got to show," O'Hara boasted, "none of you could afford more than a mere passing glance at. Fact is, that's how I made my loose change at the seminary. Speaking of which--" He took out his punch-line paper, and then he told them his seminary story.

After everybody was done laughing until they near-cried, Jacques said he couldn't help but feel that the instant he left the whole place would disappear, just go up in smoke behind him, he couldn't hope to tell anybody at home about it and be believed, there was not a soul in Venezuela nor a body in France who would believe him. He said he wished he could tie a rope around M'sieuur's waist to keep him from wandering, and bring him to Paris and exhibit him, like the noble savages were paraded by the *philosophes* before the courts. M'sieur said he'd be willing except if it wasn't that loincloths were so unbecoming, and besides, he'd have to learn all those dance-steps to a mouth organ. People would sooner believe his *science friction* tales than believe his stories about the BelleVilleans, Jacques went on. "A whole state full of people who think there's oil buried somewhere in the backyard. And so Protestant you can't get a drop of wine on Sundays, but with the City of Sin locked in its bosom. And so naïve they didn't catch that misprint in the newspaper that said President Kennedy attended the Inter-American Economic and Social Council in *Puta* del Este."

If that boring meeting was held in such a place, O'Hara said, even *he* would go have a look-see.

And then in honor of Jacques, who loved it so, Peerer brought out his recording of the "Mild und Leise" aria from *Tristan und Isolde.* And they-all sat in a circle and held hands in their last communal coming.

Jimmy Landry said he could not for his *lahfe* predict what-all was about to come out of John Kennedy's sleeve. She and Mark were entertaining the Landrys and the Mannheims at a dinner party. There was chicken jambalaya and there was candlelight and there were babies soon to be born, Camille Landry was blond and lovely and blooming, in the seventh month of her pregnancy, and Moira was carrying Teddy's brother or sister. Jimmy Landry and Mark both acknowledged they were feeling very expansive.

Felix confessed he was feeling expansive too. Hannah had gone to the State Capitol last week, and had put all the state legislators to shame. She had stood up before them not long after the demonstration there, when parents of children from the two integrated schools had carried a miniature black coffin with a blackened effigy of the U.S. District Judge into the building, and the members of the House had given them a standing ovation. "The Judge is dead!" a woman had shouted. "We have slaughtered him!" The demonstrators were wearing Confederate insignias, and they were carrying black flags, the little girl at the head of the procession was carrying a black cross. There had been placards reading THANK GOD FOR THE STATE LEGISLATURE. And Hannah had stood up there and informed the legislators that her neighbor had been inflamed by this display of hatred and was going around talking about killing a judge, about murdering him, about throwing a bomb into the Fifth Circuit Court of Appeals. And the legislature, Hannah said, was in large part responsible for this ugly mood of defiance of the law and of hatred of those who upheld it. She asked them to consider what it was they were unleashing. She had stood up there in the State Capitol, proud and scolding, all four feet ten of her round, determined little self, her voice ringing through the chambers: "You are behaving just as the Nazis behaved. I know. I was there." She told them that they, who had been elected to serve as leaders, elected to set an example of decent and reasonable behavior, were behaving like thugs, like common criminals. And they had put their heads down, they had been humbled. "My dear wife," Felix said, "can be formidable."

Jimmy Landry told them he would have to put his money on federal intervention. That there didn't appear to be anything to be hoped for from the state except more of the same. "More legislate-and-litigate. More *massive resistance.*" He reminded them that the home of the A.F.of L.-C.I.O. head man had been dynamited after the fellow made a statement *mildly* supporting school integration. "Look at the deaths in just this past year, and these are the ones we *know* about, the Negroes who tried to register to vote, the organizer of the sit-in demonstration, and now the two Negroes beaten and shot just off Dubonnet Drive last month." Jimmy Landry reminded them of the *civil defense drills* being held now in Belle Ville, and of the mounted deputies coming in to *guard the peace,* driving in with their horses in trailer trucks. He reminded them of the four-foot-tall cross the Klan had burned on the grounds of the State Capitol last fall. He said the mood was very defiant, very violent, at the Secession ceremony this past winter. He reminded them of the bomb threats called in to the schools. "The Klan is crawling out from under the rocks again. Do you-all know how much some people hate John Kennedy down here? It's not just his politics, it's his religion too. Remember that the Klan had its first big comeback in years back in '28, when Al Smith was running for President. And here they are out ridin' again, bolder 'n' ever. And they're not the gentlemen they used to like to think they were. Those with any *pretenses* at bein' civilized are in the Citizens Councils now. Ones in the *Klan* are downright savages."

Felix asked him if people really took the Klan seriously.

"People," Camille said, "are good and scared, Felix. They're goin' around more tight-lipped and worried than I ever can remember seein' them in all my life. And the Negroes are movin' into *their* own world more 'n' more. And the whites are just *full* of suspicion. It's all gettin' polarized. Lines bein' drawn like for all-get-out-war."

Only one thing can take the wind out of their sails, Jimmy Landry claimed. And that was klieg lights and lots of exposure. And bringing in federal marshals and FBI agents to see to it that the Negroes did *get* registered. And to put under arrest the local law enforcement officials who attacked the civil rights workers. To bring the Justice Department into every corner of every Parish, into every little country road in the piney woods. So that these criminals would know they couldn't get away with what they were doin' anymore. It was not for nothing that in every cabin up and down the back roads there's a picture of John Kennedy cut out of the newspapers and pasted up on the wall. "But why don't they *move?* They've got everything *goin'* for them, so why are they so *slow?"* Jimmy Landry asked them what they thought it was John Kennedy had tucked up in his *sleeve.*

Felix pointed out that they mustn't forget what was going on in the rest of the world, they mustn't forget that it was a Russian who had been the first human being in space.

"Not likely I'd forget, sir. Only a few days after this Great State seceded from the Union in the Senate Chamber of the Old State Capitol, it was this-here Jimmy Landry who composed the headline for the article in the *Herald* you-all read under SPACE-POKING 'HAM' BACK SAFELY AFTER ROCKET RIDE OF 420 MILES. Not exactly Pulitzer-Prize wording, but it got me a lot of compliments from people who told me they needed some respite from the local scene."

Perspective, Felix said, that was what everyone needed. Just think, that little boy sleeping in the next room might go to the *moon* in another twenty years.

"And if some people around here have their way," Jimmy Landry laughed, "they'll be markin' space capsules WHITES ONLY and COLORED. Yessir, they will build themselves separate-but-equal space capsules."

Khrushchev had said they will bury the people in the West, Felix said. Kennedy had *that* to consider. And the Bay of Pigs invasion was a disaster Kennedy had yet to come to terms with. And Kennedy was committed to the freedom of the people of West Berlin. "There is a whole world out there."

The world was far away, Jimmy said. It came in to them all on television, and it looked like it was just one big show after another. There was the space show, and the show where two teams rattled their rockets at one another, all mixed up with *Gunsmoke* and the like. And the federal government was far away from those little places where the newspaper photos of John Kennedy were pasted up on the wall, on the very same spot where the old folks used to paste newspaper photos of FDR. Kennedy was a hope for many people, he was like their bridge to the rest of the country. Because of what Kennedy said, people had faith that when sheriffs turned fire hoses on them and put cattle prods to them and when the night riders came down from the hills to whip and to burn and to kill, there were people out there who were stronger, more powerful, who would intervene on their behalf, people who would see to it that at long, long last they'd be granted the freedom that was their birthright. "So what's he *waitin'* for? A man who seems to have everything. A war hero, and so young and so witty. Radiates a kind of *personal* magnetism. Looked Khrushchev straight in the eye and stared him down. But then there are all those judges he appointed."

That evening, Camille Landry said very gently there were things only a native could understand completely, certain things you missed seeing unless you happened to be born here. "I am referring to the pain some of our finest people feel right now, in this growin' climate of fear, the pain of havin' to depend on federal intervention, on the goodness of forces from the outside." Felix replied quietly that this was a sorrow he and Hannah understood very well.

That evening, Hannah and Camille recruited Moira as a new member of their inter-racial group who met in downtown Belle Ville in an abandoned store. "Did you know," Camille said, "that way, way back, in 1930 or thereabouts, women in the South organized an Association of Southern Women for the Prevention of Lynching? Only women were in the position of bringing sweet reason to all this ugly fuss."

Outsider Outsider She stood in the shadowing yard And all that she loved lay enclosed In a small and fragile craft On the high and turbulent seas of a changing world And the moon bled white On the striped-tent-roof of the sandbox And lay its white wand on the bright red ball at rest Under the pecan tree And there was a stirring A false coolness Soft-blowing her gown and fevering her skin And the swordleaves of the banana plant rustled And a sound flashed in the night That might be nothing That might be everything That might be innocent That might be breathing evil intent And with her eyes, with her will She drew a magic ring of protection Around their house

The rains that night were washing Belle Ville away That night Hannah came for her To drive her to the inter-racial meeting And she stood at the screen door waiting for Hannah And Mark was holding Robin in his arms And his eyes were saying *"You are a mother now, you have all this to care for first"* There was reproach in his eyes And fear And the bitterness of their quarrel was in her mouth *"It's not safe anymore,"* he said; *"It's not a game, Moira"* But she answered, *"It's* never *been safe And I must go, I must do* some*thing The world is wider than our little house"* And Mark argued *"You are risking so much for nothing Your life isn't your own, now Remember it was* you *who wanted a family How can you leave them? Tomorrow you can have your life back again They'll be grown sooner than we know* Tomorrow, *Not today Not tonight"* She said, *"They're safe with* you, *I leave them with* you" He asked her to let him go in her place But this was impossible, she told him This was *woman's* work

"So long as we live down here, I am part of it all. And what I do is so little, Mark! Think of what *others* are risking!"

"But this isn't our *home!"*

"Home? Where is home for us, then? If not here, where?"

He said then, "We are only passing through."

But she demanded to know, "Since when? And *until* when?"

Since Jacobs had made his public statement criticizing the legislature, he said, the statement in support of desegregation of the schools, and then the legislature had ordered an un-American activities probe of the university because, they said, Jacobs was un-American and un-Louisianian, and then O'Hara, howling with the insanity of this, had been the first to sign Mark's petition in support of their colleague Jacobs, and then M'sieur had signed it, shaking his head over the *fuss and feathers,* and Felix Mannheim had signed it, and Arturo had signed it, and Peerer had put down his fork next to his plate of red beans and rice and signed it, and before too long there were forty-seven names on Mark's petition to get the legislature off Jacobs's back, and after that the legislature was saying they needed $50,000 to probe the subversive activities on the campus, beginning with a probe of these forty-seven who were *corrupting the youth of this Great State,* and the legislators were furious because a branch of the university up north had been granted $50,000 for mosquito control, the legislators would *have people to realize* that it was far more important to ferret out subversive elements on the campus than to ferret out mosquitoes, and O'Hara had offered to go to the State Capitol and spray them all with the newest insecticide, and in the midst of all this uproar Jacobs had resigned, even though Mark had pleaded with him to hold out, and M'sieur had said, *"Michou, you mustn't allow yourself to be overwhelmed by such, or the angels will weep for you"*

"We are only passing through until *when?"* she demanded once again, and she did not wait for his answer, she said they never would leave, that this was their home now, that they even spoke with Southern accents now, that they had forgotten the look of snow, the feel of autumn, of winter, that they had learned how to *be* with other human beings, direct and personal and unhurried, that "we aren't strangers here anymore."

And Mark said, "A Jew is *always* a stranger."

It hurt her and thrilled her to hear his words, to see the ancient sorrow come into his eyes, his voice.

It was through Hannah she had learned of what happened during Eichmann's trial. Some students had made a huge poster, and suspended it outside one of the windows on the second floor of Brooke Hall, a poster with a six-pointed star and the words WE LIKE EICH. Professor Cohen had asked Mark if he would like to accompany Felix and himself to see the President about that poster. "Donald Cohen told your husband people thought of him as Mr. Jew on the campus, that was why he took it upon himself to go. It was Felix who suggested that your husband should be invited to go with them. And so Mark did. And the President was incensed to hear about that poster. He was a war hero, you know, my dear. He has no love for Nazi Germany." When she had asked Mark about it, he'd said he had nothing to add to what Hannah had told her. "Except why *you* didn't tell me," she'd said. "It was in November," he'd told her. "What kind of an answer is *that?"* she'd demanded. *"November,"* he'd repeated. "You could hear the yelling at the pep rally. November, what else was November besides football?" She had stared at him, uncomprehending. "November," he had said a third time. "The day of the Great News, remember?" *The surprise dinner by candlelight, the bowl of yellow and white chrysanthemums, Ted running out the front door to greet him, Ted's eager shout, "Daddy! Daddy! Mommy says we're having a baby next spring!"*

After that, he told her there had been talk at the time he circulated the petition, talk about Jews on the campus, how *Jews conspire.* And he had received one of those *crazy letters* that said there were Jewish doctors in *that secret hospital up in Alaska where they take kidnapped Southerners and have lobotomies done on them that change them into Communists and race-mixers, and those doctors are all Jews, just like all the psychiatrists are Jews, just like Communists are Jews, and they get their orders straight from Khrushchev, Khrushchev runs the NAACP.* He showed her the letter, he told her O'Hara had laughed himself sick over it, and so had M'sieur, but Arturo had blushed with the shame of it. *"Maybe it's time to think about moving out, Moira."* But soon after, Robin was born. M'sieur brought her a silver cup with her name engraved on it, and said, "We have a lirrel Tessa, now, cha, and a lirrel Michou." There was a parade of friends old and new coming with their gifts and best wishes for their baby daughter, and Hannah and Felix became honorary grandparents all over again, and now here they were standing at the screen door arguing about where *home* was, with the rain rushing down.

And Hannah's car was in the driveway, Hannah was honking her horn. It was time for Moira to go.

And Hannah drove around the lakes They saw the water was rising up to the level of the road Soon it would wash over the roads, soon there would be flooding Hannah's windshield wipers scraped back and forth, twin metronomes marking time as Hannah hummed cheery German folk songs

The downtown was deserted. There were less than two dozen cars parked outside their meeting-place. Hugging one another under the umbrella they shared, they scurried inside. The women were seated on folding chairs facing the small circle on the dais. Camille Landry read the minutes of the last meeting when they resolved to officially join the movement to keep the schools open. Then Hannah reported on the probe the legislature wanted to make of their activities. While she was speaking, the phone rang. Bernice Cohen was stationed to answer it that evening; she listened for a moment and then began reciting into the mouthpiece, "Though I walk through the valley of the shadow I will fear no evil...," and after a moment she replaced the receiver. Mrs. Hattie Moore reported on the desegregation plans of the Catholic schools in New Orleans and six adjoining Parishes. Mrs. Catherine Kent reported on the past month's activities of the local chapter of the NAACP. After the formalities ended, the women gathered in a circle and clasped hands and sang, "Pass Me Not O Gentle Savior." During their coffee-and-cookies social time, Moira thought about asking Bernice if they might suggest a non-denominational hymn for their next meeting, and decided to call her and speak with her privately about it. They swept up and turned out the lights, and went out into the downpour.

The men were waiting for them, waiting with their flashlights, shining them into the eyes of the women, blinding them. "Y'all thought nobody knew who you were and what y'all were up to. Well, you just take a look-see in the papers day after tomorrow. And you kin read your names there, and your husbands' names too, they'll be there for all of Belle Ville to see, we got the license numbers on the cars of every last one of y'all. By tomorrow, we'll have that list drawn up. Can't say nobody didn't warn y'all, not that you'd listen."

Hannah shouted they were cowards, shining their flashlights in people's faces so that no one could identify them. Cowards, attacking women, just like the Nazis did. And she offered herself, Hannah Mannheim, as the culprit and the instigator and the agitator, she offered her name and address loudly and clearly, and asked that the other women be left out of it. Because Hannah knew who would be the victims of reprisals, reprisals certain to come after their list was published.

Moira's name was not on that list, because Moira was a passenger in Hannah's car. The list was published in the *Herald* two days later. With Jimmy Landry's own wife's name on it. And Jimmy Landry called the staff a passel of cowards for knuckling down to the Klan. And he walked out of the office and went on a binge. And Camille told Moira over the phone the day after that what Jimmy had said, "Ever since the riot in Oxford, the Klan is gettin' bolder. Only way to kill a poisonous snake is to up and *kill* it. But ever' time it rattles, ever'body jumps back."

Nothing happened to the Negro women who'd been at that meeting but crazy phone calls and crazy letters. Even so, they were afraid their group was as good as finished now.

Mark was saying again, "It's time to go home." Arturo had told him he'd been offered a good position in a private school, and he didn't think he could afford to turn it down. This might could be his last year here, he said. And then M'sieur had to take sick leave, to go to the clinic in New Orleans.

She felt it was all coming apart. It wasn't as bad as the way she'd felt when Kennedy ordered the Navy to blockade Cuba, when he called up thousands of Air Force reservists to active duty and for seven days and seven nights everybody waited for the world to be blown apart. That time, Felix and Hannah had come to visit one afternoon and Felix had told her, "We are very close to the edge of the abyss. Much too close. It all could go up at any moment. Kennedy wants to call their bluff, but the stakes are too high." Jimmy Landry had called and said it all would settle down, that nobody would want to push the button if *both* sides would go up in smoke. Kennedy knew what he was doing, Jimmy Landry claimed, Kennedy knew the shape of the devil just like he knew it when it showed itself in Oxford, Mississippi. "Only way to meet it is to confront it and stare it down." She had allowed herself to be reassured then, allowed herself to believe the world would go on. But she felt it all was unraveling, it all was coming undone.

M'sieur came back from the clinic jubilant. "All that money and all that time," he laughed. "All those degrading tests. Cha, they even strap you in a chair, and then turn the chair *upside down,* those dirty people! All that, and they told me what I've got is a bad case of athlete's foot!"

Ted asked her where the rain comes from, and where you go to wait for each other after you die, and about his two grandfathers back in Illinois. Robin pulled herself up and started to walk. Soon it was time to go to the Farewell Party for Arturo, a Sunday brunch. O'Hara laced the orange juice with vodka, and Olive Oil scrambled the eggs with Benedictine. Arturo's apartment in Cougar Alley was three flights up, right over the bend in the creek. And after the party, as they made their way back down the steps, reciting Baudelaire and Rimbaud, singing and laughing and out of their senses entirely from the sun and the heat and all that hootch, M'sieur stumbled, and they almost lost him in the waters below. Moira thought of how long it had been since she wrote her last poem, she mourned her lost poet's voice. A few weeks after the party, O'Hara's wife had a miscarriage in the middle of the night, O'Hara called them in a panic, and Mark went over to O'Hara's to stay with the kids while O'Hara drove his wife to the hospital. Not long after, Mark told Moira he had heard of a search by the English Department of a college in New England for a James Joyce man.

The two camps confronted one another. "We're just not gonna do it," the commander of one shouted. "Nevah! *Nevah!*" And those in the other camp walked toward their adversaries, singing *"Ain't gonna let nobody turn me 'round."* Massive resistance, mounted and armed, met passive resistance walking in procession over the bridge. Massive resistance stood, arms folded, in the schoolhouse doors. Passive resistance walked bravely toward them. When the doors of the bus swung open and passive resistance came down the steps, massive resistance was waiting for them armed with iron bars. And outside the jails, the crowds gathered. And in Birmingham, armed men in uniform mounted on horseback drove back the marchers, using cattle prods and fire hoses and police dogs. Early in the summer Medgar Evers was shot from ambush. And then, after a long wait, the leaders of the March on Washington were given the President's blessing as a "peaceful assembly calling for a redress of grievances." And the press reported that 250,000 people marched to Washington to show the whole world the urgency of their good cause. And Martin Luther King lifted up his voice and sang, *"I have a dream"*

And Jimmy Landry said, "The lines are drawn now, *cher*. It's really movin' now." And on Monday, Mark said they were strangers here, and on Tuesday he called her Tess, on Wednesday he said Maybe, on Thursday he said Maybe not. And a Sunday School was bombed, and four children were killed. Hannah said that history was repeating itself. And Jimmy Landry asked did she hear that *ol' Neanderthaloid* was building concentration camps for the Freedom Riders? And Hannah asked Camille Landry could It happen here?, Hannah said, "Up to now, I would never have believed it." And Camille Landry said, "There are just too many good people down here for that to happen." But Hannah replied, "There are always good people. Europe is a cemetery of good people."

Moira had what they-all called *Kennedy fever.* Kennedy was her idol. "It's his youth," Mark decided. "And that Irish charm of his." Mark said he had never believed in saviors. She said to Jimmy Landry, "Thank heaven for Kennedy." But Jimmy Landry confessed he wasn't so sure about Kennedy anymore, that it might be a case of too little too late. "People down here who hate him so much are outright *blind,* it's maybe *Kennedy* who's holding in the force of this freedom movement, ever thought of that? Trying to drive it off the streets and into the courtroom. Wasn't for John Fitzgerald Kennedy, there'd be some *real* explosions, yessiree. And a lot of people in the freedom movement say that he's usin' them. Like they've been used so many times before. You know, there's a power in that ol' charisma that could drive a lesser man than King crazy with ambition. But down here, *cher*, the old wounds are all open, the old agony's laid bare. You watch, now, there *could* be all-out war." But Felix reminded them of Kennedy's words, "Kennedy pointed out that the two countries still have very different views of the world and of the *future* of the world. And these differences set limits on how much they agree about an issue."

Kennedy had said these things in October, and Mark commented, "Maybe he's right, maybe there's nowhere to run." Mark showed her the letter he had composed to the head of the department in the college in New England. She looked up and said, "If we leave here, I won't leave here whole, Mark. I feel we came of age here, I feel we belong here."

She felt that the tide of her life was at the full.

Then, in November, on a rainy Friday, Mark took Ted to his first movie. And she heard church bells tolling, and wondered why. And Mark came home with Ted riding on his shoulders, and set Ted down, and looked and looked at her. And then he said, "He's dead, Moira. Kennedy is dead. He was shot. In Dallas."

Their neighbor's daughter went to the football game that Friday night at the high school nearby. She came by to show Moira the Sparkle she was putting in her hair, because her boyfriend was *partial* to Sparkle in a girl's hair. The television set was on, playing the film while her neighbor's daughter was talking. On the screen, Kennedy smiled, he waved, and then he fell against Jacqueline Kennedy, and Jacqueline Kennedy cradled his head in her arms. Then the film switched to the local station where local politicians were talking. One of them said, "If it weren't for all these extremists this violence never would have happened, extremists like Martin Luther King."

The rains poured down, they beat against the windows of their house, they ran down the slope out back and filled the ditches. And the cypresses shuddered, and the winds keened in the cypresses, and rain-rushes flowed through the trailings of gray moss. And Jimmy Landry came over, and Jimmy Landry was crying. That night she heard Kennedy's voice in her dreams, then his face appeared, then all of his person. She saw him jabbing his finger at a questioner, she saw he was laughing.

"What rough beast?" Mark asked, and she echoed, "What rough beast?"

The November rains were warm, they had the salt-taste of tears.

"This will be our last year here," he said.

"Yes," she answered.

"Our last November without an autumn."

"I know."

They began keeping the long vigil, then, they began the mourning.

* * * *

She was running alongside a canal, the water in the canal was silver. She was holding something precious in her hand, was it a book?, she knew it was something prized. She was hurrying now through the labyrinth of catacombs. She knew they were almost upon her, her pursuers. And the glittering water dazzled her eyes, she thought it might blind her.

She opened her eyes.

She was alone in the house. How long had it been since she had murmured, her eyes still closed, "What time is it?" and he had answered, "A quarter to eight, go back to sleep," how long had it been, what did it matter?

Last night he had told her, "You have to get through this thing by yourself." He had spoken as one who had come out the other side of it. Whoever it was who *had* come out she could not guess, she only knew it was not Mark.

Ah, well, think of the august company they were in. John Donne, keeping his "midwinter vigil." And Tolstoi. And Chateaubriand, enraged by it. And Whitman, the heroic sufferer. And Swift, roaring-mad.

The least the two of them might do is try to keep their wits about them. And a shred of humor. She doubted they could keep one another.

The qualities of silence in the other rooms. The pleasance of the clime in Ted's, the cross-grained currents eddying in Robin's. Only yesterday, her cheerful "Good morning, darling!" as *la belle dame sans merci* passed by on her way to take a shower had won a guttural "Hi" upon which the bathroom door was shut decisively. Half an hour later, the young and lovely Terrible Daughter had appeared in the doorway, holding up the overnight bag she wanted to borrow again. "Mind? I need two changes of shirts. Unless you'd rather I use a shopping bag." It was time for the "checking-out" ritual as Robin so antagonistically called it, and she would not give an inch: she had to be *asked* where she was going, how long she'd be away. This time there was a bike hike and then a dance and then a sleep-over, so she wouldn't be back until late tomorrow. "See ya." At thirteen she had been tempestuous, but still carefree. At fourteen the defiance began. Now her rejection was absolute.

How much Mark's ever more frequent and extended absences were owing to this metamorphosis of their fun-loving gamine, how much to his own, how much to *her* own, she could not sort out. There were moments when she felt it already had happened, that he had come back for the last time, that he was gone for good.

All this past year, Ted's last year at home, she had thought she was preparing for this time, she had made little partings. The break-up of their family was coming, it could not go on forever, *all things have their season.*

She lay her head back on her pillow. Last night she had been *there* again, at St. Bridget's High School in Chicago. She had looked through a dream-window and she had seen Moira standing on the street-car island on a Friday evening, her white shoe-skates yoked across her shoulders. Then there was a quickening, she felt the pulsar of the dream. And then she saw the cubes of sun burning the polished wood of the floor in the corridor, and she used them for stepping-stones into the chapel. The pews were sticky as caramel from the varnish. She could taste the Communion wafer, feel it melting on her tongue, she could hear the clatter of cutlery on the trays in the cafeteria downstairs, the nuns were setting up breakfast of sweet rolls and cocoa.

Worlds forming and vanishing under the eyelids. The rich chocolate aroma filling the air of the cafeteria on the First Fridays of the month when they said Mass for the conversion of Russia. "Or *some* such modest proposal," Tess would tell the ex-Catholics at the lunch table. *"Cha, everybody* knows *the nuns have black habits, that's why our Tess-girl decided to live in sin with Michou instead of joining the convent. Besides which, Michou has eyes."*

And Moira had a *doppelgänger* even back then at St. Bridget's, a Tess who used to tell her circle of friends at the lunch-table, "First I'll become a great whore, the most celebrated whore of the Nineteen Fifties. Then I'll see the world with all the money I earned. And if I'm still alive after that, I'll repent and then I might even join the cloister and pray for the souls of the rest of you sinners." Up and down the little white bows on the chins of the nuns' headpieces would bob, up and down, as they gave you your algebra and Latin and English assignments.

The nun-dreams were black-and-white, the fear-dreams were black and silver, but the dreams of Louisiana were *in living color. In one of these she was fording a river in a pea-green boat, her green robes billowing about her, and she came ashore and glided over the emerald brightness of the grass. "My Queen Maeve,"* Mark once called her. *"My sweet rebel, my witch-of-the-woods."* Was it when she lay down to bring Ted into the world that the Other lay down to take her leave of it? Yes, that was it, "Blessed are the meek; she shall possess the Other./The race is to the survivor, the wife, the mother." Yes, it was when her hour had come, in that hour that the Other passed into legend. A legend for Ted, orphaned beyond the male's imagining by the death of the maiden in the mother. A legend for Robin, who saw, when she looked at all, this wan, anxious, hag-ridden Demeter.

Now she remembered another of last night's dreams. She had been driving the car, a silver car, in a dream-black night, with Ted in the passenger seat beside her. And a woman in white was walking on the road ahead of them, her white veils fluttering about her slender form. The mist-figure would not turn to look, would not hurry, although their car was bearing down on her. She pleaded with Ted to take the wheel, she said she was losing control. But Ted neither moved nor spoke. And then she was alone in the car, driving *around* the luminous figure--

The telephone was ringing.

No, it was the doorbell.

The living room was still in shadows. Mark hadn't even opened the drapes before going out. She unlatched the front door and opened it. There were two young women on the doorstep, offering her a *Watchtower.*

Early March. Still wintry. The lawn frosted with last night's light dusting of snow. It would be hours before the sun could melt it. Standing at the kitchen window, sipping coffee from her old mug, she thought of the tulips, how they had begun to blossom in the false spring they'd had in late February. Three days after she and Mark and Robin had an impromptu picnic supper in the yard, there had been a snowstorm.

This year she would have to do the gardening alone. Up until now, Robin and Mark had made a religion out of gardening. Winters they fussed over seed catalogues, calling one another "farmer," drawing up long lists of the supplies they planned to lay in for the year. Summers she often came upon them holding hands strolling about their flower beds. It pleased them to hear her mock exasperation, *"The two of you."* She and Ted warned them they'd form an exclusive society of their own, just to get even. Ted, his hands in his pockets, stood in the doorway laughing, saying all he heard were promises, promises. It wasn't that there were happy and unhappy *families* so much as there were these...spells. These consolations.

She thought she could hear strains of piano music, of Ted playing Mendelssohn's *Secrets.*

She went to his room. It would be her study now, except during his vacations and parts of the summers.

A long epistle to Hannah lay on the blotter, the last page yet to be written. Robin had interrupted her, furious because she could not find her new belt, and by the time she had thought where it had to be, the thread had been broken. She sat down at the desk and read the three pages that had lain there since that interruption late Friday afternoon:

"Dearest Hannah,

"I began to think that I'd dreamed I wrote to you, that's how long you made me wait this time for an answer to my last letter. You are the only correspondent I have left from the old days, and all the more cherished for that--no one from that time, or from this one that never can take the place of it, *no* one seems to believe in writing letters. When I opened your envelope, all sorts of remembered fragrances floated up in a bouquet of sweet olive, ligustrum, jasmine, and flowers whose name I never learned. And then I heard you humming one of your folk songs, and then I saw your merry smile.

"You found me, you write, in your *unBeantwörted* file. And I'd been in that particular limbo for three months, unless you count your Christmas *Rundbriefe!* It is almost spring, almost the season for the forsythia to bloom, and the daffodils, the apple orchards. In Belle Ville, it is almost azalea time. How many lifetimes ago was it that on an afternoon this time of year we would be having High Tea at the Mannheims, you would be whistling as you wheeled in your little white cart bearing strawberries and little cakes, and Herr Professor would be sending the cups around to our gathering on your front porch? You ask if our town has F.I.S.H. Yes, the Friends in Service

Helping has a branch here in Palatine, and I volunteered to be of help to the blind. My current assignment is to perform secretarial duties for an elderly lady in a nursing home. She wears a sign lettered LEGALLY BLIND depending from a cord looped around her neck. For whose notification? I wondered when we met--I'd been told by the Director that she rarely leaves the place and is one of the Regulars in the Community Room, where she plays checkers and cards and watches the soaps on TV apparently unhindered by the disability her banner proclaims. During that first meeting, it emerged that when she heard of F.I.S.H. she hit upon this means of ensuring herself a weekly visitor willing to serve as her amanuensis (I have learned the job description is such that the Dictionary of Occupational Titles ought to cross-list this one with "confessor.") Mrs. N dictates letters to her daughter, *sermons* actually, all of them commentaries on the Commandment to honor thy parent. So far as I can determine, these are never answered. Nor, for that matter, can I be sure any has been posted--she tells me she likes to take care of addressing the envelope and affixing the stamp. She likes me to read these homilies back to her, and listens, her clever crow's face intent upon mine: a release for her, and a cautionary tale for me for the time Robin is my age, and I yours.

"I am keeping my vow not to engage myself in any political activities, even at the local level, until Robin graduates from high school. Work at the newspaper keeps me busy enough. I am staff reporter of the proceedings of the village and town board meetings, cover many local events, such as the Heritage Day festivities, and have a plum assignment tossed in my lap now and then. The most recent of these was to write a feature about ecumenism in our community. Our editor finagled an invitation for me to attend one of the third-Wednesday-of-the-month luncheons attended by interested clergy from Palatine's houses of worship; there was one condition, that I "merely observe" (!) and refrain from taking notes. Apparently, this was a privilege accorded only to members of their group! At this luncheon I learned that the pocket notebook is as much an insignia of the clergy as of the journalist--throughout the meal, one or another of the reverends would consult his notebook or jot down some little memorandum. (When they discussed what the agenda for their next meeting ought to be, there was a prolonged Quaker-meeting moment of silence after each suggestion, as they all scribbled in unison! I marveled at this harmony and good will among inheritors of the religious wars you and I never tired of talking about when I was preparing for my conversion to Judaism. Hannah, there is indeed Progress. But it seems humanity first must learn to banter before we learn how to convert swords and spears to ploughshares and pruning hooks. A delicious morsel I'm not permitted to include in my feature: One of the ministers promised that the next time he despaired for the human race, he would carry a ten-foot cross up and down Center Street. The Catholic priest asked whether he intended to wear it on his back or on a chain around his neck. When the laughter subsided, the minister said he thought his answer would depend to some extent on whether the Roman Church planned to canonize their revolutionary clergy *before* or *after* their excommunication.)

The 1970s are over by more than half, she had thought as she opened her friend's letter. *I have been living in exile for more than a dozen years now.* Then her eye had caught Hannah's postscript: "So much has changed down here, my dear. And I am growing quite old."

As she lay the basket of laundry down under the clothesline, still another of last night's dreams came to her, a dream of grief, of Robin lost, lost forever. In the beginning of the dream, she was holding the infant Robin in her arms. She could feel the warm weight of her now as she set the bedding asail in the March wind, she could taste the soft and fragrant skin under her kisses, *Gonna get me some sugah* the Southern Mommas say. She and Robin were on the back porch of a tenement, they were in Illinois. She knew this building. It was the building in the photograph taken by her aunt in 1931, the photograph of herself being held in her father's arms. They were laughing, their faces had the *special lighting* of a father and daughter between whom there is pure and perfect love.

The bag of clothespins fell. Kneeling to collect the spilled pins, she saw a string of laundry under that back porch and herself looking down at it, holding Robin. She was telling someone she knew very well, a shadow close to the shadow she and Robin cast, that her little girl would be lost to her, that it was foreordained, that this was the last time she would hold her in her arms. And she asked the shadow for a souvenir, a photograph of the two of them like this. She saw the dream-scene in a longing that was incandescent.

The telephone was ringing. She picked up the basket and hurried to the back door. The feeling was following her with her moving shadow. Robin was gone, Robin had been kidnapped, taken hostage. She had prepared herself, knowing this was to happen. Now she could only pray no harm would come to her daughter.

"Hello? *Hello?*"

She could see him grinning into the mouthpiece. He was chewing gum, he was tapping the fingers of his free hand on the wall.

"It's much warmer now than when I left. I'm in a drugstore."

"Why didn't you wait for me?"

"Would you've come with me?"

"Probably not, you win."

"I'm wearing my Oriental birth sign. Power, remember? I'm all Power this morning."

"Show us," she had teased him when he opened the gift package last year, what could she give him for his birthday this *year? "Show us. Stand up and let us hear your armor clanking!" Mark had fallen from* his *steed, too, at last. Had taken to sitting on the floor in a circle of groupies-for-human-potentiality. Touching and being touched, giving and receiving foot rubs, back rubs. Visiting one another's grottoes, chanting instant devotions before the images of one another's instant saints. Whatever they were "into" at the moment, it wouldn't be long before they'd be into one another.*

"You *go," she'd say. "Humanistic Psychology's not for the likes of me."*

"You sound like a professional Midwesterner."

"More like a refugee."

"Suit yourself. See ya."

"Well, Power, do you want me to make Sunday dinner for us?"

"Maybe for tonight. If Robin'll be home. Otherwise, why bother?"

Yes, they would sit in a circle on the floor and tell one another of matters so private and personal one scarcely acknowledged them to one*self* before the Seventies came along. Midwesterners make the poorest hippies, she'd told him, even the *Southerners* could make a better showing, even old New England ladies who have long freckled necks and live *forever.* Although Easterners and Far Westerners, she thought, have no serious contenders for first place from any other region of the country.

"*You're* full *of censors, you're a walking* republic *of censors!" he had laughed. She had replied that what she was learning was that Midwesterners don't transplant. "You managed it in Louisiana," he had retorted. "You were something else, then."*

"I'll be back in a while. Maybe."

"All right, Mark."

Now his hair was longer than hers and his smile was one she could not recognize. He had been long gone from her, his soul snatched away by some strong and clever god who was returning, now, to claim Robin's. *"What's happening to this family, Mom? What's* happening *to us?"* She had not the words to tell Ted he too was held captive, even as she herself was held captive. In thralldom. By the enchantment of the young dead.

In her dream it had not been Robin who was lost, but her own self, the lost one was the little girl laughing in her father's arms who'd come back to inhabit her grown body during that brief season of defiance. The Other, knowing who she would become, had gone down into the bayou, under the cypresses, leaving her to find her own deliverance. The day and the month and the year of the Other's passing were part of the historical record now: November 22, 1963. The day that other dying was recorded on film, on sheets of cellulose acetate or was it cellulose nitrate coated with a light-sensitive emulsion for making passports to Remembrance. How well Oliver Goldsmith had said it: "That strain once more; it bids remembrance rise." Memory came, at least for her, in musical phrases, musical thoughts played by string instruments or chanted by a choir, then falling into the sleep and the forgetting. Returning in the *très riches heures* of solitude that Mnemosyne grants to mortals whose souls are stilled to listen in serenity. Then those passages reveal themselves to be movements in a prelude to a composition. A suite for strings or an oratorio, whose theme unfolds in a *Magnificat* to the redemptive power of the Titaness who bore Zeus the nine daughters, the Muses.

The reel curled like a spiral-shelled conch in the folds hidden back of her eyes began unwinding on the turning spool: the arrival of the plane at the Dallas airport, her arms filled with roses, his quick, light descent--

Something was moving at the bourne of the field of her vision: a car was moving up the street. The slow-motion scene was framed in the kitchen window next to the wall phone where she stood, still holding the receiver to her ear, although the line had gone dead.

The procession of the fateful motorcade...the workers on the scaffold above the street, waving, smiling...and then he turned his head to receive his death.

It was Robin coming home, one of Robin's friends had given her a ride, now where did Robin leave her bike *this* time?

There was the sudden swerving of the cameras, the crazed veering away and then back...then the stricken faces of the people gathered outside Parkland Memorial Hospital...then someone was saying, "The President is dead."

The car door slammed. "Bye!" someone shouted. "Bye, Robin!"

Yes, it was then, on that early Friday afternoon, that Tess *lay down in darkness,* her laughter dissolving in the soft rain falling on the mourning cypresses, her bright laughter darkening inward from the edges of a time that, scarcely born, was passing into eternity. The church bells were tolling, tolling. Losses. She would have the rest of her life to grieve.

The porch door swung open.

He had come in with Ted riding in his arms. And looked and looked at her. And then he had said, "He's dead, Moira. Kennedy is dead. He was shot. In Dallas."

Robin came into the kitchen. "Hi, Mom, I'm home."

* * * *

"I'm still dazzled by that silver band of the tracks in his *Railroad Sunset."*

"Mom, the sunlight in that painting's a *miracle!* Have you ever seen *any*thing more vibrant?"

"Yes. Your face just now."

"Stop! No, wait, *don't* stop, I *love* it!" Robin leaned across the table and whispered, "This is the third time that man has lowered his MLA program so he can look at us. Have you noticed?"

It was the high forehead that had led her astray; most of his ruffly brown hair had left his head entirely. But behind the bifocals were the seawater eyes. And under them the unmistakable schnozzle, the broad humorous mouth.

"O'Hara!" she called, rising, starting toward him. "It's *you,* is it, bedad!"

He leaped to his feet and held his arms out to her, and she hurried into them.

"Moira. Moira Fishbein, lirrel ol' Tess. I don't believe this."

"Come, let me introduce you to Robin, all grown now. If I can stop crying. Robin, this is a very, very old friend your father and I knew in Louisiana, in Belle Ville, this is O'Hara."

Robin was laughing and saying she'd been about to have him arrested, O'Hara was remarking how charming a young woman she was, the living image of their Tess of Auld, he was asking what in *hell* the two of them were doing in Lindy's, they *had* to be here for the MLA circus, why weren't they with Michou, did Michou still have eyes? "I tracked his name to your burg in upstate New York, but I gave up looking for him in the rosters years ago, he never showed up at these shindigs before. You guys can't be more than a couple of hours away from the wicked metropolis, what've you been *doing* with your life?" And she was asking where *he* lives now, and he said "Oregon," and she echoed "Oregon," and the two of them were laughing and laughing, and Robin wanted to know what was so hilarious about Oregon, or had they laced the cheesecake with rum, or was it Irish coffee O'Hara had been drinking? "When did you and Mom last see each other?"

"Who can keep up with the years, those *great black oxen* treading the world, remember, Tess? Was it sixty-three?"

"Yes, I *do* remember, that's from the last lines of *The Countess Cathleen,* no, it couldn't have been sixty-*three,* that was the year Kennedy was assassinated, our last year in Belle Ville, Lord, *Lord,* those great black oxen! November twenty-second of sixty-three, O'Hara do you realize that two years from now, November twenty-second of eighty-eight'll be the *silver anniversary* of Kennedy's assassination?

"Your mother hasn't changed, young lady, I'm here to testify because I knew her when. The World was *always* too much with her, at least that's what your Old Man used to complain. Where *is* he, by the way?

Robin was looking at her intently.

She smiled at her daughter. Her eyes said, *You* tell him.

"I've a dinner date with my father tonight. Mom's taking the bus back upstate at 2:30, she has to get the paper out. She's owner and editor-in-chief of the town newspaper. And she's working on a *very* big feature series! You *must* have heard about the Howard Beach tragedy. Well, in one of the towns near ours there've been racial--"

"Sweetheart, I've gone on and *on* about it to you, let's not subject poor O'Hara to the sorry tale of the latest incidence of the disease of racism in upstate New York! Not that it would surprise anyone who knows the history of our area, by the way, it was a stronghold of the Klan not so long ago."

O'Hara shook his head. "Remember when we thought only white Southerners had that particular disease? That was before you introduced us to that newspaper guy you worked for, whats his name--"

"Landry," she said quietly. "Jimmy Landry. But enough of the talk about what's beginning to look like an incurable disease, 'tis the season to be jolly, right? Tell me about your family. What is Marilyn doing these days, now that your bairn are all grown-ups?"

Marilyn's a computer programmer, he said, earning almost the same salary *he* earns, and he will be retiring in another few years. One of his sons was in the medical supplies business, another was an orthodontist, one of their daughters was in a theatre group that just put on one *hell* of a performance of *Long Day's Journey,* the other two kids were teachers, the son a high school Spanish teacher, the daughter an adjunct at three different colleges. All five of them were married and busy fulfilling the commandment to increase and multiply the next generation of O'Haras. "And *you,* lovely young lady, praise the Lord but you're the reincarnation of your mother, known as Tess in the dear dead days beyond recall, not that she'd ever let on to you, *you're* married, I'll bet, the guys wouldn't let the likes of *you* get away!"

"*Thank* you!"

"Robin is *al*most married. *That* great event takes place this coming spring. As a matter of fact, what brought me to this wicked metropolis was the party her Ben's folks, the Cohens, held for the two of them on Saturday night."

"And it's ten past one on the following Monday, so did the festivities just bust up?"

"I talked Mom into staying over until today. She and I had a private festivity last night of our own, a *feast* at New York Deli!"

"So *that's* where the Old Man is, sleeping it off, eh?"

"Mark and I were divorced a few years ago, O'Hara. He's still at the College in Palatine, so we live in the same town although we go our separate ways now."

"Oh, hell. What the hell, Moira. I'm sorry."

"Thank you," she murmured. "It's all right. Thank you."

Robin asked brightly what they called the campus town in Belle Ville, she'd forgotten the quaint name. "Cougar Alley," Moira and O'Hara said in unison. O'Hara wished he had the lowdown on the old gang. She told him M'sieur had retired a long time ago and as far as anybody knew, he was blissfully shrimping in his pirogue in Bayou Bleu, "putting in *permanent* residence now. And Peerer was named President of a College somewhere in the Southwest. Can you feature Peerer eating his red beans and rice at his Coronation dinner? Olive Oil still holds the fort in her secretarial pool. And Jacques simply vanished."

"How do you *know* all this?"

"Hannah used to write me all the news faithfully up until nine years ago. Age, she said, silenced her. I called her up the year she stopped writing and asked her why. 'It left me,' was all she said. But Arturo scribbles me a note every Christmas. I have one at home with a photograph of him holding his first grandchild, a little girl. He was married soon after we left Belle Ville and fathered a daughter who became a bride right out of high school. Can you imagine Arturo a *grandfather?"*

"Hell, I've done *that* one eleven *times* by now. You guys had a son... Ted...."

"My brother is in Illinois. He's going to graduate next spring with a Ph.D. in History! He's writing his dissertation on the Civil Rights Movement, I couldn't get a *word* in when he was home for the holidays last week, not with him and Mom comparing notes on The Great Days Before."

And Ted loved Mannyheimy And Ted was afraid of The Fog Man

"Illinois, eh? Native grounds, eh, Moira? Do I get to meet him?"

"I'm afraid not. He came in with us for the party, but he flew back yesterday."

"*You're* a Mover and Shaker too, I'll bet."

"No," Robin laughed, "far from it. I'm taking graduate courses in Art History. My fiancé is an artist. Good *thing* I'm not, either! The last time I mentioned Irangate to Ben, he thought I was talking about a Persian miniature of a *moon*-gate!" She looked at her watch. "I'm sorry to break this up, but I promised Mom I'd walk her to Port Authority, and we'll have to leave in the next five minutes if she wants to make that 2:30 bus."

"Tell you what, we'll *both* walk your mother to Port Authority. I wouldn't miss one second of the pleasure of the company of either one of you."

"I'll make a quick stop downstairs at the Ladies, want to come with me, Mom?"

"We'll wait, darling."

O'Hara rose chivalrously as Robin slid out of her side of the booth.

And now they were alone together.

She looked and looked at him. She told him she could not have enough of looking at him. She asked him mindlessly where he was staying. "The Sheraton," he told her. Then she asked him if they had a deep purple suite in the place. He wanted to know what kind of crazy talk this was. "My heart is red," she sang *sotto voce,* "My heart has dishpan hands." "That cheesecake must've been *soused* in rum," he laughed. She asked if he still carried that filthy piece of paper in his wallet, his punch line paper. "Keep a civil tongue in your head," he replied.

Then he turned himself into Humphrey Bogart. He belted his imaginary trench coat, pulled the brim of his imaginary hat down over his eyes, and lisped out some smart remark about plugging her. Then he pointed a finger at her and shot her dead.

She was rattling around in this three-quarters-empty bus at this mid-afternoon hour, all the traffic in New York seemed to be pointing the other way. O'Hara still was too much with her, she was *thinking* in O'Hara-ese.

The bus just now was passing the turn-off to the Cloisters. *"Sing, choir of angels."* "And a Happy Chanukah to *you,"* she muttered to the wraith in the window.

"Robin's bringing me back to the fold, Moira," Ben had laughed, his arm going around her shoulders. "Just as she said *you'd* done with her father!"

These heroic and truly Christian souls, cher, Jimmy Landry had said to her, had he no thought of how deeply that had offended her? He *could* not have known, he never would have forgiven himself if she had told him.

Had he no thought of how deeply she was falling in love with him?

Ah, but he knew, and she knew that he knew. Yet never had there been one look, one word between them.

"I could not love thee, dear, so much,/Loved I not honor more."

Who among them would have believed there would come a day when they would retrace their steps to that one, in search of some source of light?

She closed her eyes.

She and Robin had been sitting side by side on one of the benches at the IBM Center yesterday evening. "When I was little, you took me around," Robin mused. "Now *I* show *you* the sights."

She opened her eyes. The eyes of her Double in the window were asking, asking.

She closed her eyes again. She saw the bright maraschino cherry in the noddle pudding on her dinner plate at the New York Deli, she saw the bright red ball at rest under the pecan tree in the back yard of their home in Belle Ville. She saw the soul of the derelict passing by the window of the Pancake House that morning, she saw his hunger, his cold, his homelessness, a swirling cloud, and her own soul filled with his want, his soul flowed into hers, silver waters mingling. And then she saw the silver eyes of the infant daughter she had held in her dreams last night, the third child she had dreamed was just born to her. And then she saw the silver band of the tracks in Hopper's *Railroad Sunset,* she and Robin were standing, their arms linked, before Hopper's masterpiece that very morning, in the north gallery of the Whitney Museum of American Art at Equitable Center, but a few hours ago....

"'Could we both discard...,'" O'Hara had murmured, as though in self-communion.

But she had remembered. "'This beggarly habiliment,'" she had continued softly.

O'Hara had said no more, tears were standing in O'Hara's seawater eyes.

She opened her own eyes again, and saw the eyes of the wraith in the window looking gravely into hers. And she could hear the first phrase of the invitational music. Then she saw the azaleas blossoming, red and white and yellow and purple and pink, she saw the whole of Belle Ville, a garden of azaleas

"The brute fact of physical death is not enough to consummate death in people's minds: the image of the recently deceased is still part of the system of things of this world, and loosens itself from them only gradually by a series of internal partings."

--Robert Hertz, "The Collective Representation of Death"

AFTERWORD

Echoes of the fatal shots fired in Dallas on November 22, 1963 still reverberate in the memory of Americans whose historical consciousness was profoundly stirred by the assassination of President John Fitzgerald Kennedy during the years of the civil rights movement. For the rememberers among the cast of characters in *The Kingdom Where Nobody Dies* as for many of their human counterparts throughout the country, the "brief and shining moment" of Kennedy's Presidency was transmuted over time into the Fata Morgana of a bright road-not-taken. For them as for others I have since encountered in life as well as in books and in my own mirror, the road that *was* taken in the aftertime of the Four Days in November 1963 "has made all the difference" for the remaining third of "the American century" and beyond.

"My souls (or characters)," August Strindberg wrote in his preface for *Miss Julie,* "are...scraps from books and newspapers, fragments of humanity, torn shreds of once-fine clothing that has become rags, in just the way that a human soul is patched together." So too are the composite characters (souls) in these seven short fictions, for whom making sense of the meaning of the assassination became a crucible for making sense of the meaning of their lives at that historical moment. Some are natives of the South; others moved to "Belle Ville," Louisiana from another state or region of the country. The Chicagoan awarded a Fellowship in the Art Department of the state university, the schoolteacher readying herself for a party after the football game played on November 23, the cripple witnessing the killing of Oswald on the television screen, the lawyer--who is the son of a marriage between a Midwestern farmer and a native Southerner--as he mourns the assassination of the President, the woman praying to her dead mother in the church where her husband is the preacher, the woman driving her family away from the South in 1964 just after the bodies of the three murdered civil rights workers were found in Mississippi, the memoirist whose backward look from the 1980s reveals the "Belle Ville" of 1953 to 1963 to have been a microcosm of the region of the country at which critical issues of the times converged and deep change was in the making--each has his or her own story to tell of their lives during the social upheaval of that place in those times.

A native of Chicago, I lived in Baton Rouge, Louisiana from 1954 to 1964, first as a graduate student, then briefly as a faculty member at Louisiana State University. After I left Louisiana, the souls (characters) in *The Kingdom Where Nobody Dies* became ghosts calling to me ever more insistently from the pages of a novel I wrote in Baton Rouge from November 22, 1963 to the summer of 1964 when I moved back for a time to the Midwest. My novel, *A Time To Rend,* which remains unpublished, was a fictional exploration of the impact of the assassination on my characters (souls) living in a small urban community, and in the academic community nested within it, in the Deep South.

"Chance is always powerful," Ovid said. "Let your hook be always cast. In the pool where you least expect it will be fish." By the lights of these words from the pen of the illustrious Roman, in 1975 I applied for a Creative Writing Fellowship from the National Endowment for the Arts in Literature to provide release time from my part-time teaching post at the State University College of New York in New Paltz. My Fellowship proposal was to shape *A Time To Rend* into a well-integrated collection of short fiction about life in a community in the South at the time of the civil rights movement and the assassination of President Kennedy. Although I was certain that my chances for the award were remote, I believed that my proposed collection could represent a many-faceted view of a Southern community at a turning point of far-reaching social change in 20th-century American society. I believed that it could prove to be of enduring historical value as well as of interest to readers from every region of this country and from all walks of life.

In June 1976, I was stunned by the news that I had been awarded a Creative Writing Fellowship by the National Endowment for the Arts in Literature to write this collection. That year, Fellowships of $6,000 each were awarded to 165 creative writers (Nelson Algren among them!) from a total of 2,436 applicants. The news was exhilarating--and unexpected. At the time, I was virtually unknown as a writer of literary fiction, having published eighteen stories and a few essays and poems in the "littles," but no book-length work except for *Custom: An Essay on Social Codes. Custom,* a translation of *Die Sitte* by sociologist Ferdinand Tönnies, had been published by The Free Press of Glencoe in 1961. The translation, for which I received an honorarium of $100 from the publisher, was the outcome of my study of German, undertaken in graduate school to fulfill the foreign language reading requirements for the Ph.D. degree I was awarded in 1958. Rudolf Heberle, Boyd Professor of Sociology at LSU, had encouraged me to try to find a publisher for my translation as a contribution to the field of Sociology.

A writer since childhood, primarily of poetry then, I have been writing and publishing in a variety of literary genres since the 1960s. I received my Bachelor's and Master's degrees at the University of Illinois, and the Ph.D. degree at Louisiana State University. My major field of study was Sociology; my minor fields of study for the A.B and M.A degrees were Philosophy, Law and History; and for the Ph.D. degree, Anthropology. It happens that I am a writer who elected to study the social sciences rather than a sociologist who elected to study literature. Other than a course in playwriting which I took as an undergraduate, I had not then, nor have I since, participated in any program of study at any writing school. Then as now, I had no connections in the literary or publishing worlds, nor did I know any of the members of the Literature Program's selection committee for NEA Fellowships that year (or indeed any year before or after 1976.) In any case, when I applied in 1975, no letters of recommendation or reference were required of applicants for these NEA Fellowships.

Next to good fortune, I could think of few reasons other than the quality of my writing, and the theme of the work I proposed to write, to account for having been one of somewhat less than 7% of the applicants awarded a Fellowship that year. I assumed I had been chosen primarily on the merits of the quality of the eighteen stories I had published up to the mid-1970s in the "littles," among them *The Carolina Quarterly, The North American Review, Nimrod, The University Review, Scholia Satyrica,* and *Ascent;* and because two of my stories had received special recognition--"The Visions," in the Summer 1973 issue of *Kansas Quarterly,* is listed as one of the "Distinctive Short Stories, 1973" in *The Best American Short Stories 1974,* edited by Martha Foley; and "Rachel In Search of Her Breasts," in the Autumn 1966 issue of *Zeitgeist,* had been awarded First Prize for Fiction by that literary magazine. I thought that perhaps another reason I was awarded the Fellowship may have been that at the time I applied, I noted on the application form that I had completed *Tell No More of Enchanted Days,* a fiction collection (that remains unpublished) and was at work on a manuscript, a book of essays exploring the common ground between the uses of the imagination in literature and social science. My book of essays, *Redeeming the Sin: Social Science and Literature,* was published in 1978 by Columbia University Press.

I completed *The Kingdom Where Nobody Dies* in the spring of 1977, the same year during which I also completed *Redeeming the Sin*. Therefore, I expressed gratitude to the NEA for its support from June 1976 to June 1977 in my Prefatory Note and Acknowledgments in *Redeeming the Sin*. (I did not have then--and do not have now--a literary agent. It happens that in 1975 I had submitted the title essay of *Redeeming the Sin* to the *Antioch Review,* where it was accepted and subsequently published in the Spring issue of 1976. In October that year, the editor-in-chief at Columbia wrote to tell me that he had belatedly read this essay and that, "I like your work and am writing to ask if we may see the manuscript of which this will be a part.")

With the proliferation of writing schools and writing programs at American colleges and universities after World War II, more and more trade houses, and many university presses and small presses as well, have come to adopt a policy of excluding "unagented" manuscripts from consideration. Some also will not consider any unsolicited manuscripts. I knew all this well in 1977; and for many years after I completed *The Kingdom Where Nobody Dies,* I sought representation by an agent for this book. A number of them did not trouble themselves to respond to my inquiry. Every one of the dozen or so who did, among them the few who took it on for a time without success, advised me of what I already also knew well, that it is extremely difficult to place a collection of short fiction by a writer who has not yet published a novel. Every one of them recommended that I represent myself in seeking publication of the collection. They also advised me to seek "national exposure" of the individual stories and the two "novellas" (some referred to the title story and the long story I later changed from "Or the Angels Will Weep" to "Creatures Of a Day" as novellas); and, to that end, to submit them individually for publication in magazines along the way.

So it was that in 1977 I sent forth *The Kingdom Where Nobody Dies,* both as a collection and story by story, in my quest for the writer's Holy Grail, namely, publication. Eventually, two stories were published; but their companions have fared no better than the collection as a whole over the past three decades. Since 1977, I have sent inquiries about it to a total of 135 publishers, a number which includes seven different occasions when I entered it in competition for a book-length work of fiction. Of the 135, fifty, including the seven entries of it in contests, invited me to submit it for consideration. Some asked for the whole manuscript, others only for a portion thereof. Most of them offered to read it only on condition that I not submit it elsewhere during the reading period, a condition I felt honor-bound to meet. The remaining 85 whom I queried were almost equally divided between half who declined my request for a reading (some with a form letter stating that they do not consider unsolicited, "unagented" manuscripts, and the majority stating they were inundated with manuscripts to consider and small lists from which to choose for publication), and the other half who never responded to my initial and follow-up inquiries. The 135 to whom I sent inquiries about the collection include editors at 35 trade houses, 70 small presses, 19 university presses, the publishers of winners of the seven contests in which I entered it; and four publishing houses in other countries (Canada, Germany, England and Belgium.)

Since 1977, the collection lay in hopeful waiting, often for long periods of time, at a number of presses; some editors held it for a year or more before deciding not to publish it. During the years before I had access to a word processor near my writing-desk, a number of times the manuscript was returned to me in such poor condition that I had to make freshly typed or photocopied portions of it; in one case, I unwisely submitted my one ribbon copy, and because it was returned with so many pages wrinkled, smudged and with the margins scribbled upon in ink, I had to type a fresh copy of the entire work. One editor returned it after holding it for one and one-half years, finally responding to my repeated entreaties with a letter stating that the delay was due to her embarrassment for having spilled insect repellent on some of the pages.

The reasons most editors gave for deciding against offering to publish the collection were that they had far too many manuscripts to consider for the few places they had on their lists for works of fiction; and the difficulty they encountered in marketing short story collections "successfully" (which I have long thought works as a self-fulfilling prophecy.) There were few negative criticisms of the work, and even these were mild (one editor found my style "too impressionistic for my taste.") The words of praise in a fair number of their letters persuaded me that the quality of my writing was not a critical issue in most decisions to return it. "I really admire your lyrical and fluid prose style," one commented. Another commended me for writing "with intelligence and with a pleasing and rare attention to detail," and wrote that he "enjoyed the meticulousness of your novellas."

Collective folk wisdom in the publishing world was invoked in many editors' comments; some that were made in the first person plural perhaps were meant to remind me that very few editors at trade houses and university presses are empowered to make an independent decision to accept or reject a book manuscript. An editor who graciously invited me "to favor us" with the manuscript, wrote that, "There is indeed much to admire throughout the collection as a whole; the rich language, the way details of landscape are catalogued with such clarity. There was not, however, quite enough editorial support for the collection as a whole to warrant an offer of publication at this time." Letters offering something more than the standard "not for us" and "good luck with it elsewhere" cited budgetary constraints and the appropriateness of this particular collection for their lists, in addition to the difficulty in marketing fiction, particularly collections of short stories, as reasons for returning it. An editor at a small press wrote, "You don't need me to tell you (I hope!) you're a fine writer; but be that as it may, unfortunately, this work would not fit in with our list." Still another, in a letter accompanying the return of the manuscript in 1986 after holding it for eleven months, wrote, "After much too extended a consideration-period, I'm afraid that in the end we're not to make an offer on your volume of short fiction, THE KINGDOM WHERE NOBODY DIES. As I've written to you before (in a response to an inquiry I had made earlier), short fiction is something we do here once a season only; the feeling was that your book--although it embodies a time and place quite strikingly--was too limited, lacked enough range, to be that one book....Please accept our apologies for the long time in finally responding--and good luck with this book; we hope it finds the kind of publication it deserves." In 1990, an editor wrote, "We felt that the collection was quite strong and unified, competently written. We accept very few manuscripts for publication, and in the final analysis, sadly decided that this work was not quite right for our list."

As the years turned into decades and no offer to publish *The Kingdom Where Nobody Dies* was made from any quarter, I found a measure of consolation in some letters in my voluminous files of correspondence about it. I prize one in particular, from a senior editor at a university press, who wrote in 1994, "I'm sorry to be the bearer of a potential disappointment.., but I am unable to offer you encouragement of publication.., despite the fact that I admired many aspects of your stories--the vivid evocation of remnants of the old south, in particular, of New Orleans; the interweaving of particularized characters' lives/hopes/desires with the historical events of the 60s; the limning of a nation's loss of innocence with the assassination of John Kennedy.... It is because we have been receiving so many excellent manuscript submissions vying for one of our few fiction slots that we are pushed to make difficult choices about which of the projects will best complement our fiction list. I'm sure we sometimes make wrong decisions. It is with regret that I am returning your manuscript and a sincere apology for the many months it has taken me to get to your collection."

"Loving our children and calling them our second selves because we have begotten them leads us...to consider another sort of procreation whose offspring should no less recommend itself to our love," Montaigne wrote. "The works our soul engenders, the issue of our understanding, heart, and abilities, spring from nobler parts than our body, and are more truly our own....We are both father and mother in this act of generation." So it was that the characters (souls) in these stories haunted me relentlessly as I strove with a terrible patience and tenacity to find a home for them between the covers of a published book. I can say with Montaigne that "what I have given" to *The Kingdom Where Nobody Dies* "I gave absolutely and irrevocably, as men (and women) do to their human children." But after I completed it, I went on to write new works, to which I also gave myself as absolutely and irrevocably as to this book.

By 1976, when I was awarded the NEA Fellowship, I had published poetry, essays, and eighteen short stories. All these manuscripts as well as the stories, essays, manuscripts of Journal entries and poems I published in magazines and anthologies after 1976, were unsolicited and "unagented." From 1977 on to the present day, I wrote new essays, poetry, manuscripts of Journal entries and dozens of new works of short fiction. Another eighteen of my stories were published in literary magazines and anthologies; two of them were nominated for a Pushcart Prize in Fiction.

By 1977, I had completed *Tell No More Of Enchanted Days,* a collection of short fiction about life at a private college in the Midwest during the "Sixties Revolution." After 1977, I began gathering a collection of a number of my published and unpublished short stories in a volume I eventually entitled *Evanescence: Stories, 1950s-2000.* My strenuous efforts to find publishers for both collections were as unsuccessful as those I made on behalf of *The Kingdom Where Nobody Dies*. My equally unsuccessful efforts on behalf of my novels written during the past thirty-three years also serve to have put to a severe test the collective wisdom of agents and editors that it is extremely difficult to publish a collection of short fiction without first publishing a novel. During the 1970s, I completed two novels in addition to *A Time To Rend;* all three remain unpublished. During the 1980s, I completed a trilogy of novels-in-the-round about three alternate lives of a woman living in the 1980s in "Palatine," a historic community in the Hudson Valley that was founded by French Huguenots in 1677. I published excerpts from my trilogy in magazines and anthologies. But my efforts to find a publisher even to consider, much less to publish any or all of the novels were fruitless. In 1991, in the desire to preserve at least a portion of my trilogy, and in the spirit of triage, I published fifty copies of one of them myself, and donated copies of it to libraries throughout the United States with special collections of Jewish Americana.

In 1977, virtually unknown in the academic world as well as in the world of writers but by then a faithful follower of Ovid's maxim, I applied for a Rockefeller Foundation Humanities Fellowship in support of my research project, "the older woman as seen through literature and social science." In 1978, I was awarded this Fellowship. Two books were the outcome of my award, both of them "unagented," and one of them solicited but later rejected, were published in the 1980s, but only after a fierce struggle that deserves a story, memoir or essay in itself--*Chimes of Change and Hours: Views of Older Women In 20th-Century America,* by Fairleigh-Dickinson University Press; and *Older Women In 20th-Century America: A Selected Annotated Bibliography,* by Garland Publishing, Inc., as Volume 2 of their Women's Studies Facts and Issues Series. As was the case for my translation, *Custom,* and my book, *Redeeming the Sin,* both also "unagented" and one solicited, I received no advance for either of the books I wrote with the support of the Rockefeller Fellowship, or for the other three unsolicited and "unagented" books I published after 1978, *Through The Years: A Chronicle of Congregation Ahavath Achim, 5725-5750,* which I co-authored with my life partner, Professor Walter Borenstein (we had 200 copies printed by Franklin Printing in New Paltz, New York and donated the proceeds from sales as a gift to the Congregation in honor of their 25th anniversary); my novel-in-the-round, *Simurgh,* which I produced and published myself in 199l; and *One Journal's Life: A Meditation on Journal-Keeping,* published by Impassio Press in Seattle in 2002. Of my published books, only one of the seven is fiction. Of the seven, I received royalty payments only for the (very modest) sales of *Redeeming the Sin,* the annotated bibliography published by Garland, and *One Journal's Life.*

"The days turned into the Past," as Harold Bloom has the narrator say in *The Book of J.* I knew at firsthand that for some Americans, the civil rights movement and the assassination of President Kennedy were watersheds during "the American century." I also knew from editors' comments that, year upon year, as *The Kingdom Where Nobody Dies* journeyed on in search of a publisher, there were other Americans for whom these were happenings "a long time ago," and that for those who spoke of the need to "move on," they seemed to be fading swift as dreams. The times were changing; many said as much even in the 1970s, in returning these stories. I thought, but knew it would be futile to respond, that this is what Time does because this is what Time *is,* that Time *is* Change, that Time is a god who devours his children. I thought, but knew it would be futile to respond, that I was well aware when I was living in Louisiana from 1954 to 1964, that the times indeed were changing, and that I felt called to render a living portrait in words of what I witnessed there and then so as to make of it an offering to the world. I wanted to persuade them to contemplate historian Daniel Boorstin's words, that Americans have "wandered out of history," and are therefore in danger of "imprisonment in the present."

From 1977 to the end of this year of 2008, while *The Kingdom Where Nobody Dies* was sent out, (presumably) considered, then returned and then sent out again, I have been as indefatigable in my efforts to publish the individual stories as to publish the collection. I knew from experience in submitting my fiction to the "littles," that, in addition to readers' idiosyncrasies in literary taste, length would be a problem for me in trying to place the title long story (or novella); indeed, already in 1977 it was returned with the note that it is "too long" (with the added gratuity that "your narration has a tendency to become rather breezy.") Also very early on, I had intimations from the comments of one of the twenty-six editors to whom I submitted it over the past thirty-three years, that there could be more to the decision for turning back this work than word limits, over-extended publishing commitments, and financial constraints. In 1978, I received a letter from the owner, publisher and editor of a small press who had considered publishing it as a "chapbook": "There is so much that is good about 'The Kingdom,'" he wrote. "Especially descriptive passages. The theme of the story in the end undoes it for me. Fifteen years later is hard.... We are all wiser than to be sentimental about a politician. Kennedy is tarnished. And although the story may be accurate reportage, it is not accurate in retrospect. At least for me. However, your language is beautiful. But I'm afraid we can't do it." *We see what we bring,* I thought, *as The Education of Henry Adams reminds us.* Not long after it came back, I decided to include it in a collection of both my published and unpublished fiction as an entry in competition for a national award for short fiction. It came back with an unsigned note penned by a member of the editorial staff: "This manuscript was in the top twelve, but unfortunately didn't make the final cutoff. Your work is rich and moving. As you must know, judging can be so subjective, arbitrary." From the 1980s on, I continued to send it to literary magazines and to enter it in literary contests where its length was within the word limit for submissions. In 1984, an editor of a magazine to which I sent it as an entry in their 1984 novella competition returned it with a note that it had been a "close" contender for the award. And in 1987, it was a finalist in a fiction award competition.

Over the past three decades, "Passing the Goal" was submitted to editors of 23 literary magazines and competitions. (It remains one of the few manuscripts never returned to me in the self-addressed stamped envelope I enclose with my submissions; the editor wrote that he had lost it.) This story was a Finalist in the competition for a Katherine Anne Porter Prize for Fiction in 1982. In 1990, an editor of a magazine in the South returned it with the note, "You're obviously a fine writer but I can't use 'Passing the Goal.'" In 1992, an editor of another magazine wrote that she enjoyed this story "a great deal. I like the characters you develop and your use of imagery and setting."

"Blue Sunday," written in 1976 and rejected by eight literary magazines during its first three years of life, was accepted in 1979 by *Webster Review,* and published in Volume VI, Number 1 (Spring 1981.)

"A Time To Be Far From Embraces," originally entitled "Into the Middle Mere," was completed in 1977 and revised in 1986. This story has been considered by editors and readers of fifty literary magazines and competitions in short fiction. In 1987, one editor returned it with the note, "I enjoyed your story but ultimately thought it would not quite work in our Arthurian issue." Another returned it in 1991 with the comment, "Lovely writing--but we receive a surprising amount of JFK material and, though the tone is very well sustained throughout, it is a 'sound' that we use very rarely--almost never."

"Sowing In the Shadows," completed in the Spring of 1977, was rejected by four literary magazines before being accepted in 1979 for publication in *Bloodroot,* The Special Fiction Issue, where it was published in Number 7 (Spring 1980.) Among its companion stories, "Sowing In the Shadows" had an exceptionally interesting history of rejection before it was accepted by *Bloodroot.* In 1978, in the cover letter with which I sent it to one of the co-editors of a proposed anthology of fiction about the 1960s, I wrote:

"In Bob Adelman's *Down Home,* there is a photograph of a black woman standing near a church, smiling at the photographer, and holding up a poster, 'Freedom Fighters,' with the three men, Martin Luther King, and John and Robert Kennedy, looking out at us. This is how they were seen and revered by so many. The caption under the photograph reads, 'A funeral at the Dixie Grove Baptist Church, Catherine, 1970.' Some pages later, there is a photograph of a black woman, Mrs. Rosanella Powell, Whiskey Run Road, Camden, 1966, with a quotation of what she had to say to the photographer: 'It's been sad times. Jack and Bob and King are dead. They killed them, because they didn't want the Negroes brought out from under their foots. That's how come they killed them. I don't see nothing else.'

"'Sowing in the Shadows' is meant to tell, with quiet force, the quality of faith there was in those times, and the anguish of those whose young gave themselves in body and spirit to the struggle to 'reddish,' (register to vote) for such it demanded of them. Had I not lived in the South during those years, I could not have understood these things enough for this woman to speak through my story. 'Sowing in the Shadows' reaches, too, beyond politics, beyond race and religion, to something universal in that tabooed terrain of a mother's feeling for her grown son."

In the letter accompanying the rejection of this story, the other co-editor wrote, "Thank you for letting us read 'Sowing in the Shadows.' It's a strong story, but I'm afraid I have an unreasoning antipathy to the odor of sanctity that has come to surround John and Robert Kennedy since they were murdered, and your story seems to derive much of its considerable emotional power from what I regard as a myth about the two men who were as power-hungry and ruthless as they were charming." He added a "P.S. It's only fair to mention that...my collaborator, who does not share my political bias against the Kennedys, was impressed by your story, without reservation." *We see what we bring,* I thought yet again.

In 1986 I changed the title of "Flight From a Phantom" to "Leaving Louisiana in 1964, a Cautionary Tale," but then restored the original title in 2003. I submitted this story to 27 literary magazines and short fiction competitions. When he was editor at Houghton Mifflin, the late Seymour Lawrence wrote, "It's a beautifully crafted story that continues to resonate long after the final page is turned."

"Creatures Of a Day" is a revision of a work of short fiction in this collection that I completed in 1977 under the title, "Or the Angels Will Weep," and then revised and made considerably longer in 1987, re-entitling it "Creatures Of a Day" in 2003. This novella has been considered by editors and readers of a total of 13 literary publications and short fiction competitions. An earlier version was submitted in 1977 to the Harvard Program in the Short Novel, but was returned because it did not fulfill the Program's length requirement. A member of the editorial staff wrote, "I am sorry that we must return your manuscript merely because it is too short. It looks like a well-written story of life in a southern town during a time of turmoil and change." In 1982, an editor of S.O.S.Books wrote of this earlier version, which I'd asked her to return six months after I submitted it so that I might enter it in a literary competition, "How does one praise a manuscript without publishing it? I am sure you will place this soon, and with a good house. Out of the many manuscripts we've received, this was one of the most involving and (personally) moving I've read. When you place it and its companion pieces, and other fiction by you--please let me know where it will be available." This manuscript was a Finalist in a 1986 novella competition. In 1982, when still entitled "Or the Angels Will Weep," it had been routed to the late John Gardner for a final reading by the editors of *MSS* shortly before his untimely death. Members of the *MSS* staff informed me that it subsequently was mixed in with his papers, which later were sorted and organized by the University of Rochester private collection library, where it became part of that archive.

In *Redeeming the Sin,* I noted the high ratio of published books of nonfiction to published books of fiction in this country. That was not exactly news--John Dos Passos had remarked it earlier in the last century--nor has it changed; indeed, I am certain that the ratio is much higher today than it was in the 1970s. My own experience confirms it. It has not escaped me that my book of essays was published one year after I completed writing it, and that *The Kingdom Where Nobody Dies* completed that same year, is only now in its thirty-third year of life, appearing for the first time in print, and that I am publishing it myself. I am well aware of what my own personal experience as a lifelong writer suggests about my chances for finding a reading public for my fiction. I have found publishers for six books of nonfiction, but none for this or my other two collections of my short stories, or for my trilogy of novels, one of which I produced and published myself, in 1991.

This Afterword could serve as a cautionary tale for American writers of what editors have referred to in letters to me as "serious fiction" or "literary fiction." It also could serve as material for a case study in the field of American Studies on the subject of American fiction that may be predestined to sink into the oblivion of "lost literature" by the workings of *de facto* censorship in "the American century." While I have other promises to keep than to write such a study, I find a mother lode of testaments to perseverance and to the passion for preservation of writers' unpublished works in my Commonplace Books and in a trove of my correspondence with my friends-in-writing and my Journal-keepings from 1964 to the present. In 2004, I co-founded the Life Writing Connection (lifewriting.org) with LWC Director Olivia Dresher, who created, compiles and continually updates an online registry of listings of annotated 20th-century privately-held unpublished American life writings. The Life Writing Directory registers journals, diaries, letters, autobiographies and memoirs written in English by people from all walks of life whose authors or custodians list them so as to make them accessible to readers and researchers who otherwise might not even know that they exist, and, in this way, preserve them. To read a work is to keep its light in this world. Perhaps a lover of American fiction who has some sense of the fighting heart a writer of "serious fiction" needs in order to persevere on behalf of "the works our soul engenders, the issue of our understanding, heart, and abilities," may find inspiration in the Life Writing Connection and adopt it as a model. Perhaps there will one day be someone who will create and maintain an online annotated registry of works of unpublished American stories and novels to serve the good cause of providing writers and readers access to hidden treasures of fiction written during (and perhaps beyond) "the American century."

In a Journal entry he made on 8 February 1868, Edmond Goncourt wrote, "One of the proud joys of the man of letters--if that man of letters is an artist--is to feel within himself the power to immortalize at will anything he chooses to immortalize. Insignificant though he may be, he is conscious of possessing a creative divinity. God creates lives; the man of imagination creates fictional lives which may make a more profound and as it were a more living impression on the world's memory." For me, it is a great happiness to create a work of fiction, a happiness unparalleled in the creation of all other works of literature since I lost my poet's voice thirty years ago. Undeniably, the ghosts of my characters (souls) in *The Kingdom Where Nobody Dies* know that I have given them pride of place at the top of the list of all my unpublished work in providing for their life beyond my own. In my imagination, I hear them rustling about in the papers in my overstuffed and near-toppling filing cabinet. In my imagination, they have unearthed clear evidence, in two letters I wrote over thirty years ago, while I was working to give them "a local habitation and a name," that I knew very well the challenges I would face in my efforts to bring their stories to the light of print, and that I would be undaunted by them. In my imagination, they are well acquainted with my fighting heart.

In February 1976, four months before the selection of that year's Fellowship winners was made, the NEA's Literature Program Director Leonard Randolph sent applicants a copy of the Autumn 1975 issue of the *South Dakota Review* together with a letter requesting recommendations for future Programs the NEA might institute. My response was a long letter the poor gentleman might still be trying to finish reading. After expressing my thanks for the *South Dakota Review* I wrote, "While I make every effort to keep abreast of the 'littles,' and subscribe to a number of them, it is impossible to follow all the fiction, poetry, and special issues that a writer/reader ought to be aware of, and this particular issue on 'The Writer's Sense of Place,' is one that I would not have wanted to miss. Had it not been for you, though, I would not have seen it."

I suggested "that, in part, the Literature Program try to build a little bridge between the writer and the small press. How? By, in some way, bringing them together--the writer in search of a publisher, and the small press in search of the writer. This excludes writers who *have* agents or publishers or presses, and it excludes small presses that publish writing that falls into set categories ('gay' or 'women's' or 'black' or whatever literature only) and it excludes small presses that already have a surfeit of, or a small circle of, writers they intend to publish. Perhaps that means that what you would have would be a very large number of writers whose work has been languishing for some time for want of a publisher, and an incredibly small number of presses open to bringing out new works.

"I am very afraid that this is the case. I do not think that my own case is unusual, though I base this on intuition, not on any scientific survey. I have been able to publish only fragments of my work--short stories, essays, original satires, prose poems, excerpts from novels, poetry--in the 'littles,' over a period of fifteen years. The competition has been intense; I have found that every editor has his or her own tastes; the 'littles' have such a precarious existence--they come and go, even while one's manuscript is buried with a mass of others on someone's desk, while months, even years go by; there are quarrels between editors over a manuscript; manuscripts are lost; one's work is passed over, sometimes, while that of friends and of friends of friends are published; the whole involvement is scattershot; each writer, in his or her own cell, is, as one of my poet friends put it, a 'cottage industry' unto himself or herself.., 'special issues' are brought out, devoted to the very topic one has been writing about, and one had no way of knowing such an issue was planned, so that a manuscript that might have hit the mark is put back into one's files....

"In the face of all this, how can the writer find the merest public? How can the writer build even a little house of fiction--unless he convert himself from writer into publisher, buy his own press, and devote his energies to bringing out the work he has already done, and finding readers for it--energies that ought to be firing new works. Once one has written something, well, it is done, and one wants to turn to creating something else. Why should one abandon writing to become a merchant? Most writers refuse to do this; they go on writing because they can do no other, though the manuscripts fill and overflow the files, and one feels a fool at times, somewhat onanistic, in the face of all this silence and refusal. I have written three novels and two collections of fiction in the past twelve years, and have been unable, despite repeated inquiries and submissions to commercial publishers and small presses, to have any of this work published. These books mock me--they sit on my shelf, stillbirths, like those fetuses one sees in jars in the histology labs of hospitals. They are not living, yet they are not dead; they are in some kind of limbo...and every so often, the writer takes heart, and sends them forth again, though the journey always seems to come full circle.

"I do not have a conspiratorial theory about a 'literary-industrial complex'; it would be consoling to believe in it, but I can't. Rather, I think that what we have is a very large number of gifted writers in search of a public--in search of a chance to *build* a public, rather.

"Having served for a few years as a fiction reader for *The North American Review,* and having read through many 'littles' over the years,

I am aware that much is being lost, much work of meaning and value; and I feel that those who come after us will not have a fully rounded or clear grasp of our time because of the loss of these sensibilities, these perspectives, to our literature. So long as women publish only women with the 'correct' ideological orientation, and blacks do the same, and Chicanos, and those under thirty, and prisoners, and Californians and Christians and motorcyclists; so long as editors turn back works because the return address is unacceptable or anathema to them, or because the style does not conform to their conception of literature, or the ideological content is not pleasing, certain sensibilities, certain perspectives will be shut out, will be silenced; certain unique ways of seeing things will fall into oblivion...and certain understandings of our time will be lost to those who will search through the archives and records for some grasp of what we were really about, of what our 'age' really was.

"I think that the discipline in which I was trained, Sociology, has contributed much to this corruption, to this sorry state of affairs, and I am writing an essay about this so will say no more about it here. But what can be done is this, I think: a small beginning can be made, in the interests of bringing out unusual or different or dissenting works, or works that are, by default, destined to be buried. A small press, or more than one, might devote itself to bringing out chapbooks or collections of writings, short stories or fragments of novels, *that writers themselves select as the one work that they want to be redeemed from oblivion.* That is, writers can be offered the opportunity to submit the one work of fiction that, of all they have done, they do not want to be lost; and these can be gathered up by a small press and published--as a chorus of voices that might otherwise go unheard. Announcements of such a venture could be made in *Margins,* in *Coda,* in *Poets & Writers Newsletter,* and such publications as serve as little clearinghouses; eligibility requirements might be structured as they are by the Fellowship Program which you administer; and in this way, editors of small presses and writers of fiction might be brought together to bring out a book (maybe even a series of books) of fiction writing that might otherwise never have been brought to light. And who knows? We as readers might all be the richer for it. For some writers, it might be the first door opening.

"I hope all this isn't too hazy; had to dash it off. Reading it over, it occurs to me that the toughest part of the whole under-taking would be to find editors ('judges') who are fair- and open-minded, who don't have some axe of ideology or literary style to grind. Best wishes,"

I knew one year after receiving the NEA Fellowship, when I completed the first draft of *The Kingdom Where Nobody Dies,* what challenges I would be facing in my efforts to publish the collection. I knew also that the odds against placing the individual stories and novellas in the "littles" were nearly as formidable. The few attempts I had made even that first year as I completed writing each of them had been unsuccessful. One editor wrote that he already had accepted a story about the assassination, another that he didn't care for the theme of the story, still another that he felt the story I sent him was part of a longer work, and yet still another that she was looking for a story from a woman's point of view, but that the story I had submitted was from a man's point of view.

In July of 1977, NEA's Literature Program Director Leonard Randolph sent the 1976 winners of the Fellowships a questionnaire we were asked to complete that it was hoped would be of help in evaluating the Creative Writing Fellowships and thus of great benefit to the future of the Program. "The most serious problem the writer faces today is simply, *being published,"* I wrote in the letter enclosing my completed questionnaire. My letter, dated 25 July 1977, continued, "This is especially true for writers of fiction and poetry. There are too few publications; and every editor and reader has his or her own prejudices about style, theme, and so on. Therefore, when I imagine or dream that I am the editor of a literary journal, I decide that after an initial screening of manuscripts by a group of readers, I would hold a lottery to determine which manuscripts would be published. There is, it seems to me, more justice in a lottery than in the decisions made by many a reader or editor."

I suggested in my letter that the NEA have its own press for publishing and distributing the works of Fellowship winners. "Not every writer will want this; some have an agent, or a publisher, and therefore this is not an issue for them. For the rest of us, it is the *burning* issue. If the Fellowship had given me the option of returning a portion of the grant to the Endowment for publication of *The Kingdom Where Nobody Dies,* I would have seized upon the opportunity at once, and most gratefully. The business of marketing is distasteful, disheartening and distracting beyond reckoning."

Once, to quiet them, I read to my ghosts the entry *From the Goncourt Journals.* I wanted to assure them as I have countless times during these past thirty-one years that in a directive to the executors of whatever literary estate I can claim as my own, I have chosen *The Kingdom Where Nobody Dies* to be given first priority in bringing to light the unpublished works I have left ("mind, not for want of trying") to Posterity. But the sight of them lying in wait inside a manuscript box has become my most powerful *memento mori.* And they have become ever more restless and demanding of my attentions. I have counselled patience; I have quoted Ovid to them. Did they not know my fortitude, I chided them, did they not trust me to soldier on, as I have done for so long? But they are not appeased. In making their case that I must see them into print in my own lifetime, while I still have the eyesight and sensibility to accomplish this, they rummaged among my Commonplace Book papers and found a passage written by another writer from a time much closer to theirs and mine. Last month, they lay it on my writing-desk to read in the Novemberlight:

In his *Remembrance of Things Past,* Proust reflects that, "What artists call posterity is the posterity of the work of art. It is essential that the work (leaving out of account, for brevity's sake, the contingency that several men of genius may at the same time be working along parallel lines to create a more instructed public in the future, a public from which other men of genius shall reap the benefit) shall create its own posterity. For if the work were held in reserve, were revealed only to posterity, that audience, for that particular work, would not be posterity but a group of contemporaries who were merely living half-a-century later in time. And so it is essential that the artist.., if he wishes his work to be free to follow its own course, shall launch it, wherever he may find sufficient depth, confidently outward bound towards the future."

During this past month of November, I happened to be reading Ted Sorensen's *Counselor,* I happened to watch "The American Experience: 'Oswald's Ghost,'" on television, I happened to awaken day upon day, knowing I had not dreamed of the inexpressible joy of the celebration in Chicago's Grant Park on the evening of Election Day. I knew these were Signs that harvest-time had come for the seeds that were sown in the shadows those many years ago, I knew these were Signs that it was time for me to offer *The Kingdom Where Nobody Dies* to the world.

The Kingdom Where Nobody Dies commemorates the dream proclaimed by Martin Luther King in Washington, D.C. in August of 1963, and the ideal of public service inspired by America's youngest President, whose loss we suffered in November of that same year. For the torch-bearers of that dream and that ideal in the name of our common humanity, the hope that Americans may one day fulfill the promise of the civil rights movement that had been gathering strength during Kennedy's Presidency was rekindled on Election Day in November of the 45th anniversary year of his untimely death.

Audrey Borenstein
9 December 2008

www.ingramcontent.com/pod-product-compliance
Ingram Content Group UK Ltd.
Pitfield, Milton Keynes, MK11 3LW, UK
UKHW041829200726
13854UKWH00002BA/892